PRAISE FOR THE
STEEL BROTHERS SAGA

"Hold onto the reins:
this red-hot Steel story is one wild ride."
~ A Love So True

"A spellbinding read from a
New York Times *bestselling author!"*
~ BookBub

"I'm in complete awe of this author. She has gone and
delivered an epic, all-consuming, addicting, insanely
intense story that's had me holding my breath, my
heart pounding and my mind reeling."
~ The Sassy Nerd

"Absolutely UNPUTDOWNABLE!"
~ Bookalicious Babes

FATE

FATE

STEEL BROTHERS SAGA
BOOK THIRTEEN

HELEN HARDT

WATERHOUSE PRESS

For everyone who asked for Brad and Daphne's story

PROLOGUE

B r a d

Present Day...

Prison is hell.

I gave up my right to go to a white-collar crime facility so that my accessories could walk. They'd worked hard for me, and they were young. They didn't deserve incarceration. It was the least I could do.

I always knew I'd end up in prison. My money could only buy freedom until my reasons for hiding ran out.

Once they did, I was ready to go.

Ready to answer for the life I'd led.

Ready to pay.

Yeah, prison is hell.

Not because of the constant inmate fighting. I may be in my sixties, but after a lifetime of watching my back, defending myself, and protecting those I love, I can fend off even the worst of them.

Not because of the disgusting slop masquerading as our meals. I'm used to fine dining, but what is food other than fuel for a body? I can change my thinking, imagine a Steel rib eye in place of the glop they call beef stew.

Not because of the asshole guards. They all know who

I am, know I have access to wads of cash. They pretty much leave me alone.

The real hell is the time.

All the fucking time in the world with nothing to do but think.

Think about the life I chose, the roads I traveled, the choices I made. The mistakes—and what they'd cost me.

I chose to fund the Future Lawmakers . . . and the money they made was used for unthinkable activities.

I chose to marry Daphne . . . and though I loved her and love her still, my choice harmed so many.

I chose to sleep with Wendy . . . and though I had my reasons at the time, things between Daphne and me were never the same.

I chose to raise Wendy's child as mine and Daphne's, telling no one the truth . . . and my youngest son will never forgive me.

I chose to leave my children . . . and though my reason was noble—to protect their mother—they felt abandoned.

I chose to fake my own death—not once but twice—and though my children forgave me the first time, they'll never forgive me now.

I chose to protect my wife and children at all costs . . . and now I'm paying the ultimate price.

Time is a formidable enemy. Time to think of the chaos I'd caused.

Time to imagine how everyone's lives may have been had I acted differently.

Time to create every viable scenario in my mind.

Could I have prevented Wendy's obsession with me?

Daphne's madness?

Talon's abduction?

What could I have done differently?

Hindsight is twenty-twenty.

But what could I have changed? The outcome might have been far worse had I acted differently.

The past is mine to live with, as it is for my wife and my children.

At least Daphne is safe. All the threats to her have been eliminated, and her children will care for her. She will live out her days comfortably, with her doll for company, in the world she created because she couldn't exist in the world I gave her.

And I wanted to give her so much! Daphne was fragile, more fragile than I knew when we met and made Jonah. And I loved her. I loved her nearly from the beginning, and I love her still. She was and is my soul mate. If only I could have been worthy of her. I watched my own mother's abuse by my father, stopped it when I was large and strong enough, but still she suffered the effects. I wanted so much more for Daphne, for our family.

And my children . . .

Jonah, Talon, Ryan, Marjorie.

They've all found happiness, and I'm the grandfather of five so far with another on the way.

I can't ask for anything more. I don't deserve to find joy in my children or grandchildren because I denied Daphne the joy in hers. In ours.

Happiness was never in the cards for me. Yes, I had moments here and there—Daphne's smile, the births of my children, teaching my sons how to work the ranch, my baby girl looking up at me with those big brown eyes and demanding I teach her everything I taught her brothers.

But each moment was only a tiny oasis in the hurricane I constantly sought shelter from.

The hurricane has finally turned to nothing but a cool breeze, but it left so much damage in its wake.

Life was forever altered for each of my children.

My children who, though they bear no responsibility, have suffered endlessly for my sins.

My children.

My life.

I'd been furloughed for Marjorie's wedding, and she'd allowed me to walk her down the aisle when she married Bryce Simpson, but she hadn't forgiven me. She made that clear after the ceremony.

I wanted to give you this, Dad. I wanted to let you walk your only daughter down the aisle. I selfishly wanted it for myself, too. But I'm not ready to let this go yet. I don't know if I'll ever be ready.

Her brothers were harsher, especially Ryan. I don't blame him. I lied to him from his birth about his true parentage—only one of my many sins against my children.

Time.

Just time.

Time to ponder.

Time to ruminate.

Time to relive.

Time to self-loathe.

But never enough time for what I want most in the world.

Redemption.

CHAPTER ONE

Daphne

Forty years earlier...

I had the dream last night.

Two months had gone by since the last time, and I'd allowed myself to think I was better.

My heart beat like a bass drum against my sternum.

You're just nervous about leaving home, Daphne. College will be fun. The best time of your life. No reason to be scared. No reason. No reason. No reason.

A knock on my bedroom door, and then my mother's voice.

"Wake up, sleepyhead!" She cracked the door, peeking in. "Breakfast is ready. We need to leave soon. Are you all packed?"

"Yeah," I said softly.

She opened the door and walked in, her forehead wrinkled. "You okay?"

I nodded. She worried so much. Between my half brother, Larry, and me, my parents had more than most to handle.

I hardly knew my half brother. He was three years older than I was, and he lived with his mother—Lisa, my father's first wife. I'd never met her. Larry was almost done with college and planned to go to law school. He'd mastered his demons, apparently—those things that had sent him into therapy at a young age and seen him through countless arrests as a teenager.

Now if only I could master mine.

The dream. The damned dream.

I couldn't tell my mother. She'd freak out, worry herself sick. My beautiful mother had permanent bags under her eyes thanks to me, and I wasn't about to add to them today.

No, today I was leaving her.

She deserved to live in peace.

★ ★ ★

My dorm room was small but cozy. My roommate, Patty, hadn't arrived yet. We hadn't communicated at all. I just got a postcard in the mail from the university telling me her name and that she was from Iowa. I'd lived in Denver all my life and was going to college in Denver as well.

I couldn't go far away from home, not after what I'd been through. I needed a safety net.

"I'll help you make your bed up," my mother said.

"It's okay, Mom. I'm capable of making a bed."

"Then why don't you ever do it at home?" She laughed.

It was a nervous laugh.

She considered me fragile, and she worried, but she was trying to give me something normal. After high school, you went to college. That was normal.

But I wasn't fragile. Not anymore. I kept up with my high school classes despite my hospitalizations. I'd always learned quickly and easily, and that was a godsend when I ended up missing most of my junior year. I worked hard and was able to graduate on time.

I returned for senior year. Everyone at school believed I'd spent junior year abroad in London. Everyone at home walked on eggshells, wondering if I'd break again.

But I hadn't.

I hadn't broken.

I was okay. Okay enough to leave home and begin college.

I remembered everything now. Never lost time, and never escaped to an imaginary world in a cloudy haze of medication. I knew what was real and what wasn't. I'd worked hard with my therapist to put the pieces of junior year back in place, but in the end, the puzzle remained unfinished. I just didn't remember most of the year.

Everything else was good, so it was time to accept that my amnesia wouldn't be cured.

The dream I'd had last night popped into my head.

The images always began to form but never completed. Maybe this time—

The door to the room swung open. "Hi there! I'm Patty. You must be Daphne Wade." The bubbly redhead stuck out her hand to me.

"Oh, yeah. Hi. These are my parents." I took her hand and gave her a firm handshake, like my father always taught me.

"Mr. and Mrs. Wade, great to meet you. This is my mom, Lila Watson."

Lila was an older and slightly overweight version of Patty. The same red hair, bubbly personality, and everything.

"Are you ready to go?" Patty asked me.

"Go where?"

"To the mixer, silly. It's a welcome-back thing, and upperclassmen guys always go to check out the freshman girls."

My father wrinkled his brow. "Upperclassmen are here already?"

"Yeah. Well, a lot of them anyway," Patty said. "My older brother graduated last year. He told me most upperclassmen come back early to party for a few days before classes start."

My father's brow stayed wrinkled.

"You should go, honey," my mother said. "Get into the spirit. Orientation starts tomorrow."

I looked in the mirror. My long dark hair was pulled back into a braid hanging down my back. I didn't wear a lot of makeup. I'd gotten out of the habit of painting my face after another hospital patient painted a canvas of me. I'd had no makeup on, and he made me look so beautiful that I began seeing myself as beautiful without it. I was lucky that I had dark brows and long black lashes. I liked a little lip gloss, though. My lips were a nice pink, but I liked the shine.

I looked down at my jeans and sandals. "I guess I should change."

"It's casual," Patty said. "You look great. You're a natural beauty."

My cheeks warmed a little. "So are you."

"I do okay. Too many freckles. Not you, though. That's a peaches-and-cream complexion if I ever saw one."

I looked a lot like my mother, and I was lucky I never had an acne problem. My brother, Larry, had terrible zits, or at least that was what my father said. I'd only seen him a few times over the years. I used to wonder why . . . until junior year. After that, I had enough of my own stuff to deal with, and I rarely gave my seemingly invisible half brother a thought.

My father cleared his throat. "We should be going, Lucy."

My mother nodded, her eyes a little sad. "You okay, Daphne?"

"Yeah." I went in for a hug.

My mom was always available for a hug. I'd put her through so much, I was surprised I hadn't hugged her out.

Dad kissed me on the cheek. "Give 'em hell, little girl. Be strong."

Be strong.

The same words he'd used every time he came to visit me at the hospital. At least the times I could remember.

I'd heed them.

I'd be strong for my parents. I'd put them through more than enough.

★ ★ ★

The mixer was held in the huge courtyard in the middle of campus. A keg of beer was set up. I was only eighteen and had virtually no experience with drinking. Patty pushed through the crowd and came back with two red plastic cups filled with beer.

I wasn't a huge fan of beer, but I wanted to fit in, so I took it. I'd been cleared for alcohol consumption once I went off all my meds, but still, I planned to be smart about it. I wouldn't have more than this one cup.

I was shy by nature, but Patty was the opposite. She dragged me all around, introducing the two of us to pretty much everyone who crossed our paths. We met some girls from our dorm and quite a few others as well.

I finished my beer and felt a little more at ease.

"You want another?" Patty asked.

"I shouldn't."

"Sure you should. Let's go."

We made our way to the keg and held up our red cups.

The auburn-haired guy manning the keg filled Patty's and turned to me. "Empty, sweetheart, but a new one's coming. Hold on a minute. Here he comes."

A muscular man hauled another keg toward us.

He turned and met my gaze.

And I nearly melted into the darkest brown eyes I'd ever seen.

CHAPTER TWO

B r a d

"Thanks, Steel," Murphy said.

But I barely heard him.

Next to him stood the most beautiful girl I'd ever laid eyes on. She was perfect. Fucking perfect. Dark hair pulled back and accenting her perfect oval face. Pink cheeks and lips. Gorgeous big brown eyes with the longest black lashes. Like a curtain of ebony.

Since when did I think in such stupid poetic words?

I hadn't seen her before, so she was probably part of the new crop of freshmen.

Also, I had a girlfriend. Sort of.

Wendy and I had been together since high school. She was a junior at a different college, and I was a senior here. We were on-again, off-again, and right now we were in an off-again phase.

Which was fine with me, especially now that I'd laid eyes on this beauty.

Murphy got the keg tapped and filled the girl's cup. "There you go..."

"Thanks," she said.

"You didn't catch that, did you?" Murphy said.

Her red-haired companion laughed. "He paused at the

end. That means he wants to know your name."

"Oh, sorry." She blushed adorably. "Daphne. Daphne Wade."

"Nice to meet you, Daphne." Murphy held out his hand. "Sean Murphy."

She took his hand, and a strange pang hit my gut. Probably ate some bad shit last night.

"I'm Patty Watson," the redhead said, "Daphne's roommate." Then she turned to me. "And you are ...?"

"Brad Steel."

Patty held out her hand, and I took it, but my eyes never left Daphne.

Was this Larry's half sister? Larry Wade and I had gone to Tejon Prep in Grand Junction together. I knew him well. Better than I wanted to, honestly. He'd told me about his sister, said her name was Daphne and that she'd be starting college here this fall. She didn't look anything like Larry, who was blond and blue-eyed. Of course, they had different mothers.

"You're not Larry Wade's sister," I said.

"Yeah, I am."

Shit the bed.

"I went to high school with Larry," I said.

She nodded. "He's a senior at CU, plans to go to law school."

"Yeah, I know. Good for him, huh?"

What did I just say? Did I really have nothing else to say to this girl except talk about her half brother? Besides, Larry and I weren't close. We'd run in the same circle in high school, but he was a lot closer to Theo and Tom than to me. The three of them were like peas in a pod.

Somewhat strange peas in a pod.

Then there was Wendy.

She had her own quirks, but the two of us had a physical thing that we could never quite get over.

Looking at Daphne Wade, though, I could forget Wendy in a heartbeat.

I was ready to dump a girl I'd been with for years for the first pretty face—

No.

That wasn't it at all. Beautiful women threw themselves at me on a daily basis, and so far I'd been able to resist. Even when Wendy and I were off-again, I dated gorgeous model types, but I never felt what I was feeling at this moment as I stared into Daphne Wade's eyes.

Daphne didn't respond to my remark about Larry going to law school.

Luckily, her roommate seemed eager to get to know Murph and me better. "So . . . where's a good place to get pizza around here?"

"Angelo's is the best," Murph said.

Unfortunately, the roomie was eyeing me, not Murph. Though she and Murph would make a striking couple. Both good-looking gingers. They'd have a gaggle of pretty little ginger kids.

"You ladies have any plans for dinner?" Murph continued. He was eyeing Daphne.

Yeah, we had a problem.

"We sure don't," Patty said. "At least I don't. I can't speak for Daph."

Daphne hadn't said much since Murph had handed her the beer. Finally, she took a drink. "No plans."

"You're in luck, then," Murph said. "The two best-looking

guys in school want to take you for pizza."

Daphne blushed. Actually, she hadn't stopped blushing since I'd begun staring at her. I couldn't tear my gaze away.

Yeah. She was *that* beautiful.

"That's awesome," Patty gushed. "Daph and I are in Hodgekins, Room 209."

"Great," Murph said. "What do you think, Steel? About six?"

"Sure, works for me," I said, still staring at Daphne Wade.

"Great!" Patty raised her red cup and took a drink. "We'll see you then. Daph and I have to bolt now. Need to mingle, you know?" She grabbed Daphne's arm and led her away.

I regarded my friend, who was filling up the next red cup. "Daphne's mine," I said in a low voice.

"Aw, man! She's fucking hot."

"So is the other one."

"You know I don't go for redheads."

"Dude, you *are* a redhead."

"That's why I don't go for them. Too much red, you know?"

"Maybe she's a true redhead."

"Most of them aren't."

"She might let you find out tonight."

"Fuck it, Steel. Why do you always get the gorgeous ones?"

In truth, the gorgeous ones usually went for me. Not that Murph didn't get his share of gorgeous women, he just got the less gorgeous one when he and I were together.

Which was A-okay with me.

Because frankly, Wendy and I were more off than on lately, and I was beginning to question certain things about her. She was still in business with Larry, Theo, and Tom. So was I, for that matter, but I was a silent partner if there ever was one. They'd taken my silent investments and done some serious quadrupling and then quadrupling some more. The four of them were millionaires now, though they kept that hidden from their families. Mommy and Daddy were paying for Wendy's college, even though their daughter could buy and sell them.

I knew they were millionaires because they'd paid me my profits. Nice seven-figure profits.

Not that I needed the dough, but I'd put up the cash, so I took my reward. Now? They no longer needed me, but I continued to invest. They had a basic buy-low-in-bulk-and-sell-high thing going, and they did it with serious volume. They'd started with popular toys and made a freaking mint last year when Theo got his hands on a warehouse full of Cabbage Patch dolls at bare minimum price.

"I have a feeling you'll get all the gorgeous ones from now on, Murph," I said.

I wasn't sure why I said that. I only knew that Daphne Wade was someone special, someone I wanted to know better. Something about her eyes. They hid things. Things I wanted to bring to the surface.

She was someone I already felt connected to.

Someone who might be able to help me break the toxic cycle I had with Wendy once and for all.

★ ★ ★

She didn't say much.

Her friend Patty was a nonstop talker, though.

"Just a farm girl from Iowa," she said. "Denver is the

biggest city I've been to so far."

"What kind of farming?" Murph asked.

She laughed. "You won't believe it. My daddy raises pigs."

"Hey, Steel," Murph said. "You and Patty have something in common."

Yeah. I saw what he was doing. Since I lived on a beef ranch—the biggest and most successful in Colorado, which also included an orchard and a budding vineyard—he thought Patty and I were more suited for each other.

Not happening. Daphne was still mine.

"We do? Where do you come from, Brad?" Patty batted her brown-red eyelashes at me.

She was quite striking, but not my type. I had a feeling no one else would ever be my type again.

"Ever heard of Steel Acres?"

Patty shook her head, but Daphne's eyes widened.

"It's my father's ranch on the western slope. We raise prime beef, and we grow apples and peaches."

"Biggest ranch in Colorado," Murph said.

Nice try, Murph. Still not happening.

"Really?" Patty smiled. "Our farm is just a small operation. We raise about a thousand pigs for slaughter each year. But we eat a lot of really great pork. My dad has a smokehouse, and we smoke our own hams and bacon."

"Interesting," I said. "Pig farming and beef ranching are two completely different animals. No pun intended."

"Good one, Steel," Murph said, giving me an evil eye.

Actually, my words were true. They *were* very different operations, so Patty and I had nothing in common other than our families both raised animals for meat.

"I was big into 4-H in high school. Three champion sows."

"Good for you," I said.

"I made Daddy promise they wouldn't ever be slaughtered," she continued. "They're going to live long lives and have lots of babies."

"And the babies will be slaughtered?"

I lifted my eyebrows. The words had come from Daphne. Was she an animal activist? I might not have a chance with her after all.

"The babies?" Patty said. "Well, a lot of them will be, yeah. People have to eat."

"I know," Daphne said softly. "I just hate the thought of animals in pain."

"I see you're eating that pepperoni pizza, though," Murph said jovially. "I'm thinking the pepperoni didn't grow on a tree."

Daphne blushed. "I'm no vegetarian. I just don't like to think about where it all comes from, you know?"

I *did* know, actually. When I was a kid, I got too attached to a couple of calves. My father made me go with him when they went to the slaughterhouse. A lesson in manhood, he'd called it.

More like a lesson in cruelty.

I was the only child of a majorly successful beef rancher. The ranch would be mine soon, for my father's health was failing. He still worked seven days a week, but he struggled with emphysema from all his years of smoking. He'd taught me well, and I could run it better than he could. I was learning more about the business side here in college. In a year, when I graduated, I'd be more than ready to take over.

"I know," I said softly, replying to Daphne's question.

I wouldn't tell her the calf story. At least not right now in front of Murph and Patty.

I didn't like talking about it. All these years later, it still hurt.

I never got close to another animal on the range again, though.

"These aren't pets, son," my father had said. "We treat them well, but they're our livelihood. They're meat. They're a commodity. You want a pet? Get a dog."

So I had. Misty had passed away a couple of years ago. I'd cried—the first time I'd succumbed to tears since the calves. Now I had Ebony and Brandy, two labs—one black and one chocolate. I missed them every day. I often thought about bringing them here to live at my condo, but they'd miss the wide open spaces. Wouldn't be fair to them.

Daphne met my gaze. In her brown eyes, I saw something I didn't recognize at first.

A few minutes later, though, I knew.

This girl had been through something. Something big. A new feeling landed in my gut, something I hadn't felt since that day my father made me drive those two calves away to be killed.

It was a profound urge to protect.

CHAPTER THREE

Daphne

He was looking at me again.

I was used to men looking at me. Sean Murphy had been eyeing me since he poured me a beer from the keg on campus. Most men looked at me the way Sean did—they thought I was pretty, so they were interested.

Brad Steel was different.

When his gaze met mine, I felt stripped naked, as if he could see everything inside me. Everything I hid so deeply.

As if he were looking into my soul.

I was being silly, I knew. No one could see inside me. He was probably just looking at a pretty girl like they all did.

Still, I couldn't shake that there was something more to his gaze.

Something a little bit scary, but in a good way.

I knew all about the Steels. I'd grown up in a Denver suburb, and the Steel ranch distributed beef to most restaurants in town. They were in the news a lot, and everyone knew it was the biggest and most successful ranch in Colorado. The fruit from their orchards ended up on produce shelves all over the state.

Which meant one thing.

Brad Steel was filthy rich.

I didn't care about money, though. I lived a modest life. Having a sound mind was the most important thing to me. I had one now, and I wouldn't give it up for all of Brad Steel's money.

Funny how most people took their minds for granted.

I'd never do that for the rest of my life.

"So, not a vegetarian," Sean said. "You just don't think about where your meat comes from."

I sighed. "It may not make sense to you, but I really love animals. I get that we're at the top of the food chain and all, and that we're omnivores and are meant to eat meat. But I don't like to think of an animal suffering just so I can have pepperoni on my pizza."

"If it helps," Brad said, his voice low and soothing, "we treat our animals really well. They're pastured and fed with local grasses, and we don't sell our cows to dairy farms just to get hooked up to a milk machine. Our steers and cows have a great life, even if it is a short one."

"We treat our pigs really well too, Daph," Patty said. "Because we're such a small operation, we focus on quality."

I smiled at both of them. "I'm glad. Thank you for telling me that."

"Your pepperoni probably came from some disgusting place, though," Sean said.

"Jesus, Murph," Brad said.

"Yeah, that was kind of rude," Patty agreed.

Sean swallowed a bite of pizza. "The truth hurts, guys."

Brad threw a wadded-up napkin at him. "The truth is you're a douche."

Sean laughed. "Takes one to know one."

Then Brad laughed. "Tell me again why you're my best friend?"

"Because I find all the hot women."

I warmed, but Patty, of course, spoke right up.

"You found *us*? What a crock. Daph and I found you, right?" Patty nodded to me.

Several times, I'd started to open my mouth to tell Patty that no one had ever called me Daph, but now I stopped. It was growing on me.

"Right, Pat," I said.

I finished my diet soda and wiped my lips on a napkin. The two beers from the kegger on campus had worn off, so I was feeling shy again.

"Is this the best pizza you've ever had or what?" Sean said.

"Can't say I've ever had better," Patty said.

"It's our favorite," Brad said. "Beats anything on the western slope too."

Normally, I'd go along with what the majority said. Life was easier that way. But though this pizza was delicious, it wasn't the best I'd ever had.

"Sorry," I said. "It's great, but not the best."

"You torture me," Sean said dramatically. "We haven't done our jobs, Steel. Now we're going to have to find a better pizza for Daphne."

"You don't have to," I said. "The best isn't too far from here. It's a little mom-and-pop Italian place near where I live in Westminster."

"We've got cars," Sean said. "Let's go."

"Sounds great," Patty agreed. "Except I'm stuffed."

"Tomorrow, then." Sean grabbed the last slice. "That work for you, Steel?"

Brad smiled at me, and his eyes seemed darker than before. "That works great."

"Pat and I have orientation starting tomorrow."

"The evening stuff is crap," Sean said. "All social stuff. You can skip it and have pizza with us."

"I don't know..." I said.

Brad touched my forearm.

Sparks shot through me. His hand was so big, and he wore a gold ring with a strange symbol on it. It was intricate, and I didn't recognize it. I loved the tan of his skin against my fairer flesh.

"Please," he said. "I really want to see you again."

I wanted to see him again too, but no way would I say that. I'd be too embarrassed. I settled for, "Okay. I guess we can miss the evening stuff. Is that okay with you, Pat?"

"Absolutely! If you know pizza that's better than this, I want to try it."

I smiled, meeting the dark gaze of Brad Steel, and something dawned on me.

I'd smiled a lot in his company, more than usual, and that made me feel good.

I liked that feeling.

CHAPTER FOUR ·

Brad

Murph seemed to accept the fact that he was with Patty, because he asked her to go on a walk around campus when we got back from dinner. She'd quickly agreed, which left me alone with Daphne.

She was so quiet, but silence with her didn't seem odd. In fact, it seemed perfectly normal. So she wasn't a big talker. I wasn't either, really. The quiet between us was comfortable. In fact, I hadn't felt this comfortable with a girl in a long time.

Wendy and I had been together for so long that there was a certain level of comfort with her, but it didn't feel like this. More often than not, I was treading on eggshells with Wendy because she seemed to snap at the slightest provocation. She could snap at something that hadn't bothered her days ago. She blamed it on her hormones.

But I was beginning to think a twenty-year-old woman couldn't possibly be so hormonal. She seemed to snap more often every time we saw each other.

Something else was going on—something I wasn't sure I wanted to be a part of anymore.

If things worked out the way I hoped they would with the beautiful young woman whose hand I was holding, I'd end things with Wendy once and for all.

I'd grabbed her hand impulsively after Murph and Patty had left us. Daphne was tall, and her hands were larger than most women's, but her hand felt perfect in mine, as if they were meant to entwine together.

"Thank you for dinner," she said shyly as we stood together outside her building.

"You're welcome."

I wasn't usually at a loss for words, especially with women. Why this one, who'd so clearly captivated me?

Again, the desire to tread softly with her rose within me. I wasn't sure why. What was so different about her? Was she truly hiding something, or was that just my own head playing tricks on me because she was so quiet?

And because I was so attracted to her?

"I'll walk you to your room," I said.

"Oh. Thanks." She sounded slightly disappointed.

"Unless you want to do something else? The night is young." I smiled.

She smiled back, her full pink lips bowing into the most beautiful smile I'd ever seen. Her whole face shone brightly under the lights outside her building.

"If you do," she said.

"Come to think of it"—I squeezed her hand—"I'm not quite ready to say good night yet. I hate to copy Murph, but we could take a walk around campus. It's big and it'll take you a while to find everything on your own."

"Or we could find a bench and sit under the stars," she said.

I stopped my jaw from dropping onto the ground. This girl was an angel. An angel who'd dropped into my life just when I needed her most.

"I know the perfect place," I said, still holding her hand. "Come on."

We walked, mostly in silence, to the manmade lake at the far end of campus. It wasn't actually part of campus. It was a public park, but the lake was kept stocked. During the day, kids sometimes brought their fishing poles, and walkers and runners did laps around the water.

At night, though, it was peaceful and serene. I led Daphne to a bench overlooking the moonbeams shining on the water.

"Wow." She sat down. "It looks like stars fell onto the water. It's beautiful."

I looked at her. "Yeah. It is."

As gorgeous as the moonlight on the lake was, it didn't hold a candle to the woman sitting next to me. She was ravishing on the outside, but whatever she held inside put her outer beauty to shame.

She was something, Daphne Wade. I wanted to know everything about her, all the secrets inside her.

I wanted to . . .

I reached toward her and trailed my fingers over the graceful line of her jaw. Her lips shone in the soft light of the moon. Slightly parted, they glistened.

Glistened.

I wanted to . . .

I leaned toward her and brushed my mouth against hers in the softest kiss.

Just a kiss. A peck, really. No tongue or anything.

And I swore I felt more in that one kiss than I had in all the making out Wendy and I had done over the years.

I never thought I was a romantic, but it was a beautiful kiss.

A perfect kiss.
So perfect that it was enough.
For now.

CHAPTER FIVE

Daphne

My heart jumped, and the place between my legs fluttered.

I'd been kissed before, but never like this.

It was so simple. No one trying to probe my tonsils. Just a simple kiss.

A perfect kiss.

And I wanted more.

The few other times I'd been kissed, during my freshman and sophomore years in high school, the guys had scared the crap out of me with their aggression. Everyone wanted to shove his tongue in my mouth or grope my boobs.

I was honestly surprised Brad Steel didn't try for more. He was over twenty-one, eons apart from the high school boys I'd been with.

But no, he seemed to sense that I wasn't quite ready for anything more tonight, and he respected that.

Except that I *did* want more.

For the first time, I wanted more.

His gaze never left mine. "You're beautiful."

"So are you," I replied.

He smiled. Perhaps he thought my words silly. But to me, he was beautiful. He looked like a pagan god in the moonlight. Perfect in looks with just the right touch of darkness.

I should know.

I was used to darkness.

I'd learned to live in it when I had to. It was just part of my life. Something that was a piece of me.

I had the feeling Brad Steel knew what darkness was as well.

My therapist had told me I'd overcome my fear of men. I had no basis for that fear, but so far, everyone who'd kissed me had been so pushy.

Didn't want to go there right now.

All I knew was one thing.

Brad Steel didn't scare me.

And now I wanted more. More than just the chaste kiss he'd given me. I wanted to feel his tongue trace my lips, enter my mouth, twirl with my own.

I wanted to feel his large and beautiful hands again on my face, on my neck, on my body, on my breasts.

I wanted to feel his lips slide down the side of my neck and over my bare shoulder.

And that secret part of him . . . I wanted that too. In fact, I ached for it now. The fluttering between my thighs continued, became more resonant.

Brad would go slow. Brad would make it good for me.

I hardly knew him, but I knew that as well as I knew my own name.

Brad Steel was the one.

"No one's ever called me beautiful," he said.

"Then no one's ever seen you," I said. "You're more than handsome."

"My God, Daphne." He cupped both my cheeks and brought our faces together. Our lips touched softly, and then he traced my lips with his tongue. "Open for me. Please."

I hadn't had the best of luck with French kissing, but already I knew Brad Steel would be different. I parted my lips.

He didn't plunge his tongue into my mouth. No, he tasted me slowly. First my lips, then the inside of my mouth, my teeth, my gums, until finally his tongue touched mine.

And I was lost forever.

It was soft. It was sweet. It was amazing.

But much better than all that?

It was right.

It was *so* right.

I parted my lips farther, letting him sweep into my mouth and kiss me with passion. Yeah, it was passion. I felt it. And within a few minutes of the kiss, after stroking my tongue against his, I wanted to explore his mouth too.

So I did.

His teeth, his gums, the velvet of his tongue.

More passion, more need.

More.

More.

More.

Until I was suffocating, suffocating...

The dream... The dream I never recalled but knew only in feelings.

I pushed away. "No!"

"Daphne? Sweetheart? What happened? Are you okay?"

I was far from okay. How could I want something that scared me so much?

I wiped my mouth and nodded.

"I'm sorry. I know you're young and—"

"You didn't do anything wrong," I said. "I wanted that kiss

as much as you did."

"Then what happened?"

"I got scared, is all."

He nodded. "You're what . . . eighteen?"

"Yeah."

"Not very experienced."

"Not exactly. Just not any experience that's good."

He stroked my cheek, and I turned into his warm palm.

"We'll go slowly, then."

I widened my eyes. "You mean you want to . . . try again?"

"We already have a date tomorrow," he said. "You're not getting out of that. You promised me the world's best pizza."

Without thinking, I pressed my lips into his palm. "I never break my promises."

CHAPTER SIX

Brad

The chaste kiss I gave Daphne when I saw her to her dorm room door was better than third base with Wendy or anyone else.

I smiled as I walked to my car. Smiled as I drove home. Smiled as I parked the car in the garage and unlocked the door.

Murph and I lived in a condo my father owned just off campus. It was a sweet two-bedroom. I had the master, of course, and Murph the second bedroom. We had two sleeper sofas where our friends crashed pretty often.

Yeah, it was kind of a party house. But Murph and I both had 4.0 grade point averages. We got our work done before we partied.

I opened the door from our garage into the kitchen and yelled, "Murph?" before I switched on the light.

"Not home yet," said a female voice I knew well.

Shit. Not tonight. Not fucking tonight.

I switched the light on and walked toward the voice.

Wendy Madigan sat in the living room in my leather recliner—stark naked.

"For God's sake, Wendy, Murph could walk in any time."

"And I'm sure he'd scream if he saw anything he hadn't seen before." She stood and walked seductively toward me.

"What are you doing here?"

"Getting laid, I hope." She wrapped her arms around me and gave me a hard kiss on the mouth.

I pushed her away. "You told me to fuck off the last time I saw you."

"I've had a change of heart," she said. "Right now I definitely want you to fuck *on*."

Wendy Madigan had been my kryptonite for six years. She had mesmerizing blue eyes and a killer body, but the real attraction was her mind. She had a ridiculously high IQ with just a touch of cuckoo. A lethal and seductive combination.

I looked at her standing naked, her pussy shaved the way she knew I liked it. Her nipples were hard, and her breasts fell gently against her chest.

If this were any other night, we'd be heating up the sheets by now.

But I wasn't in the mood.

I wasn't sure I'd ever be in the mood again. At least not for Wendy. Or any other woman who wasn't Daphne Wade.

I did have a giant hard-on, though. One kiss from Daphne and I was a fucking rock. Wendy was already wet for me. I could smell her own brand of musk.

"Get on the bed, bitch," I said through clenched teeth.

Wendy liked it rough. Rough and turbulent. She let me do anything I wanted, and what I wanted right now was to tie her up, put a blindfold over her, and pretend she was Daphne Wade.

Maybe this was a good thing. Maybe a good fuck with Wendy would erase Daphne from my mind. As high maintenance as Wendy was, I had a sinking feeling Daphne might be even more so. Maybe I should strip her from my mind right now . . .

... before she edged into my heart.

I wasn't in love with Wendy. Not anymore, at least. We had a physical connection, one that wasn't good for either of us. I'd been thinking about that a lot lately. This was my senior year of college, and maybe it would be best to end things with Wendy once and for all.

I'd loved her once—as much as a seventeen-year-old boy was capable of love. We'd fallen out of love long ago, but we always seemed to find our way back to each other. Our chemistry was addictive.

Despite the chemistry, though, we were horribly bad for each other. Our personalities clashed, and her temper was notorious.

The sex was pretty damned good, however.

I stalked into the bedroom. Wendy had taken her place on my queen-size bed, grasping two of the rungs of my headboard. I riffled through my top drawer and found the leather bindings I hid under my boxers. I held them for a moment, letting my fingers trace the roughness of the leather, the smooth chill of the silver chains.

Yeah, I was still hard. Fucking hard.

I was still fully clothed as I walked to the bed and bound Wendy's wrists to the headboard.

"Good and tight, Brad," she said. "I want them good and tight."

"I always do," I said.

Then I gave her boob a light slap.

I never left a mark. Well, almost never. Wendy actually liked it when I did. I gave her tits another quick slap and then her pussy.

She squirmed, and her scent wafted toward me. She was

ready. Wet and ready.

I could fuck her quickly. We didn't stand on ceremony anymore. Back in high school, we'd steam up my windows with marathon make out sessions, but these days, we were both in it for the fucking.

I'd never been able to resist her, and I wasn't going to start tonight.

I'd met an angel. An angel who could be my future. An angel who was hiding something underneath her almost untouchable beauty.

Didn't mean I couldn't enjoy a fuck with Wendy.

"Tell me what you're going to do to me, Brad," she said.

"I'm going to shove my cock into you. I'm going to fuck you."

"How are you going to fuck me?"

I slapped her tits once more. "Hard. I'm going to fuck you so hard, you won't be able to walk out of here."

She squirmed, pulling at her bindings. "I like it hard, baby. I like it really hard."

Worked for me. I could never deny the physical chemistry Wendy and I shared. No, I didn't love her.

Like I said, she was my kryptonite. My weakness.

But Daphne...

I'd met an angel who'd affected me deeply in a way that shocked me. I didn't want to ruin what that might become.

If Wendy was my weakness, maybe it was time to find my strength.

I regarded her, naked and tied up, ready for me to do whatever I pleased.

I was still hard as granite, hard as steel. The bulge under my jeans was clear, and Wendy knew it. I wanted her.

I always wanted her.

But maybe, just maybe, it was time to think not of what I wanted, but what I needed.

I'd dated on and off when Wendy and I were off-again, but never had I found someone I truly felt a possibility of a future with.

My future wasn't with Wendy. I'd known that for a long time now. In her own nutty way, Wendy knew it too. She fascinated me. Her mind was one of a kind, but lately she seemed to be going down a dark path, a path I couldn't follow.

In fact, I was beginning to wonder about Larry, Theo, and Tom as well. They were loyal to Wendy and the club above all else.

It was a little creepy.

"You going to fuck me or what, Brad?"

I jerked out of my thoughts. I was still hard.

Until—

"Hey, Steel!" Murphy's voice boomed. "You home?"

"Shit. Murphy's home," I said.

"So? Like we haven't fucked with someone else in another room a thousand times."

She was right. We had. Our physical chemistry always found a way. Plus, this was *my* room in my condo. The door was locked. Murph and I fucked women while the other was home all the time.

So why did it bother me this time?

"What a great condo!" came Patty Watson's voice.

Yup. That was why.

All it took was her roommate's voice to remind me of Daphne Wade. I had no idea what the future held for Daphne and me, but I knew one thing.

I was done fucking Wendy Madigan.

Daphne seemed to be the antidote to the kryptonite, and whether we ended up together or not, I'd be forever grateful to her for that.

"Brad," Wendy whined, "I'm so horny for you. Come on. Fuck me, baby. Hard and fast."

My dick had lowered to half-mast. I wasn't going to fuck anyone tonight.

I braced myself.

When I told Wendy, it wasn't going to be pretty.

CHAPTER SEVEN

Daphne

Patty hadn't returned to the room yet. She and Sean had been gone for over an hour on their walk. I knew nothing about my new roommate. Would she sleep with a guy she just met? I had no idea.

I looked at my watch. Nearly midnight.

I didn't want to go to bed yet. The first night in a new bed—a new place altogether—was the perfect storm for my nightmares.

Part of me wished I'd told Mom about the dream, but she might not have let me come to college. She was pretty protective.

I wanted to be here. I wanted a fresh start.

No one knew me here. No one knew I'd been sent away for most of my junior year of high school. I wasn't strange Daphne here.

I was Daphne Wade. College freshman, just like everyone else.

I wasn't overly social, but I couldn't bring myself to undress and get into bed. I'd go to the lounge on the first floor. Maybe I'd meet a few people.

Maybe Brad Steel would be there.

No, he wouldn't. He'd told me he lived off campus in a

condo with Sean. Even if he hadn't gone straight home, he wouldn't be hanging out in a freshman dorm.

Voices and laughter rang out as I neared the lounge. Definitely a party going on. With booze. Everyone here was a freshman, though. How did they get alcohol?

I walked in, and a good-looking young man approached me with a red cup like the one I'd drunk beer from earlier.

"Welcome," he said in a British accent. "Try this."

"What is it?"

He smirked. "Hell if I know. Some bloke's brother brought it over. But it's fucking delicious."

"Uh . . . okay. Thanks."

"No problem. I'm Ennis Ainsley."

"Hi, Ennis."

"That's when you tell me your name, love."

"Oh, sorry. Daphne. Daphne Wade."

"Lovely to meet you, Daphne Wade." He took a drink from his own red cup. "I'm on an exchange program, and let me tell you, it's weird not being able to buy my own drinks here."

"What's the legal age in the UK?"

"Eighteen. I'm nineteen, nearly twenty."

"What are you doing in a freshman dorm, then?"

"I'm a sophomore, technically, but since I don't know anyone, they put me in here so I could meet people and go through orientation." He took another sip. "You going to try that?"

"Yeah. Sure." I brought the plastic cup to my lips and let a little of the pinkish liquid spill into my mouth. Sweetness with a tinge of pungent alcohol slid over my tongue and down my throat. "Wow. Delicious."

"Told you. I'm not sure what the hell's in it, but go slowly, love, or you'll be sozzled before you know it."

"Sozzled?"

"Pissed. Sloshed."

"Drunk, you mean?"

"If you want a more mundane way of saying it. Sure."

I smiled. "Thanks for the warning."

"No worries. Want to find someplace quiet to talk?"

"I don't think there's any place quiet around here. This place is packed."

"My roommate isn't here yet, which means there's no one in my room."

"I don't think—"

"I'm a gentleman, love. I'm not looking for a quickie. Just a friend."

A friend?

How long had it been since I had a real friend?

A lifetime?

Had I ever had a true friend?

Only once, it seemed. Sage Peterson had moved the summer after sophomore year of high school, and we lost touch.

Maybe Ennis Ainsley could be my second friend.

"I'm not comfortable going to your room, but we could go to mine. My roommate isn't back yet, but she'll be home in a while."

"Works for me. Lead the way."

"Okay."

"Let's replenish first."

He grabbed my cup, which, oddly, I'd drained just standing there talking to him. I felt at ease with Ennis. Was it the drink or him?

A little of both, probably. I loved his accent, and he'd been nothing but friendly and gentlemanly.

He was handsome, too. Light-brown hair and blue eyes. Tall. I liked tall, since I was tall. He wasn't quite as tall as Brad Steel, but he was tall enough. I didn't feel a spark, though. Not like I'd felt the first time I'd locked eyes with Brad.

We walked back to my room, and I unlocked the door.

"Come on in. We haven't really gotten settled yet."

"None of us have."

"We can sit on my bed, I guess. Patty has the top bunk. Or the desk chairs."

"Bed's fine. A little more comfortable, I'd say."

"Okay." I sat and patted the spot next to me.

He sat as well. "So where are you from, Daphne?"

"Westminster."

"You don't have the accent." He smiled.

"Westminster, Colorado, silly. It's a suburb of Denver."

"Ah. Didn't know that."

"Well, now you do."

Okay, now what to say? I came up with nothing, so I took a big gulp of my drink. It seemed to get sweeter the more I drank.

"What are you here to study?" he asked.

"I don't really know yet. You?"

"Literature, I think. It's my first love. I'd like to write and to teach."

"Cool."

Cool. *Great, Daphne. Now what?*

"I seem to be empty again." Ennis pointed to his cup. "You want another?"

"I'm not sure."

"Okay. I'll be right back." He stood.

I impulsively handed him my cup. "Yeah. Another, please."

"Will do."

I waited on my bed for Ennis to return. My mind was a little muddled, but I was okay. I actually liked the feeling. It made me forget...things. I stood to make sure I wasn't drinking too much. I walked across the room to my desk in a straight line without stumbling, though it took some work.

"Knock knock," Ennis said, entering. "Here you go."

I took the red cup from him and swallowed a mouthful. Yeah, definitely getting sweeter.

"So why did you come to Colorado?" I asked.

The words sounded like they came from somewhere other than my mouth.

"Always wanted to see mountains. I've been to the US several times, but always the East Coast. Your country is so huge. I'm not sure I could see all of it in a lifetime."

"I'm not sure anyone who actually lives here could," I replied. "It's so vig and bast."

"Sorry?"

"It's so big and vast."

"Right. You first said vig and bast."

A huge laugh erupted from my throat. "I did not."

"You did, love." He took my cup. "I think maybe that's enough for you."

"Give that back!" I grabbed it from him, spilling a few precious drops onto the floor. I was almost tempted to suck them out of the carpet. Instead, I brought the cup to my lips and poured the rest of the contents down my throat.

Then I hiccupped. "Oops," I laughed.

Ennis took my cup and tossed it into the wastebasket by Patty's desk. "Sozzled, Miss Daphne. I'm cutting you off."

I stood...and the room moved. Sort of. "The hell you are." I dug through the trash and grabbed my cup. "I'm going to get more."

"You're not."

"Just watch me." I pushed Ennis out of the way and stumbled down the hallway to the lounge.

Almost there. Almost there.

Until I fell in the hallway.

"I've got you, love." Ennis pulled me into his arms.

Nausea. *God, I'm going to—*

I threw up on his chest.

"Fuck!" he said.

"I'm so sorr—"

Again. More pink puke that would surely stain his white cotton shirt.

"Come on. Bathroom for you." He hauled me to the nearest bathroom door and got me into a stall.

"That's it," he said. "Get it all out."

I heaved a few more times before I was done. I wasn't crying, but tears rolled down my cheeks.

I turned to Ennis, who was still holding my head. "I'm okay now. I think."

"It's my fault. I shouldn't have given you that last cup."

"I'm eighteen years old, Ennis. I should know what I'm doing. I'm really sorry about..." I looked at his shirt.

"This old thing? Not a worry. I was going to throw it out tomorrow."

"Bull. It looks brand-new."

"It's trash."

"Yeah," I agreed. "It is now, anyway."

He smiled at me then. A friendly smile.

I'd ruined his shirt, but I'd found something amazing. A friend.

CHAPTER EIGHT

Brad

"Let's go, baby," Wendy said, feigning a struggle against the bindings. "I'm so ready."

I walked to the head of the bed and detached the binding on her right hand. "This isn't going to happen."

"Bullshit," she said. "This always happens."

"Not tonight." I walked around the bed and released her other wrist. "And not ever again."

"You've said that before, Brad."

She was right. I had. More than once, for sure. This time was different, though.

"I mean it this time."

"You've said that before too."

"So have you."

We'd had knock-down-drag-outs about never seeing each other again, about ending it once and for all, but neither of us ever held up that bargain.

"You know I never mean it, baby," she said. "I love you. It will always be you. There will never be anyone else for me."

Again, words I'd heard many times before. Words I'd stopped saying in return about a year ago. Had she noticed I didn't say "I love you" anymore? She certainly didn't act like she had.

"I need you to leave," I said.

"My clothes are in the living room."

Fuck. Murph and Patty had walked right into—

Fuck it all. Patty had seen women's clothes. Women's clothes that were not her roommate's.

"Damn it all to hell." I raced out of my bedroom to the living room.

"Hey, Steel." Murph held up Wendy's push-up bra. "Looks like you're having a good time in there."

"Not what it looks like." I gathered up the rest of Wendy's clothes and yanked the bra from Murph's hand.

"You've got a naked woman in your room, bro."

"Yeah, and you'll notice I'm still fully clothed."

"Hey, you don't owe me any explanations."

He was right. I didn't. I didn't owe him or Patty anything. Or even Daphne Wade.

I couldn't explain it, but I didn't want Patty running home and telling Daphne I'd been with another woman. Even though I hadn't actually been with her.

All this time, Patty didn't speak. Should I say something to her? Beg her not to tell Daphne? Tell her nothing had happened between Wendy and me? Other than a few slaps and tickles, but that was nothing.

Nothing. Best not to say anything.

"Fuck you!" Wendy's voice carried from the bedroom. "You can just fuck off, Bradford Steel. I don't care if I never see you again!"

"Yup," Murph said, "that's Wendy."

"Who's Wendy?" Patty finally asked.

"Steel's girlfriend."

"*Not* my girlfriend," I said adamantly.

"Okay, his on-again, off-again girlfriend."

"We are permanently off-again," I said. "Excuse me."

I went back into my bedroom and threw Wendy's clothes on the bed. "Get dressed."

"You're a cocksucker, Brad. A prick. A fucking prick."

Words. Just words. I'd heard them all before.

Wendy had an amazing mind, and I'd realized recently that with genius came crazy, at least for Wendy. Not just a little cuckoo as I'd always known, but big crazy. Big out-of-her-mind crazy.

I couldn't fix Wendy Madigan, and I was done trying.

She'd be out of my life for good now.

"You got nothing to say to that? Not going to call me a crazy-assed bitch like you usually do?"

"Not this time," I said quietly. "This time, I'm done with all that. You're toxic, Wendy, and we're toxic together. It's over."

"Fuck you. *I'll* decide when it's over."

"Get dressed," I said again.

She stalked toward me, pulled my head to hers, and kissed me. Hard.

I kept my lips sealed shut and pushed her away. "It's over. Over and done, and I don't want to see you again. Ever."

She stepped into her panties. "We'll see about that."

Yeah, she wouldn't go quietly. I'd always known the final breakup with Wendy would be long and painful.

But I was ready now. Finally.

Ready to say goodbye forever.

And hello to a new life with someone else.

A normal life with a normal woman.

Man, wouldn't that be something?

"Fuck you, Brad. You think you can erase me from

your life? It'll never happen. We're connected, Brad. We're connected, and we always will be."

"You're wrong. I don't love you, Wendy."

"You just wait. You won't be able to exist without me. You'll return to me again and again just like you always have." She finished dressing and grabbed my chin, drawing me down to meet her fiery blue gaze. "You'll never be rid of me, Bradford Steel. Never."

She walked out of my bedroom.

I stayed for about five minutes until I heard the front door slam.

Murph and Patty must have left. Who could blame them? Or they went to Murph's room, though Patty Watson, Iowa pig farm girl, hardly seemed the type to put out on the first date, especially after Murph had been kind of douchy at dinner.

Then again, I could be wrong.

Distinct moaning wafted from Murph's bedroom. I smiled. At least *he* was getting some.

My erection had subsided during the battle with Wendy. I could get it back, but did I want to?

I scanned my watch. After midnight. Would Daphne Wade still be up? The partying never stopped during orientation week, so she might be.

It was worth a try.

CHAPTER NINE

Daphne

A judge was pounding his gavel inside my head.

"You need a shower, love?" Ennis asked.

"Yeah. But first I need to brush my teeth." I stood, still pretty wobbly.

"I'll get your stuff," he said. "Just tell me where it is in your room."

Had I even unpacked my toothbrush? I couldn't remember. "I have no idea."

"All right. Stay here. I'll get some toothpaste and gargle. That'll freshen you up."

"My clothes…"

"You got a robe?"

"Yeah, yeah. I know I hung that in the closet. It's burgundy terry cloth."

"I'll get it for you. Get in the shower, and I'll bring a towel from my room and get your robe."

"But the toothpaste…"

"Get your shower. Then we'll clean your teeth."

"Thank you, Ennis. Thanks for taking care of me."

He nodded and left the bathroom. I stumbled to a shower stall and peeled off my clothes. My first instinct was to burn them, but I'd been wearing them when I met Brad Steel. For some reason, that was significant to me. I didn't have shampoo, but someone had left a well-used bar of soap in the stall, so I could at least get clean. I brought my blouse into the shower with me to rinse off the puke before the pink from the drink could stain it.

My hair was falling out of its braid, and I tugged the rest out of the band and unwound it, letting the water run over it and plaster it to my shoulders and back. I grabbed the soap, lathered my whole body, and rinsed, feeling not exactly clean but better.

I washed my blouse as best I could, though a light-pink tinge still remained. I sighed. This was one of my favorite blouses, and I couldn't ask my parents for money for another. They were struggling as it was, with all my doctor's bills and now additional expenses associated with my college.

My first day at college . . . and here I was, drunk and alone in a shower stall, having ruined my favorite blouse.

Nice job, Daphne. Nice job.

I exited the stall and found a towel and my burgundy robe sitting by one of the sinks. Thank God for Ennis Ainsley. I dried off and put the robe on, wishing I had a brush to run through the tangled mess of my hair.

But I didn't, so I left the bathroom.

Ennis stood outside. "Feeling better, love?"

I smiled . . . or at least tried to. "A little."

"Here." He handed me a toothbrush and toothpaste. "I found it in your room. Get the taste out of your mouth."

I nodded, walked back into the bathroom, and brushed the heck out of my teeth.

Ennis was still in the hallway when I returned. "I'm sorry. I tried to warn you to go slowly with that drink."

FATE

"You did. It's my own fault."

Take responsibility for your actions, Dr. Payne always said. *No one controls you but you.*

"You'll be fine by morning. There's a big day planned with orientation festivities."

"Ugh," I said. "The thought of orientation festivities makes me want to get sick all over again."

"It'll be fun. You'll see."

We stopped at the door to my room.

"Get to bed, now. A good night of sleep is all you need."

"My head hurts."

"Do you have anything for a headache?"

"In one of my boxes somewhere."

"I've got some in my room. Go ahead in. I'll bring it to you with a large glass of water. You'll be good as new come morning."

I nodded and let myself into my room. Thank God for the bottom bunk. I couldn't handle climbing at the moment.

A few minutes later, a knock sounded on the door. I hoped it was Ennis, because I was too exhausted to get up and look.

"Come in," I said.

The door opened.

But it wasn't Ennis.

"Hi, Daphne," came the deep voice of Brad Steel.

Oh, God. I knew I looked like hell. My long hair was tangled and plastered to my neck and chest. I wore nothing but the burgundy robe.

"Shit, are you all right?" he asked, walking in.

No, I was so not all right. I was embarrassed beyond all get-out. The most amazing guy I'd ever met, who'd given me such a tender kiss earlier tonight, was seeing me at my worst.

50

"What happened?" he asked again.

"Nothing. I'm fine."

"You're not fine. You've been drinking."

"So? You and Sean drank at dinner."

"Sean and I are used to alcohol. What were you drinking?"

"I don't know. Some pinkish punch someone made."

"Most likely Everclear. That shit's a hundred and twenty proof at minimum."

"What's that mean?"

"It means you were drinking sixty percent alcohol. It's banned in some states."

"But not here?"

"Nope. Oh, man. Who gave you that stuff? I'm going to kick the shit out of him."

"Ennis."

"Who's Ennis?"

"My friend Ennis."

"Did I hear my name?" Ennis walked in the door, carrying the promised glass of water.

"You Ennis?" Brad asked.

"Yeah, who are you?"

Brad didn't answer.

Instead, he punched Ennis in the jaw.

CHAPTER TEN

Brad

The glass of water the guy carried fell from his hand and shattered on the tile floor of the hallway when he toppled against the wall. I raised my fists, ready to pounce—

"Brad, no!"

I turned.

Daphne stood right outside her door, her robe falling precariously and baring one milky shoulder.

"Please," she said. "It's not his fault. *I* drank it."

"He gave it to you."

"He simply brought me a drink," she said, her eyes glistening.

God, please don't cry. Please don't cry.

Daphne didn't cry.

The guy stood, rubbing his jaw. "Mate, I didn't do anything to her."

British, apparently. Great. I should apologize. That was what a gentleman would do. But the words didn't come.

"Did she get sick?" I asked him.

"She did. I took care of her. I was bringing her some aspirin and water."

I regarded Daphne Wade, and an overwhelming desire to protect her from every evil in the world surged through me. Maybe she reminded me of my mother. Her coloring was similar. I hadn't been able to protect my mother from everything. But I sure as hell wanted to protect this woman in front of me—this woman I hardly knew, but who had the softest lips I'd ever kissed.

"You owe Ennis an apology," Daphne said softly.

I did, but he wasn't going to get one. My old man had taught me never to apologize. It was weak.

Of course my old man was a Grade A asshole, too.

"Not necessary," Ennis said.

Good. I was off the hook, until Daphne's eyes darkened with anger.

"Say you're sorry, Brad. He deserves that much."

"Please, Daph, let it go. I'm bowing out politely." Ennis walked down the hallway.

"You're a prick," she said to me.

I couldn't deny the truth of her words, so I didn't. "I'll get a janitor up here to clean this up." I motioned to the glass and water on the floor.

"Or you could clean it up yourself," she said. "It's your fault, after all."

Was she kidding? I'd had housekeepers my whole life. I'd never cleaned up a mess inside. I'd cleaned a lot of barns, though. Nasty shit, literally. But . . . no.

"The dorms have people who are paid to do this," I told her.

"At one in the morning?"

She had a valid point. "Do you have . . . a broom or something?"

"You have to pick up the larger pieces first." She sighed. "I'll show you."

"No, stay there. You have bare feet. I don't want you to step on any of this."

"All right. Pick up what you can see and throw them out. Then we'll need a wet-dry vac."

"Where am I supposed to find a wet-dry vac?"

"I have no idea. You've been here for three years. I've been here one day."

"Oh, for God's sake." I picked up all the large pieces of glass and threw them away in the large wastebasket at the end of the hallway. When I returned, I said, "I'll go see about that wet-dry vac."

"Okay." She yawned.

I was being an asshole like my old man. She hadn't gotten the water and aspirin for her headache. "I'm sorry. Go to bed, okay? I'll bring you the water and meds for your head. Then I'll take care of this."

"You'll have to warn people not to step on it. They could slip on the water or get a sliver of glass in their foot."

"Hopefully people aren't walking around here barefoot," I said.

"No, take care of the glass and water first," she said adamantly. "I'll be fine."

She was something else. "All right."

She went back into her room and closed the door. Before I could ponder where in hell I'd find this wet-dry vac she spoke of, her pal Ennis came loping up with something that might fit the bill.

"Figured we'd better get this cleaned up. Once the booze runs out downstairs, everyone'll be coming up here to bed."

"Yeah. Thanks, I guess."

"Don't mention it. I got this. I'm the one who made the mess."

"Because I punched you."

"True."

"Hey...I'm..."

"It's fine." He plugged the thing in and began cleaning.

Yeah, I was being a dick. But around Daphne, I didn't want to be a dick. Where could I find some aspirin for her?

"Hey," I said to Ennis. "Do you have more aspirin?"

"Yeah. Help yourself. My room's open. It's on the lower level, room 103. Sitting on the dresser."

"Roommate?"

"Hasn't arrived yet."

"Thanks, man."

I scurried down to Ennis's room and found the aspirin. I made a pit stop in the lounge where the party—and the Everclear punch—was still going strong and snagged an empty cup. I filled it with water from a drinking fountain and headed back up to Daphne's room.

Ennis and the shop vac were gone, so I knocked gently on Daphne's door.

"Come in," she said softly.

I entered. She was lying on her bed on top of the covers. Her robe had parted slightly, giving me a view of her cleavage. My groin tightened. Damn.

"I got you another cup of water, this one unbreakable."

"Thanks."

"Come on. Sit up. Take the pills and drink all the water. It'll keep you from feeling completely shitty tomorrow."

"The thought of putting anything in my mouth..."

"I know. But you need to. Come on."

"Where's Ennis?"

"He found your wet-vac thing and cleaned up the mess."

"Is that what I heard? Why did he clean it up? You made it."

"Actually, he's the one who dropped the glass."

"Because you punched him for no good reason."

"It's over now, Daphne. Here." I handed her the pills.

She popped them in her mouth and took a sip of water.

"The rest," I said.

She dutifully drank all the water and handed me the cup. "Go now. I don't want you to see me like this."

"I've already seen you like this."

"Crap," she muttered, falling back onto the bed. "Where's Patty?"

"She's at my place with Murph."

"You mean Sean?"

"Yeah, with Sean."

"What's she doing . . . ? Oh." Daphne laid her arm over her forehead, covering her eyes. "Of course. That's why you came here. You want sex."

I couldn't fault her observation, given what Murph and Patty were doing, but that wasn't why I'd come. I could have had eight different kinds of monkey sex with Wendy if sex were all I was after. "I'm not looking for sex."

"Of course you're not now. I look atrocious."

"Hey, you look beautiful," I said, meaning every word.

"I'm a mess. God, my hair is going to be in knots by morning."

"Then brush it out now. Where's your brush?"

"I don't know. Where did I put that stuff? The top dresser drawer, I think."

I stood and walked to the dressers. I had to guess which one was Daphne's. I opened the top drawer of the closer one, and inside sat a hairbrush with a hot-pink handle. "The pink one?" I asked.

"Yeah, that's the one."

I brought it back and handed it to her. "Here you go."

"I'm too tired to do anything." Another yawn split her pretty face. "I'll just deal with it in the morning."

"You just rest," I said. "I'll take care of it."

Then I did something I never imagined myself doing in a million years. As Daphne closed her eyes, I began to brush out her hair.

CHAPTER ELEVEN

Daphne

The sun streamed into the room, waking me. I'd passed out and had forgotten to close the window blinds.

Ugh. I still felt kind of queasy, but at least my head had stopped pounding. I eyed the clock far away on my desk. Six a.m. Orientation stuff started at eight, so I should get up. I had a lot to do. My hair would be a ratty mass of knots.

I rose slowly and walked over to the mirror above my dresser to assess the damage. Hmm. My hair looked fine. A little messy from sleep, but otherwise fresh and silky with no knots. Before I had time to ponder how this had happened, I jolted when the door burst open.

"Hey, Daph." Patty smiled.

"Oh, hi." Patty hadn't come home? I'd just assumed I slept through it, since I wasn't sure anything short of a tornado could have woken me last night. This meant she'd spent the night with Sean. My tummy churned a little. I wasn't judgmental by nature, but she and Sean had just met. She didn't volunteer any information, and I didn't ask.

Not my business.

"Ugh! I need a shower," Patty said. "Then we'll have time to hit the cafeteria for breakfast before orientation begins. You in?"

My stomach was still a little iffy, but breakfast would probably help that. Plus, there'd be coffee there. A definite plus.

"Yeah, I'm in." I gathered my supplies so I could take a real shower, complete with shampoo. I was already in my bathrobe. I waited for Patty to ditch her clothes from yesterday and robe up, and we headed to the stalls.

No waiting, which was nice. Six o'clock in the morning was clearly not a popular time with college students. I shampooed my hair, still wondering at its freshly brushed softness. Then I scrubbed from head to toe. I still felt a little dirty from the previous night's drinking. After my shower, brushing my teeth again was pure heaven! Finally, the last remnants of pink puke were gone from my body.

Never again.

How in the world did anyone become an alcoholic? I couldn't see it. Not from this angle.

We dressed quickly in shorts and tank tops and headed to the cafeteria. The walk was slightly brisk, but this was September in Colorado. The day would warm up soon, and we'd be happy we'd worn shorts.

Footsteps sounded behind us.

I turned to see Ennis Ainsley and another guy hurrying to catch up with us. "Hi," I said.

"Hey, Daphne."

The bruising on his jawline brought the evening back in living color. "I'm sorry. Does it hurt much?"

"Nah. I'm good. This is Dirk. He's in the room next to mine."

"Hey," I said. "This is my roommate, Patty."

We all shook hands, and Ennis said, "You ladies want to join us for breakfast?"

"Fine with me," I said. "Pat?"

"Sure. The more the merrier."

Breakfast was definitely a good idea. Scrambled eggs were my comfort food when I wasn't feeling good, and they did the trick. A slice of bacon and a cup of coffee rounded out the meal for me.

"This isn't worth eating." Patty threw down the slice of bacon she'd taken a bite of.

"We don't have bacon like this in the UK," Ennis said. "Unfortunate, because I think it's delicious."

"You should try the bacon we make on my farm," Patty said. "So much better than this crap. Plus, we don't cure it, so no nitrates. Those things'll kill you."

"What a way to go, though," Dirk said. "Bacon is the perfect food."

Ennis looked to me. "What say you, love? Where are you on the bacon debate?"

"I don't really have an opinion." Really, were we discussing bacon? This was college?

"Pick a side, Daph," Patty said.

"I like bacon. That's my side. I just don't like thinking about..."

Patty laughed. "Daphne is a carnivore who loves animals."

The two guys laughed as well. My cheeks warmed. They were making fun of me.

"Go vegan then," Dirk said. "Save the bunnies."

"I'm not against consuming meat," I said. "I just want the animals to be treated with respect."

"Hey, I totally respect the pig who gave up his life so I could have bacon," Dirk said. "Life without bacon isn't a life worth living."

Ennis and Patty laughed.

And I decided I didn't like Dirk much.

"I just mean I like the animals to be treated humanely while they're raised for meat. I know you treat your pigs humanely, Patty, but most animals raised for meat aren't treated that way."

"If it bothers you, love," Ennis said, "do something about it."

"What can I do?"

"First off, stop eating mass-produced meat. You can buy from local ranches and farms."

Dirk grabbed the remainder of my slice of bacon off my plate. "That means you don't want this." He shoved it in his mouth.

Yeah, Dirk was a jerk. It even rhymed.

"Unfortunately, you're not going to find anything but mass-produced meat at a college cafeteria," Patty said. "Tell you what. I can get my family to send us pork from the farm. We can eat that."

"How would we cook it?" I asked.

"There's the kitchenette in the dorm," she said. "Or better yet, I bet we could store it and cook it at Sean's condo."

Sean's condo was also Brad's condo. That meant I'd see Brad.

"It's not a bad idea," Patty went on. "I'd even join you. We eat vegetarian here in the cafeteria, and when we feel like meat, we get it from my family or we find other sources of humanely raised meat."

"Brad Steel said all his animals are treated humanely," I said softly. "Plus they're grass fed."

Patty clammed up at the mention of Brad Steel. I wasn't

sure what, if any, significance that had.

"Brad?" Ennis said. "The guy who used my jaw for a punching bag?"

Right. For a moment I'd forgotten. Brad had been an ass.

Still, I couldn't stop thinking about him. Did we still have a date for pizza? I had no idea, after last night's debacle.

He'd treated Ennis, my first real friend here, like crap. But he'd been nice to me.

"That reminds me," Patty said. "He and Sean are picking us up at six tonight for pizza. That work for you?"

That answered my question. "Sure. Fine."

"You're going out with that Neanderthal?" Ennis said.

"It's not a date, really," I said. "I hardly know him."

Again, Patty said nothing. This was getting weird. Did she know something about Brad Steel that she didn't want to tell me?

"To each his own." Ennis looked at his watch. "We should go. The first program starts in an hour."

After depositing our trays, we headed out.

Orientation was a whirlwind of lectures, activities, and mixers. The four of us stuck together, although I could have done without Dirk. I was glad to be rid of him when, after lunch, we divided into our dormitory corridors and Patty and I met the rest of the girls on our floor.

Our senior counselor, Mariel, led us through some "get to know you" activities and then sat us down, saying it was time to discuss something important.

"Last school year," she said, "three college girls were raped on campus. Only one of the perpetrators was caught and convicted. This is a growing problem, so please keep yourselves safe. We have an escort service available. If you're alone after dark and need to be escorted back to your dorm, use the service. A male student who has been vetted will walk you safely wherever you need to go."

My heart started to beat a little faster. I wasn't sure why. It was scary to think we might not be safe here. Her comments never left my thoughts the rest of the day.

Mariel and the rest of our floor headed to dinner, but Patty and I begged out and returned to our room to wait for Brad and Sean to pick us up. I decided to wear my hair down. I pulled it out of the braid and let its wavy length fall down my back nearly to my butt.

"You have great hair," Patty said.

"So do you. I love the color." No lie. I never liked red hair much, but Patty's was a lovely strawberry golden, and it was perfect on her.

"I wish it were as thick as yours, though." She looked in the mirror, and then she turned to face me. "I slept with Sean."

"I figured as much, since you didn't get home until six a.m."

"I know, but I want you to know that I don't normally do stuff like that."

"Was that ... your first time?"

"No. I had a boyfriend in high school, and we did it a couple times. I didn't expect it to happen with Sean last night, but ... one thing led to another."

"And ... ?"

"It was amazing. So much better than with the first guy."

"He's older and more experienced, probably."

"Definitely." Patty turned back to the mirror and applied some lip gloss. "I'm not sure where it's headed, though. College guys are different. They're just looking for sex, you know?"

I didn't know, actually. Brad Steel had been a perfect gentleman—to me, at least. Punching Ennis hadn't been very gentlemanly. Ennis had been kind as well. Even Dirk the jerk hadn't come on to either Patty or me. Mariel's rape speech crossed my mind once more.

"Maybe Sean's different."

"I doubt it. His roommate isn't."

My heart dropped to my stomach. "What do you mean?" Though I wasn't sure I wanted to know.

"He had a woman at the condo last night."

The words sliced into me. But how? He'd been with me last night until one a.m. "He did?"

"Yeah."

No. Couldn't be. "Oh."

"So . . . I mean, pizza's still on tonight. I just don't want you to go in with any expectations, you know? I don't want you to get hurt."

"Yeah," I said softly. "Thanks for telling me. But I hardly know the guy. I don't have any expectations yet."

Except that I did.

And now they'd been dashed.

CHAPTER TWELVE

Brad

Daphne Wade looked even more beautiful than she had last night.

Hell, even in a bathrobe with knotted hair and nausea, the woman had been a goddess. Of course, I'd seen beautiful women before. It wasn't her beauty that attracted me so much. It was something else. Something I still couldn't quite put my finger on.

She was quiet tonight. She sat beside me in the passenger seat of my truck, and once we got to Westminster, she guided me to the pizza place.

Murphy and Patty sat in the back seat, talking about nothing in particular and making out a little.

"Are you still mad about me decking that guy last night?" I finally asked.

"No."

Okay, then what was the problem?

We pulled into Rosetti's Pizza and Pasta, and I parked the car.

"It's a weeknight," Daphne said, "so we should be able to get right in."

True to her word, we were soon seated in a booth opposite Murph and Patty. I ordered a pitcher of Coke and then cleared my throat. "This was your idea," I said to Daphne, "so what do you recommend?"

"The New York–style pizza, with whatever toppings you want. I'm having mushroom and black olive."

"What about pepperoni?" I asked. "You ate it last night."

"I've decided to stop eating meat."

I lifted my eyebrows. "Oh?"

"Well, not all meat. Only meat that's not humanely raised."

"Yeah," Patty piped in. "I'm going to have my family send us some pork from Iowa. We just need a place to store and cook it. Hint. Hint."

Daphne's cheeks blushed a beautiful pink.

"Sure, you can keep it at our place," Sean said. "We have a huge freezer. Brad keeps us stocked with great beef. Right, Brad?"

"Not a problem," I said.

"Thanks," Daphne murmured.

The server came by and took our order. Daphne and Patty ordered pizza with mushrooms and black olives. I wasn't sure I could be a vegetarian, even for a night, so Murph and I ordered the supreme. A man needed his protein. There were limits to what I'd do for a woman, even one as beautiful and interesting as Daphne Wade.

Patty was a chatterbox and engaged Sean and me most of the evening. Daphne stayed quiet. Although she hadn't been overly talkative last night, this was a definite difference.

The server laid the check down and I grabbed it. I had unlimited funds, and I enjoyed treating my friends. They were always very appreciative.

"Thanks, dude," Murph said.

"Yeah, thanks so much," Patty said. "I have to agree with

you, Daph. This pizza was spectacular."

Daphne smiled at her roommate and nodded. "Told you."

How I wished that smile had been for me.

"It was pretty damned good," Murph agreed. "You ladies up for a nightcap back at our place?"

"Sounds great to me," Patty said.

I turned to Daphne. "You don't have to drink, but I hope you'll come."

"No thank you," she said.

"Come on, Daph," Patty urged. "It'll be fun."

Daphne arched her eyebrows at her roommate. Something wasn't right. She cleared her throat. "I promised Ennis I'd meet him and Dirk for a drink."

"Oh. Okay. I guess it's just me, guys," Patty said.

I looked Daphne straight in the eye. "Cancel."

She raised an eyebrow. "Why should I?"

"Because I'm asking you to. Because I want to spend the evening with you."

"I believe in honoring my commitments."

"You're not breaking a commitment," I said. "You're postponing it."

"I don't see why I should—"

"Do it. Please."

Her gaze never wavered from mine. She was looking at me. Looking into me. Looking for something, and I wasn't sure what.

"I . . . can't."

I got up from the booth and extended my hand to her. "Come outside with me for a minute. I want to talk to you."

"We're leaving anyway," Daphne said. "You just paid the check. Thank you, by the way."

"You're welcome. Now come talk with me."

"Go ahead," Murphy said. "Patty and I are happy to hang here for a few."

"Come on," I urged.

When she put her hand in mine, sparks shot through me. She stood and I led her outside. We found a bench a few yards away from the entrance.

"Sit," I said.

She sighed and sat down.

"What's going on?" I asked. "I thought we had something special starting."

"So did I."

"Then what's wrong? Did you change your mind?"

"I didn't," she said, "but apparently you did."

"What are you talking about?"

"Patty told me you were with a woman last night."

Shit. "That didn't mean—"

She held up her hand to stop me. "Don't. It doesn't matter anyway. We just met. You're way older than I am. I'd be a disappointment to you."

"Daphne, you could never be a disappointment to me."

"How can you say that? You don't even know me."

"I know you're beautiful on the inside and out."

"No, you don't."

"Are you kidding? You love animals so much that you're willing to give up eating meat unless it's humanely raised."

"That was Ennis's idea."

Ennis? Why the hell did she have to mention Ennis? Was she attracted to that Brit? I remained calm. "It was?"

"Yeah. I love meat. I don't want to give it up. He told me to do something about it, and Patty had the idea of her family sending us humanely raised pork from the farm."

"But the idea came about because of your love of animals."

"Yeah, but I never did anything before."

"You're eighteen. No one does anything when they're a kid."

"It . . . is a good idea."

I smiled. "It is. And I'll do you one better. You're welcome to all the beef Murph and I have. We couldn't possibly eat it all, and I promise you we treat our animals well."

"I don't want anything from you."

"I'm offering."

"Offer it to your other women."

"Daphne, I'm not interested in any other women. The girl at our place last night is from my past. She's having a hard time letting go."

Of course, I'd almost fucked her, but Daphne didn't need to know that.

She bit her lip. "Like I said, I'd be a disappointment."

"Why do you keep saying that?"

"I'm . . . I'm a virgin, Brad. I can't give you sex."

Her confession didn't surprise me. I'd known instinctively that I had to go slow with Daphne. Something about the way she carried herself. Wendy and I had taken each other's virginity long ago in high school when she was sixteen and I was seventeen. That had come with its own problems—none of which I wanted to think about at the moment.

"Who says I want sex?"

"You're a guy, and you're a senior in college. Of course you want sex."

She wasn't wrong, but for her, I was willing to forgo sex. For a while, anyway. Why? I couldn't say. I just knew Daphne was something special, and the desire to protect her coiled through me in a way I didn't fully understand.

"I'm not after sex with you."

"What do you want, then?"

"Right now? I want you to postpone your drink with Prince Charles and spend the evening with me."

She smiled at the Prince Charles remark. Her friend Ennis did sort of resemble the future monarch, with his wavy brown hair and blue eyes. He was better looking than the prince, though, which didn't sit well with me.

"I wouldn't feel right about that."

I sighed. "All right. I tried. Keep tomorrow night open for me, okay?"

"Are you sure that's what you want?"

"I've never been surer about anything."

CHAPTER THIRTEEN

Daphne

I didn't actually have plans with Ennis and Dirk. I certainly didn't care if I ever saw Dirk again, but I did like Ennis a lot. I truly felt we could be friends. He'd been nothing but a gentleman. Hadn't tried a thing with me, and so far, I wasn't interested in him in that way.

Brad Steel, though? He was perfection. Male beauty like I'd never seen. Why he was interested in me mystified me. I was attractive, I knew, but I'd just told him I was a virgin and wasn't interested in sex. From what I understood, that would send most college guys running.

I'd lied about having plans because of the woman Patty mentioned. If Brad Steel was already involved with someone, I didn't want any part of him.

Except that I did.

I wanted him badly in a way I didn't fully comprehend, which scared the daylights out of me.

Brad dropped me off back at the dorm, and Patty went home with them for the nightcap. I sighed. Had I made the right choice? Patty most likely wouldn't be home again tonight, so I was alone. Another party was already starting in the lounge, but no way was I drinking again tonight. Or possibly ever. I wasn't in any hurry to relive that nightmare.

I could call home, but then my mother would worry. I'd only been gone two days. She was such a mother hen, especially after the events of junior year.

I tried not to think about those days. I didn't remember a lot of what went on during my hospitalization anyway, so thinking about it racked my nerves something awful. Losing a block of life was freaky, to say the least.

I remembered everything now. I forced myself to, from the important to the mundane. I didn't ever want to lose a part of me again. For example, I remembered that Brad Steel was wearing a black T-shirt, jeans, and leather sandals when I met him. I remembered his feet were as perfect as the rest of him. I remembered the warmth of his hand, the feel of his firm lips on my own.

Yeah, and what I had for breakfast each day, and so forth. Never again would I lose a part of my mind. I was determined.

What would Brad Steel think if he knew I'd spent the majority of my junior year of high school in a mental hospital? Would he still be interested? That was a lot more to deal with than my virginity.

No matter how much I tried not to think of that time, when I was alone, it always crept into my mind. I could go down to the lounge, forget my woes in some more pink punch, if indeed that was what they were serving up tonight.

I forced myself to remember everything, though, and one thing I'd never forget was how I felt last night.

Never again.

But what to do?

I checked my hair in the mirror and decided to see what my next-door neighbors were up to. We'd done some "get to know you" activities today. I knocked on the door next to ours.

No answer. Same for the door on the other side.

They were probably all down at the lounge party, where I didn't want to go.

If I wanted company, that was where I needed to be. Why not? I didn't have to drink. There was certainly no law forcing me to.

I went back to the room, braided my hair, and added a touch of lip gloss. Then I went to join the party.

"Hey, love!" Ennis brought me a cup.

I shook my head. "Not going there tonight."

"Relax. It's punch. You weren't the only one who experienced the horrors of last night's brew. Tonight it's strictly add your own booze if you want it."

I sniffed at the drink. "How can I be sure? I hardly tasted the liquor last night."

"Scout's honor," he said. "I poured it myself."

"All right." I took a drink. It was sweeter than last night's, which I guessed meant it wasn't spiked. I hoped, anyway.

Sex wasn't the only thing I had no experience with. Drinking was another, obviously.

"Not with the caveman tonight, eh?" Ennis said.

"Caveman?"

Ennis pointed to his jaw.

"Oh, Brad. He's really sorry about that, by the way."

"No hard feelings. He seems to like you a lot. I'm surprised you're not with him."

"I was. We had dinner, but that's over."

"I suppose I don't stand a chance against him, do I?"

"Oh. I guess I didn't realize . . ."

"What? That I might be interested in you? Daphne, you're the most beautiful girl in this room. In any room, actually."

I wasn't sure what to say.

"You really have no idea how spectacular you are, do you?"

"I mean ... I guess I'm attractive ..."

"Attractive? You're stunning. You're tall and lean with perfect curves. You're supermodel material, love."

I warmed all over. "I just ... I don't know. I'm just me, you know?"

"I'll settle for friendship, of course. You're a lovely person."

"Thank you. You're my only friend here so far."

"What about your roommate? The cute little redhead?"

"Patty. She's nice, but she's ..."

"Off with a guy?"

I smiled. "Yeah."

"So why aren't *you*, then?"

"I'm just not ready for any of that. Nothing serious, anyway. Seems like all these college guys are after sex."

That got a laugh out of him. "Can't say you're wrong about that."

"I'm not interested in going there yet."

"No hurry. Anyone who tries to make you go faster than you're comfortable with isn't who you need."

"I know."

"And the caveman ... ?"

"I'm here, aren't I? He's not forcing me into anything, but he wants to see me tomorrow night."

"And what do *you* want, love?"

"I don't know."

Except that I did. I wanted to be with Brad Steel. I wanted to give him everything he wanted. Everything I wasn't ready to give.

"Well, hang with me. Hands off, I promise. But if you ever change your mind . . ."

I smiled. "Nice to know. You look sort of like a better-looking Prince Charles. Sound like him too." Funny I hadn't noticed the resemblance until Brad pointed it out.

"The Queen's English. I was raised in London. I'm not a lord, but my father is. Technically I'm the Honourable Ennis Ainsley." He bowed.

"Really? That's cool."

"Just means my father was granted a life peerage. I can't inherit it, though, and my children won't have any title."

"Well, it's cool anyway." I took another drink.

A cute blonde joined us. "Hey, Ennis!"

"Hi, Molly." He returned her hug. "This is Daphne."

"Hi!" Molly said excitedly.

"Nice to meet you," I said.

She turned back to Ennis. Clearly, he was the one she'd come to talk to. They chatted about nothing in particular, and I felt myself fade into the background.

Invisible.

I was invisible.

I'd felt this way since the hospitalization. Crowds like this ate me up. Consumed me. Swallowed me.

"Hey, gorgeous."

I jolted. A tall guy touched my shoulder.

"Hi," I said.

"Want to dance?"

I looked around. "Are people dancing?"

"A few."

Ennis was still chatting with Molly. My nerves skittered. Did I want to dance? I'd never danced with a guy before. I didn't go to prom. No one asked me, and I wasn't going to go alone or with friends.

Besides, I didn't have any close friends in high school. Most of them lost interest in me when I disappeared junior year.

What was the harm? He seemed nice.

"Sure."

He led me over to a small area where a few couples were dancing slowly to the music. He pulled me close, and I copied what the other girls were doing, wrapping my arms around his neck.

The music was louder over here, so we didn't talk. I just danced with a nameless stranger.

He was a gentleman. Didn't try to touch anything he shouldn't. Not that I thought he would. I wasn't sure why I was hyperaware of things he shouldn't touch, but I was.

And he didn't.

When the song ended, he said, "Want to get a drink?"

"I'm not drinking tonight."

"Oh?"

"Last night's mixture had a detrimental effect."

"Yeah, that stuff was brutal. Can't blame you."

"What's your name?"

"Leif. You?"

"Daphne."

"Nice to meet you, Daphne."

"You too."

"I'll get you a virgin."

My brows nearly flew off my forehead. "A what?"

"A virgin drink. You know, no alcohol?"

"Oh. Yeah, thanks."

What was wrong with me? I had virgin on the brain. I felt like it was stamped across my forehead in big red letters.

Leif returned with two drinks and handed me one.

"Thanks," I said.

"You're welcome. What's your major?"

Classic college question. To which I had no answer. "I'm not sure yet. I'm going to get all my requirements out of the way this year and see what interests me the most."

"You must be interested in something."

Was I? I used to enjoy writing, but I got out of the habit when I lost so much time during junior year. Writing was difficult when you couldn't remember parts of your own life.

"English, I think," I said. "Maybe philosophy. How about you?"

"Engineering. It's a five-year program, so I'll be here an extra year."

"Oh. Interesting." Though it really wasn't.

"My father and my older brother are both engineers. It's what's expected."

"Do you want to be an engineer?"

"Doesn't really matter what I want."

"Of course it matters."

He laughed and took a drink. "Dad's paying the bills, so I study what he wants. That's the deal."

"What if that weren't the deal?" I asked.

"It is."

"But if it weren't, what would you study?"

"Science."

"What kind of science."

"Biology. Zoology. I'd like to be a veterinarian."

"Then that's what you should be."

He scoffed. "Not in the cards."

"It should be."

"It's not. Want to dance again?"

"No," a voice said from behind me. "The next dance is mine."

CHAPTER FOURTEEN

Brad

Jealousy raged through me. I'd expected to find Daphne with Prince Charles. That was who she'd said her plans were with, but he was across the room making out with a blonde. This guy was new.

She'd lied to me.

"Who are you?" the sandy-haired guy asked.

"Brad Steel. Let's dance, Daphne."

"I—"

I pulled her away before she could finish. Her drink sloshed as we walked swiftly out of the crowded lounge and outside. Darkness had fallen, and stars dotted the night sky. I grabbed the red cup out of her hand. "You're drinking? After last night?"

"It's virgin," she said.

I sniffed it and took a drink. She was right.

"You have to be careful," I said. "Those guys in there will try to get you drunk and then . . ."

"And then . . . what? I'm eighteen. I can take care of myself."

God, she was beautiful. So beautiful, and so naïve. I was only four years older, but those four years made all the difference.

If anyone hurt her . . .

If anyone hurt her . . . what? What would I do about it, and why should I even care?

But I did. I fucking cared. Protecting Daphne was of paramount importance to me, and I had no idea why.

"Why are you here?" she asked.

I didn't answer. I simply poured out what was left in her cup onto the ground. "This was spiked."

Why I lied, I had no idea.

"No. He said it was virgin."

"He's a guy, Daphne. Guys will try to get you drunk so they can fuck you."

Her mouth dropped open.

Yeah, so naïve.

"He seemed perfectly nice. He's studying to be an engineer."

"I don't care if he's studying to be a brain surgeon. He's still a college guy."

"So are you," she said.

"I'm . . . different."

"How, Brad? You had another girl at your place last night, so just how are you different?"

Her lips were glistening, her beautiful dark eyes burned. She was angry at me, justifiably angry. I couldn't help myself. I grabbed her, pulled her to my body, and crushed my lips to hers.

She didn't open. I traced her lips with the tip of my tongue and gently probed at the seam.

Then I pulled back slightly. "Please," I whispered. "Open for me, Daphne. Let me show you what a real kiss is."

She sighed and parted her lips.

I forced back my instinct to dive into her mouth and explore. Instead, I entered slowly, gently, finding her tongue and touching it with mine.

Had this beautiful woman ever been kissed? Really kissed? I hoped she hadn't. We'd shared a short one last night, but I wanted to be the one to show her what a kiss truly was, what a kiss could be.

What love could be.

Her tongue was even silkier than I remembered, warm and soft against my own. I tasted the traces of her fruity drink plus another lingering sweetness. A sweetness that was all her.

She sighed into my mouth, a soft noise that I felt through my whole body.

And I quivered. I actually quivered.

Had I ever quivered from a kiss?

Ever?

Her innocence charmed me, enticed me. Gave me the insatiable urge to keep her from harm, protect her from anything that might hurt her. So the guy she'd danced with hadn't spiked her drink. He might have eventually, and I'd protect her.

I deepened the kiss slightly, taking more of her mouth. Our lips slid together in passion, and I explored her gums, her teeth, the inside of her cheeks with my tongue. When she finally moved her own tongue, twirling it against mine, I couldn't hold back any longer.

I grabbed a handful of her dark hair and deepened the kiss so that our mouths were fused.

And she jerked away, our mouths parting with a loud smack. She inhaled sharply and wiped her mouth with her hand.

"Hey," I said gently.

No response.

She'd enjoyed the kiss. I was sure of it.

"I'd really love to do that again," I said softly, trying not to scare her.

"I... No one's ever... You know."

"No one's kissed you like that before?"

"No. No one. I feel really stupid."

"Why should you feel stupid?"

"I'm at college. All these girls are so... I mean, Patty didn't come home last night."

"I know."

"I'm a mess."

"You're beautiful," I said. "You're the most beautiful thing I've ever seen."

I meant those words with all my heart, and even *they* didn't convey what I truly meant. I wasn't sure words existed to describe Daphne Wade. Not the way I saw her. Not the way I felt about her in such a short time.

It wasn't love. At least I didn't think it was. I wasn't cut out for love. But it was something. Something big and strong and full of a force I didn't understand. She needed me. I didn't know how or why. I just knew she did.

And I'd take care of her.

I needed to.

"I know you liked the kiss, Daphne."

"I... How..."

"Because you responded. Your body responded."

"Did I?" She touched her lips.

"You did."

So had I. My dick was hard as a rock, but I couldn't tell her that. She'd run away screaming. Or would she?

No, couldn't go there. Not yet. No matter how much I wanted to.

I advanced toward her slowly, taking both her hands in my own. They fit perfectly within mine.

"You want to go for a walk?"

"It's late."

"Daphne, it's eleven."

"We were warned about walking at night. There were rapes here last year."

"You'll be with me."

She nodded slightly.

"Daphne," I said, as gently as I could. "Why are you afraid of me?"

CHAPTER FIFTEEN

Daphne

Why *was* I afraid?

I wasn't, at least not in the way he thought I was. Sure, I was inexperienced, but he made me feel things I didn't think I was ready for. I wanted to trust him.

He made me melt inside. My brain was foggy, and I couldn't think. Didn't want to think. Just wanted to go back to kissing him. My breasts were heavy, my nipples tight and hard. New feelings swirled through me, landing between my legs.

I wanted it all.

I wanted his kisses, his hands on my body. I wanted to explore him with my fingers and my lips. How might his tan skin feel beneath my touch? His broad shoulders? His hard chest? His stubbly cheeks and jawline? His . . .

I zeroed in on his crotch.

The bulge.

It was there.

And it was there because of me.

Brad Steel didn't scare me nearly enough.

And that was what frightened me the most.

"I'm not afraid of you, Brad."

"Could have fooled me. Daphne, you've been alone with me three times now. Have I ever made any indication that I'm going to hurt you?"

"No."

I stroked my hair absently.

Oh, God. My hair. I'd woken up and my hair hadn't been knotted and tangled.

"Did you . . . brush my hair last night?"

"Yeah. I just . . ." He chuckled softly. "I have no idea why I did it. It's just . . . your hair is so beautiful, and I didn't want you to wake up and have to brush all the tangles out of it."

My heart nearly melted. Seriously, melted right into a puddle in the middle of my chest.

"That's really . . . sweet."

The word was minimal. It didn't say nearly what I wanted to.

"You fell asleep. I brushed your hair, and then I left."

"You didn't . . . want to do anything more?"

"While you were unconscious? What kind of a guy do you think I am?"

"That's just it. I don't know. I don't know anything about guys. I've never . . ."

"I know. You're a virgin. It's okay. Believe it or not, you're not the only virgin on campus."

"I know that. I think."

"It's okay that you don't have much experience," he said. "I just want to be with you."

"Why? Why do you want to be with me?"

He chuckled again, shaking his head. "Hell if I know. I just do."

I bit my lip. I wanted to be with him too. I just wasn't sure I should say it. Then he might think I wanted all those other things.

Which I did want.

And I also didn't want.

But the *did* was stronger.

"Aren't you going to say anything?" he said.

"What do you want me to say?"

"I don't know. Maybe something like, 'That's great, Brad. I want to be with you too.'"

I smiled this time. A great big smile. "I want to be with you too."

He wrapped his arms around me and pulled me close. "You're safe with me. I'll always protect you. I'll never make you do anything you don't want to do."

His words warmed me like a mug of hot chocolate on a cold winter day.

And I believed him.

We stood and embraced for several minutes. I was still for most of it, but finally I allowed my hands to wander up his strong arms to his hard shoulders. Steel was the perfect name for him. His hard body was made of steel. Everything about him was hard where I was soft.

Especially...

That part of him.

It pushed against my belly, but not so much that he was doing it on purpose. I knew all about how men worked. I knew everything.

I was all theory and no practice.

Maybe it was time to get some practice.

Who better to teach me the ways of men and women than Brad Steel? The perfect man?

I pulled back a little. "This girlfriend of yours..."

"She and I are over. It was mostly a high school thing."

"Then what was she doing at your place?"

"It's like I said. She has a hard time letting go."

"Why?"

"It's complicated, and I haven't helped the situation. I always let her come back when I'm not involved with someone else. It doesn't mean anything."

"How can you say that?"

"Because it's just sex."

"Nothing is just sex. Sex is important. It's the closest you can be to someone else. How can you even say it's just sex?"

"Because . . ." He shook his head. "I don't have an answer for that."

"Because I'm right."

"Yeah. You're right. I mean, men and women are a little different. Men are really physical, but sex with the right person isn't just sex."

"Have you ever had sex with the right person?"

"No," he said, "I haven't."

CHAPTER SIXTEEN

Brad

The right person was in my arms.

How did I know? I had no idea. I just knew.

Daphne was the woman I was meant to meet. The woman I was meant to protect. The woman who would someday bear my children.

Maybe I *was* cut out for love. Looking back, I'd never loved Wendy. Sure, at the time, I'd thought it might be love, but I'd never felt the wondrous beginnings of that all-encompassing emotion. But I was feeling it now for the gorgeous girl in front of me.

I kissed her gently on her lips. "Let's get you back inside."

She nodded.

When we reached her door, I brought her fingers to my lips and kissed them. "Tomorrow?"

"Okay. I have orientation stuff in the morning and then registration in the afternoon."

"How about I pick you up around five?"

"Okay. Will we be going to dinner with Sean and Patty again?"

"No. I want to take *you* to dinner. Just you and me. Wear a dress. We'll be going downtown."

★ ★ ★

"Shit."

A car sat in the street outside our condo—a black Corvette that belonged to one of my friends from high school. Theodore Mathias—Theo to us—was a brilliant guy who was in business with Daphne's half brother, Larry Wade, and another high school buddy, Tom Simpson. Wendy was involved too, and I was the bank. Worked well so far, but now that Wendy and I were finished for good, I needed to get out of the business.

Still, I liked having my own money—money that hadn't come from my father.

I unlocked the door and walked inside.

Theo, black hair hanging into his eyes and clad in all black leather, looked like a cover boy for a badass biker magazine. He pulled it off easily. He was of Greek descent and definitely looked the part. His right ring finger sparkled with the ring we all wore. Once, I'd considered him a brother. Now, he was a friend. Sort of. Honestly, I didn't know what he was. He'd gotten a little more distant each year since high school. Tom and Larry were going to law school, but Theo always did his own thing. I just wasn't sure what that thing was.

"Hey, Steel. I think Murphy's getting lucky." He nodded toward the carnal sounds coming from Murph's room.

I nodded. "Cute little redhead. Freshman. What are you doing here?"

"What do you think?"

I sighed. "How much?"

"Not much. A couple grand."

I eyed him. "I think you're wearing a couple grand, dude."

He laughed. "This old stuff? Nah. And I misspoke. I need about fifty grand."

Right. Whatever. "Are you ever going to tell me what you guys are up to?"

"I thought you only wanted to be included on a need-to-know basis."

"True, but with Tom and Larry both going to law school . . . Why do you need two lawyers? That's a little suspicious."

"You're my brother, Steel. You know I'd never put your money into anything untoward."

Interesting use of the word *untoward*. He could have said illegal. Unethical. Instead, he said untoward, which meant unexpected or inconvenient. It was purely subjective.

Mathias was an odd duck. Brilliant mind like Wendy with a subtle dark edge. Yeah, he was a friend—I was actually closer to him than to Larry and Tom—but I'd learned to guard my back around him. He'd never done anything to warrant my suspicion, but I kept one eye open anyway.

"It's been a while since I've reaped any dividends."

"Your last check was seven figures, man."

"It was also over a year ago."

"We're working on things. You know that. We just have to find the next great thing and get our hands on it. Cabbage Patch dolls won't last forever. You've always gotten your money back and then some."

He was right. I always had. I was in the black with them. I didn't need the money, but so far, their enterprise had been a solid investment. I'd be stupid not to keep it up. I'd known these guys since we were teens. Surely they wouldn't be doing anything bad with my money.

"Wendy was here yesterday. If you needed money, why didn't she ask for it?"

"This is something we're doing without Wendy," he said.

"Tom and Larry?"

"Yeah, they're with me. We stand to make a fucking shitload of cash."

"How's Wendy going to feel when she learns you dealt her out?"

"No reason she has to find out."

I scoffed. "Wendy always finds out."

"Not this time. By the way, speaking of Larry, his kid sister's here. She's supposed to be one hot piece of ass."

Red anger whirled into me like a cyclone. Within a second, Theo was pinned against the wall, my hand at his throat. "Don't ever talk that way about her again."

"Whoa. Hold up. Larry says she's gorgeous. That's all I'm saying."

"You said hot piece of ass."

"Which means gorgeous. Fuck, Steel, what's wrong with you?"

I let him go. "I've met her. She's a nice girl. She's not a piece of ass."

"But gorgeous?"

I nodded, though gorgeous didn't even begin to do Daphne Wade justice. "Keep your hands off her."

"Steel, I have no interest in Larry's sister or any woman right now. I'm building a business. I'm going to triple my assets by the time I'm thirty."

I didn't doubt it. Theo was one of the most driven people I knew, possibly even more driven than Wendy.

Or not. Wendy became possessed when she wanted something.

And the something she wanted was usually me.

She was a tomcat in the sack, no doubt. And she had a

killer body and killer mind that challenged me in many ways.

But she wasn't the one.

She'd never been the one.

The problem was . . . she thought *I* was the one.

If I was going to have a shot at something special with Daphne, I had to make sure Wendy understood we were truly over.

Nausea crept up my throat at the thought. Dealing with Wendy would not be fun.

I walked to my bedroom and into the closet, where I kept my locked safe. My dad had taught me early to keep my checkbook and other bank stuff locked up. I dialed the combination, opened the door, and withdrew my checkbook. I quickly wrote out a check to Theo, walked back to the living room, and handed it to him.

"*Muchas gracias,*" he said.

"Spanish?"

"Yeah. Why not? I'm thinking of changing my name. What do you think of Jorge Ramirez? Or Milo Sanchez?"

I shook my head. "You're nuts. You're Greek, not Hispanic."

"My coloring works. On the other hand, maybe a Greek name would be better." He wrinkled his forehead. "How about Nico Kostas?"

I shook my head again.

"Or something simple. John Smith?"

"I'm sticking with 'you're nuts.'"

He laughed. "Maybe so. Maybe not. You never know with me, do you, Steel?" He took the check and left.

CHAPTER SEVENTEEN

Daphne

Patty sneaked in again around six the next morning, waking me up. Not that I minded, really. I had to get up anyway for the day's events. More orientation this morning, and then registration in the afternoon.

Then a date with Brad Steel at five.

An actual date. Not a double date with Sean and Patty. I'd be alone with him for the evening.

I wasn't proud of the fact that I'd never been on an actual date. I'd been pretty young before the wreckage that was my junior year in high school, and my experience with boys before then was always as a participant in silly games in a group atmosphere or on group dates.

Senior year, the other students seemed to avoid me. We'd kept my hospitalization a secret. Word on the street was that my mom had sent me to London to stay with a relative that year because it would be a terrific experience for me.

I wasn't ashamed of my issues. The only thing that truly bothered me was the lack of memories. Losing months of your life was freaky, especially at such a young age. I should have been in school, joining clubs and going to dances. Learning how to date. Instead, I was cooped up and out of my head.

Severe anxiety and depression. That was my diagnosis,

according to my mother. Funny thing was, I didn't recall being anxious or depressed, because I didn't recall much of anything about that year.

And I still had the nightmares, but I kept that quiet. Nightmares didn't hurt anyone, and I didn't want my mother needlessly worrying.

Patty and I showered and went to breakfast.

"What did you do last night?" she asked after swallowing a big bite of scrambled eggs.

No bacon graced either of our plates. Boy, I missed bacon, but Patty promised some uncured, humanely raised bacon would arrive soon.

"After dinner? I went downstairs to the lounge for a while. No drinking, though. You?"

She smiled dreamily. "I had a great time with Sean."

"Are you guys a thing now?"

"I'm not sure. He may just like fucking me."

I tried not to wince at her words. They were crass, but they were also true. "Do you want more than that?"

"I think I might, but I'm not going to push it. We just met. Besides, this is college. We're supposed to have fun, and I'm definitely having fun."

I nodded, taking a sip of coffee.

"So what's up with you and Brad? Or Ennis?"

"Nothing with Ennis. We're just friends. Brad? I'm not sure, but we're going out tonight."

"Oh? Sean didn't say anything about getting together with you guys."

"Brad says he wants it to be just the two of us. He's taking me to dinner downtown."

"Really? What about the woman he—"

"It's over, he says."

"And you believe him?"

"I don't know." I sighed. "I want to."

"Then you should, I guess. A dinner in Denver sounds wonderful." Patty's eyes gleamed. "What are you going to wear?"

My stomach dropped. What *was* I going to wear? I had a few dresses, but they seemed childish when I thought about them. One was a sundress with daisies on it, and the other was a hot-pink wraparound dress. I could wear basic black pants and a silk shirt. If I had a silk shirt, which I did not.

"I have no idea," I replied.

"I'd let you borrow something, but you're so much taller than I am. I know! Let's blow off orientation and go shopping!"

"How? We don't have a car."

"The bus, silly. I have a schedule. This will be great."

"But orientation… What if there's stuff we need to know?"

"Big yawn," she said. "It's more of that team-building crap. We met everyone yesterday. We'll be back in time for registration at two. Besides, tomorrow's the big event. It's first nighter."

"First nighter?"

"Weren't you listening yesterday? First nighter is when they line up all the freshman girls and all the freshman guys by height and pair them off for a dance. They give us roses and everything."

"Just when did they mention that?"

"Yesterday morning. Plus, it's on the schedule. I swear, Daph, sometimes I think you walk around in a daze."

Sometimes I did. I forced myself to remember everything,

but I hadn't read the schedule, and if first nighter was mentioned yesterday morning, I was still a bit hungover.

I didn't have anything to wear to any first nighter either. I didn't have a lot of disposable income—read: none—but Patty's shopping idea was looking better and better.

"You've convinced me. Shopping it is."

★ ★ ★

Patty and I returned with new outfits for my dinner with Brad and for first nighter. For tonight's dinner, I'd wear a basic black wrap dress that hugged my curves. I'd thought it a little much, but Patty convinced me it was perfect. I had to admit it seemed to be made for me.

I was willing to wear the same thing to first nighter tomorrow, but Patty said that would be tacky. I wasn't sure why, since Brad wouldn't be at first nighter, and only he would see me tonight, but whatever. So for first nighter, I got a burgundy dress that was slightly less revealing—but not much. I got some black strappy sandals that went perfectly with both. Though she tried, Patty did *not* talk me into another pair of shoes.

Patty had spent most of the several hours we spent shopping complaining about how nothing went with her red hair and green eyes. I disagreed and told her she could wear anything she wanted. She finally decided on an emerald prairie dress for first nighter, and she bought a very smart mahogany number for her big date with Sean—should it ever happen. She bought two new pairs of shoes.

Pig farming must pay.

Either that or she liked to spend money.

I was naturally frugal because my mother was. These new

purchases put a serious dent in my bank account, but I figured I wouldn't need to shop for anything besides shampoo for a while.

Registration went smoothly. We each got the classes we wanted, which supposedly almost never happened for freshmen, so we were ecstatic.

Then back to the room to prepare for my date with Brad.

And I froze.

CHAPTER EIGHTEEN

Brad

My gut was full of fluttering moths. My mouth was dry. My skin felt tight.

These were new feelings. I was nervous.

Fucking nervous for this date with Daphne.

I'd never been nervous about a date in my life.

My black pants and white cotton shirt felt all wrong. I grew up on a ranch. I wore jeans and cowboy boots...and never, never a white shirt. White didn't stay white for long on a ranch.

In the car was my sport coat. The temperature was too hot for it at the moment.

I took a swig from the bottle of Coke I'd brought with me. Why did my tongue feel like sandpaper? Man, this had to stop. No woman was worth this. *Get a grip, Steel.*

I pulled up in front of Daphne's dorm at four forty-five.

Damn. Early.

I was never early.

This was insane.

I drove away from the dorm. I had fifteen minutes to kill.

My car phone rang. Yeah, I had a car phone. I was a Steel, after all.

"Yeah?" I said into the phone.

"Brad? I need you. Come quickly. I'm at your place."

Shit. Seriously? "Wendy? I can't. I'm busy."

"Please, Brad. It's an emergency. I'm in trouble."

"Fuck," I said under my breath. I hung up the phone and drove the five minutes back to my condo.

Wendy was indeed there. Her car was parked in front and she had let herself in. Time to change the locks again.

I parked and walked in.

And she attacked.

She was on me like a rabid dog.

She pressed her lips to mine and then spread kisses around my jawline to my ear, where she bit the lobe. Hard.

"I know about your little slut, Brad," she whispered.

I pushed her away. "You said this was an emergency."

"It is. If you don't get rid of the slut, you'll see what an emergency it will be."

"Don't threaten her."

"The only reason I haven't already gotten rid of her myself is because she's Larry's half sister."

"Since when are you and Larry so close?"

"Loyalty, Brad. There's this little thing called loyalty. I have it. You, obviously, do not."

"Loyalty? Really?"

"I promised Larry I wouldn't harm his sister."

"Since when are you okay with harming *anyone*, Wendy?"

"You're the one who taught me how to shoot a gun. If I harm anyone, you hold some responsibility."

I had, when we were in high school. I was a good shot, and she'd wanted to learn, so I taught her. We couldn't go to the range together without an adult, so we practiced on the ranch during the weekends. She took to it like a pig to slop.

Now, with the crazed look in her eyes, I vowed I'd never teach another person to shoot a gun.

"What the hell has happened to you?" I demanded.

"You know me, Brad. I get very testy when I don't get my way."

"No one gets his way all the time, Wendy. You know that."

"Not me. I always get my way." Her eyes misted. "Except for once."

Our child. She was talking about our child. She and I were horny teenagers, and we'd failed to use birth control once.

Only once.

Of course, once was all it took.

She got pregnant but miscarried. A blessing in disguise. Neither of us was ready to be a parent in high school.

Still, she found a way to use it against me any time she could.

I remained calm. She wasn't going to trip me up this time.

"Get out of here," I said, "or I'll have you arrested for trespassing."

"No, you won't."

"You want to try me? I'm not Tom or Larry. I'm not your lackey."

"Tom and Larry aren't my lackeys. They're my friends. They're loyal. They're better men than you'll ever be."

"Fine. They can be better men than I am. I don't rightfully give a fuck."

"Get rid of her," she said angrily, "or I will."

Rage welled in me. "You stay away from her."

"I won't hurt her. I promised Larry. But...sometimes accidents happen."

"You fucking bitch." I clenched my teeth. "If she so much

loses a hair on her head, I'll have you arrested."

"For harming a hair on her head? Fuck you, Brad. What about the promises we made to each other?"

"We were kids. We've been through this."

"*You've* been through this. *We* have never been through anything. We belong together. You know it as well as I do."

Damn. It was five o'clock now. I was late. I hadn't planned on dealing with Wendy today.

But today, it seemed, was the day. I didn't have a choice.

"Sit down," I commanded. "Now."

She sat.

She always sat.

All I needed was my commanding tone, and Wendy would do anything I asked. In the bedroom, at least. Outside the bedroom? That was always up in the air, but I could get her to obey me about seventy-five percent of the time.

This appeared to be one of those times, thank goodness.

"Listen to me, and listen good," I said. "We're over, Wendy. There's nothing more between us."

"You're lying."

"I'm not lying."

"You're really dumping me for an eighteen-year-old girl?"

"I'm not dumping you for anyone. I'm simply dumping you."

"You're not."

"Oh, I am."

"I'll ruin you."

I couldn't help a laugh at that one. "You'll ruin me? I don't care how much money you and the guys make doing God knows what. I'll always be able to buy and sell you."

"Doesn't matter. You can't hide the truth, Brad. No

amount of money can hide the truth. I'm top in my class. I'm going to be the best investigative journalist in the world, and I'm going to find every single thing the Steels are hiding."

"Go ahead. Look all you want. You won't find anything."

I hoped I sounded more confident than I felt. The Steels *did* have things to hide—a *few* things.

She stood and drove into me, hammering her fists into my chest. "You bastard! You fucking bastard!"

Yeah, Wendy wasn't above getting physical. Never in my life had I struck a woman—our bedroom antics notwithstanding—and I wasn't going to begin now, no matter how tempted I was.

"Let it go," I said. "Let us go."

"Never. I'll never let you go, Brad Steel. You and I will always be bound for life." She backed away.

"If it helps you to think that, go ahead. I'm done caring."

"You'll never be done caring. I'll see to that. I always get what I want. Always."

Her words sent chills rippling down my spine.

I wasn't sure why.

CHAPTER NINETEEN

Daphne

"Daph? Are you okay?"

My mind was mud. Sludge and mud. Someone was calling my name.

"Daph? He's going to be here any minute!"

I jerked back to reality. Patty was sitting on my bed, waving her hands in my face.

"What's wrong? Why aren't you dressed for your date with Brad?"

Oh, God. My date with Brad. What must I look like? I was going to shower, do my hair and makeup ... What happened?

Why didn't I remember?

No. No, no, no. I was not losing time again.

I stood quickly. "I'm fine. I must have dozed off."

"Daph, your eyes were open."

"Sometimes I sleep like that." I hated lying. I *really* hated lying.

She pulled my dress out of the shopping bag. "He's going to be here any minute. Come on. I'll help. Thank goodness this doesn't wrinkle much." She eyed me. "Your legs look good. You can get away without shaving. We'll brush out your hair and then rebraid it. Luckily you don't need a lot of makeup. We can do this, Daph."

I nodded, letting her take the reins. My mind was still a little fuzzy.

By five fifteen, I was ready, and I looked pretty darn good, all things considered.

I breathed a sigh of relief until something occurred to me.

It was five fifteen, and Brad wasn't here.

He was late.

Or maybe he wouldn't show up at all.

"Guys are late all the time, Daph," Patty said. "Don't worry about that. Be glad you had the extra time."

Indeed, I *was* glad. Patty clearly knew much more about men than I did. Maybe they *were* always late. I had no idea.

"I've got to run," Patty said.

"Plans with Sean?"

"Actually, no. Just some of the girls down the hall. I might meet up with Sean later, though. He said he might call."

She didn't sound overly upset about not having any solid plans with the guy she was sleeping with. If she was okay with it, I was okay with it. "Okay. See you later, I guess."

"I won't wait up!" She winked and dashed out the door.

Her comment made the skin on my arms tingle like electricity was shooting through my veins. I wouldn't be sleeping with Brad Steel. Not tonight, and not anytime soon.

I didn't particularly want to stand around, but I resisted sitting back down on my bed.

Fear edged its way into me.

I'd been about to get ready . . .

And then . . . nothing. I'd ended up on my bed with Patty waving her hands like a maniac in front of my face. What had caused me to freeze? I walked slowly around the room, looking for something, anything, that seemed out of place.

I found nothing.

I breathed in. Out. In again.

Relaxation exercises. Where had I learned them? Junior year, of course. I knew that much. I just didn't recall the actual learning.

So I stood.

Waiting.

Five thirty came around.

Five forty-five.

Six o'clock.

Finally, I allowed myself to sit.

He wasn't coming.

Brad Steel had stood me up. Given me the rabbit, as they said in France, according to my French teacher.

Tears formed in my eyes, but I sniffed them back. No reason to cry. I hardly knew the guy. Didn't matter how sincere he'd seemed last night. How sweetly he'd held me. How he'd given me my first real kiss.

I'd spent fifty dollars I didn't have on this dress, and then another thirty-five on the burgundy one for tomorrow.

First nighter.

Maybe there I'd meet the man of my dreams. At least he'd be tall enough.

Brad Steel was tall enough.

But Brad Steel was not—

Frantic pounding on my door.

I opened it.

There stood beautiful Brad Steel, looking flustered. Beads of perspiration dripped from his forehead, pasting his dark hair to the sides of his neck and face. He wore a white button-down shirt, no tie, and a few black chest hairs peeked out. Black pants and black shoes.

"I'm so sorry, Daphne. God, you look beautiful."

I warmed, fuzzy feelings rushing through me, along with a sense of panic.

And I realized why I'd frozen earlier. I was nervous for this date—this first *real* date. Here was my chance to end it with Brad once and for all. I wasn't falling for this. He as good as stood me up.

I forced myself to calm down. "What are you doing here?"

"I'm here to pick you up. We'll have to skip drinks at the Four Seasons, but we can still make our reservation."

"Really? Enjoy yourself, then."

"Daphne, I'm sorry. Something came up."

"Interesting. I don't recall getting a phone call, and I've been right here."

"I know. I just wanted to get here. I just wanted to get to you."

"You got here. It's too late."

"No." He walked into my room and closed the door. "It's not too late. It can't be."

"What kind of person do you think I am? I'm not a doormat." Something I'd learned junior year, though I didn't recall when or why.

"Of course you're not. Please, Daphne. Please." He touched my cheek.

Sparks shot through me.

The last shred of panic dissolved, and I knew, in that instant, I'd do anything for this man.

Absolutely anything.

CHAPTER TWENTY

Brad

"Please," I said again.

Shivers quaked through me. What would I do if she said no? She couldn't. She just couldn't.

If she did, things would never be the same. I'd blown it, all because Wendy had shown up.

"All right," she finally said.

An anvil crashed down off my shoulders. Thank God. *Thank God.*

What the hell was happening to me? Why did she matter so much in so little time? It was crazy. Completely crazy.

"I'll make this up to you." I stroked her soft cheek. "I promise."

"Let's just go," she said. "I mean, I got all dressed up and everything."

"I know. That dress is amazing. You're so beautiful, Daphne."

Her cheeks blushed a soft pink, a lovely contrast to her fair skin and the black wrap dress. Boy, did she have long lean legs. They went on for miles.

She didn't talk much during the drive to the restaurant, and I didn't force it. Silence was okay with Daphne. It felt good, actually. It felt right.

Tante Louise was a French restaurant in downtown Denver. I'd been there a couple of times with my family when my father traveled to Denver for business. Our place was on the western slope of Colorado, the other side of the Rockies.

"Aunt Louise," Daphne said softly as we walked toward the door to the eatery.

"I'm sorry?"

"Tante Louise means Aunt Louise in French."

"You took French?"

"Yeah, for three years."

"You stopped senior year?"

"No. Three years. Freshman, sophomore, and senior."

"Why not your junior year?"

She went rigid for a moment. "I was abroad junior year. In London."

Oh? That was a surprise. "Really?"

She cleared her throat. "Yeah. I stayed with a relative. It was my mom's idea. Get me cultured, you know."

"Wow. I've never been out of the country. You'll have to tell me more about it."

She didn't reply. The maître d' led us to our table and helped Daphne into her seat. Then he gave us some menus. "Bon appétit."

"Thanks," I said.

"I don't want you to drink tonight," Daphne said.

"I wasn't planning to, but why?"

"Because I can't. And I don't like to drive with people who've been drinking."

"You've been out with me before," I said. "I never have more than one drink if I'm driving. Or two if I'm eating. I have a solid rule never to ever drink and drive. My friend Tom got a

DUI in high school. He was a minor, and his dad got it swept under the rug. The record was expunged when he turned eighteen, but he had to have weekly urine tests for a couple years. Big pain."

"Was anyone hurt?"

"Just a lamppost," I said. "He got lucky."

She nodded.

Silence again. She scanned her menu.

"I haven't been here in a while," I said, "but last time I had the Sole Beaujolais. It was excellent."

"I don't eat a lot of fish," she said. "I like salmon, though. But..."

"But what?"

"How do I know the fish were treated humanely?"

"Just make sure you order something that's wild caught. That way they weren't farmed for meat."

She nodded. "Makes sense."

This wasn't going well. She was still angry with me, and I couldn't blame her. I reached toward her and grabbed the menu from her hands. "Daphne, look at me."

She met my gaze. Sadness laced her eyes.

"Please. Let's have a nice time. I've been looking forward to this."

She sighed. "I was too."

"Then let's enjoy ourselves, okay? I'm really sorry I was late, but I can't keep saying I'm sorry. You either have to forgive me or get rid of me, I guess."

Shit. Did I really just say that? What if she took me up on it?

"I ... I don't want to get rid of you."

Damn. Thank God. The anvil slid off my shoulders again.

"Good. Now, what looks good? Do you want a cocktail? Virgin, of course. Or an appetizer?"

She smiled, and my heart surged. At that moment, I knew I'd do anything to see her smile.

Any-fucking-thing.

CHAPTER TWENTY-ONE

Daphne

We didn't talk a lot. He asked me some questions about my home life, and I answered them briefly. And maybe not *completely* truthfully, but truthfully nonetheless. So far, the only lie I'd told was the London lie. That lie was so much a part of my life, sometimes I thought it might actually be true.

Then I caught myself.

Lies weren't truth.

Dreams weren't reality.

Lost time wasn't lost forever. I hoped, at least.

I went to therapy the whole of my senior year, and I asked my therapist, Dr. Payne, and my mother if I could take some time off to begin college. To actually have something normal in my life. They'd both agreed.

Maybe "normal" included a relationship with a nice guy. Brad Steel seemed like a nice guy so far. Yeah, he'd been late, but he clearly felt terrible about it. If he was willing to go slow with me, which he claimed he was, maybe seeing him could be a good thing. A healing thing.

"I'd like to take you to my condo," he said when we got into the car to drive home.

My nerves hit me with blunt force. Everyone knew what going to a guy's place meant.

"I don't know..."

"I just want you to see where I live. I know where you live. We don't have to do anything."

Yeah. I'd definitely heard that before somewhere, though I couldn't remember where. Probably on a TV series or soap opera. I watched a lot of TV junior year, though most of it was a blur. Things came back to me sometimes, though, like the déjà vu I was having at this moment.

I knew fear.

I wasn't sure how I knew, but I did. It was invisible knives scraping across my skin. It was a heartbeat made of thunder and breath like lightning. It was nausea clawing up my throat.

I didn't feel any of that right now.

I did not fear Brad Steel.

"Okay," I said.

He smiled. "Great."

★ ★ ★

His condo wasn't a condo at all. It was a patio home that was at least three thousand square feet. His bedroom alone was bigger than my house. Okay, I was exaggerating—but not by a lot.

My nerves pricked my arms as I looked around the massive suite. A huge bed—bigger than my parents', I was sure. Was theirs a queen? This was a king, no doubt. Oak hardwood floors covered by royal-blue rugs placed here and there. A bar. Yes, a bar in the bedroom. And a bathroom easily twice the size of my dorm room. Two walk-in closets, two sinks, two toilets.

I'd never seen anything like it other than in magazines.

"What do you think?" he asked.

"I think it's the most amazing bedroom I've ever seen."

He smiled. "Technically my father owns it, but it will be mine someday."

"What about Sean?"

"Murph? He pays me nominal rent. He's a little strapped, so I let him live here."

"That's nice of you."

"Murph's a good guy. It's nice to have a friend who's normal."

I wrinkled my forehead. "Your other friends aren't normal?"

"That's not what I meant." He laughed. "Okay. Maybe that's exactly what I meant."

"How so?"

"I have a group of friends from high school. Good guys for the most part, but the more I get to know them, the more they seem a little off."

A little off?

Whispers filled my head—whispers I'd heard last year at high school.

Daphne's back, and she seems a little off.

I'd love to ask her out. She's gorgeous, but a little off.

She thinks she's all that. Walks around, not talking to anyone. She's a little off.

"What does that mean, exactly? A little off?"

"It's not something I can pin down, you know? Just a feeling."

"What kind of feeling?"

"That something's not right. I don't know. They're a little off."

This was getting me nowhere. If Brad could explain what

the phrase meant, maybe I'd know what those kids at high school meant. I felt normal. I didn't feel "a little off."

"They're just envious," my mother had said. "You're the prettiest girl in school, and you spent junior year in London."

"But I *didn't* spend junior year in London," I'd said.

"But they think you did. That's all that matters."

Was it? Was it all that mattered?

I was tired of the lie. I wanted to shout out the truth sometimes. "Hey, everyone! I spent most of my junior year hospitalized for anxiety and depression!"

But I'd never do that. Never. What if I lost my newfound friends? Ennis, Patty, and Sean? What if I lost Brad Steel? What if they all decided I was "a little off"?

Brad cleared his throat. "Penny for your thoughts."

No way would I tell him what I'd actually been thinking about. "I think this is the most amazing home I've ever been in."

"You should see our main house on the ranch. Makes this place look like a tiny cabin."

I wasn't sure what to say to that, so I said nothing.

"Maybe you can come home with me sometime. I'd love to show you around the ranch. You could see the animals." He smiled. "Make sure we're treating them properly."

That got a smile out of me. How I'd love to see Brad Steel's ranch. How I'd love to see his animals.

"Do you have any pets?" I asked.

"We have a couple labs, one black and one chocolate. Ebony and Brandy."

"Gorgeous names," I said.

"They're awesome. Do you have a dog?"

"No. I've always wanted one, though. My mom's allergic."

"That clinches it then. You have to come visit the ranch. You can get your dog fix."

He wasn't really inviting me to his ranch. We barely knew each other. But maybe... Someday...

He took my hand.

Sparks shot through me.

"Come on. Let's go back to the kitchen. I'll fix us some drinks."

I held up my other hand. "I'm still not sure I'm ready for alcohol after the other night."

"No worries. I have all kinds of soda. Do you mind if I have a drink?"

"As long as you're able to drive me home."

"Not a problem."

The kitchen was beautiful. All black appliances, including the refrigerator, and gorgeous countertops that looked like white marble streaked with gold.

Brad pulled a beer out of the refrigerator for himself. "Coke, Fresca, Sprite. What's your pleasure?"

"Fresca, please."

"Have a seat." He motioned to the barstools set up at the kitchen island and set a can of Fresca in front of me.

"Thanks." I sat down.

He took the chair next to me, opened his beer, and took a long draught. Then he looked at me as if he were memorizing every inch of my face.

"You're so beautiful," he said.

I looked down, embarrassed, my cheeks warming. "Thank you." Then I took the sliver of courage that came to me unexpectedly. I met his gaze. "So are you."

He chuckled softly. "You said that the other night."

"Well, it's true. There's such a thing as male beauty, and you definitely have it."

His cheeks pinked slightly. I'd embarrassed him! It was adorable, almost. Brad Steel could never be described as adorable, but this was pretty close.

"Thank you," he said. "I look a lot like my mom. She's got dark hair and eyes like I do. My dad has dark hair, but his eyes are blue."

"He must be striking," I said. "I've always loved blue eyes with dark hair. I always wished my eyes were blue."

"Are you kidding? You have the warmest brown eyes I've ever seen. They dazzle. They're perfect."

My eyes weren't perfect. Nothing about me was perfect, but when Brad told me I was beautiful, that my eyes were perfect, I almost believed him.

Almost.

If this man thought I was perfect, and if I wanted a relationship with him, I owed him the truth.

The whole truth.

But not tonight.

CHAPTER TWENTY-TWO

Brad

Damn, I wanted her.

I wanted Daphne Wade in my bed, her lush body beneath mine.

I wanted her more than I'd wanted anything—any woman—in my life.

I could make a move. I was good at "the moves." I'd never been turned down. Besides Wendy, I'd had many others, mostly just sex. One or two I'd cared about.

But nothing like this.

Daphne Steel affected me like no other woman ever had.

Yeah, I was young. Only twenty-two. Who found a soul mate at twenty-two? It sounded ridiculous in my head, even though I knew the truth of it.

This woman—this young, untried woman—was my soul mate.

Don't ask me how I knew. Don't ask me what "soul mate" even meant.

But it was as real to me as the woman sitting next to me. Real. And true.

And scary as fuck.

I'd never had to go slow with a woman. Could I? Didn't matter. I had to. If I wanted Daphne, I'd go slowly. No ifs, ands, or buts.

I took another sip of my beer and trailed one finger over her forearm. I smiled when goose bumps erupted on her soft flesh.

"Tell me what your dreams are, Daphne."

"I . . . don't know. I haven't chosen a major yet. I'm going to take my requirements and—"

I pressed two fingers against her soft lips. "Not your major. What are your dreams?"

Her forehead wrinkled for a few seconds. Then, "To enjoy the little things. To take life one day at a time."

Hmm. Interesting answer. I couldn't find any fault with it. "You don't have anything you really want to do? Have you thought about how you want to live your life?"

"With love," she said. "One day at a time, with lots of love."

"God, Daphne." I couldn't help myself. I cupped both her cheeks and pressed my lips to hers.

Within a few seconds, she parted her lips, and I swept my tongue between them. She tasted as sweet as I remembered— sweet and pure and irresistible.

A soft moan left her throat, vibrating into me and arrowing straight to my cock. One touch, one kiss from Daphne, and I was as hard as these marble countertops.

Our lips slid together, and after a few more minutes, she darted out her tongue to meet mine. And then something miraculous happened. She ran her tongue over my teeth, exploring my mouth as I was hers.

She was actively kissing me, much more so than the last time.

And I couldn't remember ever having been more turned on.

A mere kiss. Nothing more. I hadn't seen her naked.

Hadn't touched her breasts. Hadn't even kissed her anywhere except on her mouth.

And I was ready to pound her into the next day.

God, how I wanted to pound her into the next day.

I deepened the kiss, groaning into her mouth, my fingers itching to trail over the swells of her breasts covered by her insanely sexy little black dress.

Instead, I skimmed my fingers down the side of her neck to her beautiful bare shoulders.

Then, she surprised me. Truly surprised me.

She took my hand and led it to the gorgeous mound of her breast.

So perfect was the shape against my palm. I brushed my fingers over the swell, and a nipple hardened under my touch.

Another soft moan into my mouth.

Fuck.

Fuck. Fuck. Fuck.

Much more, and I wouldn't be able to—

I broke the kiss, pulling away abruptly.

She inhaled sharply, touching her lower lip. "Did I . . . Did I do something wrong?"

"God, no. Nothing wrong. I swear."

"Then why did you stop?"

"I stopped, Daphne, because if I didn't, I wouldn't be able to."

"Wouldn't be able to—? Oh." She looked away. "I was following my body. I wanted you to touch me there, so I . . ."

"You didn't do anything wrong."

"I want so much when I'm with you, Brad. It scares me."

"I know, baby. I know. Believe me. I want the same when I'm with you."

"I'm not sure I'm ready."

"It's okay. I told you we'd go slow."

"Sometimes, though, I think I *am* ready. More than ready, you know?"

Hell, yeah, I knew. Her body was responding, but her mind wasn't there yet. Women were like that, sometimes. If I could convince her that sex wasn't wrong, that it was just two people exploring each other's bodies and giving each other pleasure...

Nothing is just sex.

The words she'd said earlier haunted me.

I could take her. She was in that dreamy haze, where her body was ready. I knew all the right words, all the right ways to touch her. I could easily convince her to give up her virginity right here and now. She was young. Impressionable. I could make it happen, but I'd pay the price.

It would be the only time with Daphne. She'd regret it later, and I'd risk losing her.

No.

I couldn't take her. Not tonight. Not when she obviously needed more time. Because the truth was, I also needed more time. More time with her. And if I took her tonight, I risked losing that.

"I'll take you home," I said.

"What if I don't want to go home?"

My eyebrows shot up. "You mean..."

"Maybe. Just a little. I feel so..." Her sigh was a soft breeze against my cheek. "I need something. Something more."

"What, baby? What do you need?"

CHAPTER TWENTY-THREE

Daphne

I had no answer.

I had no idea what I needed, just that my body was telling me I needed something, and I needed it badly.

My nipples were hard. The feeling was similar to how they felt on a cold day, but it was also different. It was a warm hardness, an aching hardness. They wanted to be touched, fingered, licked.

Between my legs, I throbbed in time with my heartbeat, which thundered in my ears, almost as if I were underwater. My whole body felt hot and flushed.

And my head... My head was spinning with images and feelings I didn't quite understand but that I wanted to explore more than I'd ever wanted anything.

Again, I didn't feel fear, even though I should have.

Something about Brad Steel negated all fear in me. He was like a large mountain shadowing me and protecting me from a swirling storm.

What do you need?

His question still rang in my ears.

He didn't pressure me for an answer, but he did deserve one.

Face your fears.

Wise words from Dr. Payne.

The fear of this actual date with Brad—a man I was attracted to more than I ever imagined I could be attracted to anyone—had caused me to freeze earlier, caused me to feel panic.

Right now, though? I didn't feel any panic.

If I faced my fear now, while I wasn't feeling it, perhaps I could conquer it. Being here with Brad, kissing him, letting him touch my body—it all felt so right.

I drew in a deep breath and let it out slowly. "Do you believe in fate? In destiny?"

He wrinkled his brow. "I never used to."

"Meaning?"

"I never used to believe in any kind of fate . . . until I saw you."

I smiled. Was it possible? Did he feel it too?

"Is that what you mean?" he asked.

I nodded slightly, embarrassed. "Yes. Something about you. It's like I was meant to meet you. I know that sounds stupid."

"Actually, it doesn't sound stupid at all." He chuckled. "Not to me. I think we were meant to meet as well."

"Do you? Do you really?"

"Don't be so surprised. You may be inexperienced, and that's okay, but I know you feel the connection between us."

I nodded again. Why was this so difficult to put into words? Words didn't seem to exist for what I was feeling. Fate? Providence? Destiny? All of those plus something else. Love?

Yes, I loved him. I had no experience, nothing to compare this feeling to, but it was love. I had no doubt.

Someday, I would have this man's child.

A beautiful dark-haired and dark-eyed child. Brad would be my universe and the child would be my sun. No more darkness. Only light.

I couldn't help a little laugh. I sounded mushy. I certainly wouldn't tell Brad what I'd been imagining. He'd think I was a sappy eighteen-year-old having my first crush and daydreaming about marriage and kids.

He was right, though. We had a connection made of something I couldn't explain. All I knew was that everything about being with Brad Steel felt right. Felt safe.

I hadn't felt truly safe in a long time. I wasn't sure why. Nothing horrible had happened to me, and I'd always had a home and parents who, if they weren't perfect, loved me very much.

So why had I never felt the safety and comfort I was feeling with Brad?

Did it even matter? Why not revel in this wonderful feeling that he seemed to share? Why not enjoy it?

"Yes," I said. "I feel the connection. I felt it right away."

"So did I."

"Then what now?"

"That's up to you," he said.

"What do *you* want?"

He chuckled. "Something you're not ready to give me."

Face your fears, Daphne. "What if I *am* ready?"

"Baby, you're not. I see it in your eyes. It's like I said. Your body might be ready, but you aren't. Not yet."

"I want to give this to you, Brad," I said.

"Believe me, I want to take it. But not yet."

"Please," I begged, the juncture at my thighs almost painful in its heat. "I need you."

"I need you too."

"Show me."

"Show you what?"

"How much you need me."

Fire shot into his dark eyes. "Are you sure?"

I inhaled, gathering all my courage. "I'm sure, Brad. I want it to be you."

He cupped my cheek, thumbing my lower lip. "Come on." Then he led me back into his bedroom. The door locked with a click.

What if Sean came home? What if Patty was with him? What if . . . ? What if . . . ? What if . . . ?

I'd made my decision, and I wasn't backing out now.

Brad deftly removed his jacket and then his shirt. I drew in a breath at his chest. Male perfection in all its glory. His shoulders were bronze and broad, his abs a perfect six-pack. And his chest—the perfect amount of black hair scattered over it, framing his copper nipples.

I dropped my gaze. Yeah, the bulge. The bulge he'd eventually uncover tonight. The first time I'd see, in real life, a man's penis.

I swallowed back the sliver of fear for what it was. Not fear so much as apprehension.

He took my hand, kissed the fingertips, and then placed it on his chest. His flesh was warm and hard. Tingles shot through me at this tiny bit of contact. Tingles that bubbled through me like hot lava and landed between my legs.

That feeling . . . That feeling of wanting another person, of being truly ready . . .

It intoxicated me.

I'd been intoxicated two nights ago, and before I'd

gotten sick, the feeling had been euphoric. But it was nothing compared to what I felt now. Euphoric, yes, but also an ache so pure and raw it was almost beautiful in its pain.

"God, Daphne. Your hand on me. I can't . . ."

"What?" I whispered.

"Just touch me. Touch me everywhere."

I added my other hand and slid them up and over his broad shoulders. His flesh was hot against my fingertips. Burning hot, just like that place deep in my core. I was burning for him. For his hands on my body, his tongue against every part of me.

I slid my hands up his neck and cupped his cheeks, scraping my fingers against his black stubble. I traced his full, firm lips, lips that had touched my own.

Lips that would touch me everywhere else.

God, I was on fire!

"Should I take off my dress? Or something?" I asked.

"Do whatever you feel like doing," he said. "This is your call. Your speed."

"That doesn't seem fair."

"Daphne, I'm not sure you understand everything you do to me."

"Sure I do. You want me like I want you."

He clenched his teeth, his jaw tightening under my fingertips. "I want to rip your clothes off your body, shred them into tiny pieces if that's what it takes. Then I want to sink my cock so far into you that our bodies never come apart."

A chill swept over my skin. I hadn't expected such bluntness, but it made me want him even more.

"I want you to," I said.

"Daphne, you don't know what you're asking."

"I know exactly what I'm asking, Brad Steel. I want to feel

every part of you joined with every part of me. And I've never wanted anything more."

CHAPTER TWENTY-FOUR

Brad

I was burning so hot right now, I almost felt like I could dissolve Daphne's clothes with a mere look.

She was so beautiful.

And so innocent.

She thought she knew what she was asking for, but truly, she didn't. I didn't just fuck. I took everything a woman's body had to offer me. I took control, and I liked it.

Daphne Wade wasn't ready for the kind of sex I liked, and for her, I'd make an exception.

For her, I'd do anything.

Fucking anything.

She'd asked me about fate. About destiny. Only moments before, I'd been certain she was my soul mate.

Which meant we were both thinking the same thing.

God, my cock was aching to get out of these fucking pants.

Should I? Should I give her what she asked for? I could sink into her for days and never want to come up for air. Days upon days upon days.

She stood, gazing into my eyes, her lips swollen from the kiss I'd given her earlier. That kiss. It was that amazing. That magnificent.

My balls ached. My cock burned.

I pulled her to me and grabbed the front of her dress. Such flimsy fabric. I could rip it down the front with minimal effort.

How I was tempted.

"One day," I whispered, "I'm going to tear this dress from your body."

Her brown eyes went wide.

"But not tonight."

She looked visibly relieved. "It's new."

"The next time you wear it around me, it won't last long." I eased the stretchy fabric over her shoulders, taking it down to the tops of her breasts. Her cleavage beckoned. Daphne had perfect breasts, more than enough to fill my large hands.

I met her gaze, and she nodded ever so slightly.

I untightened the tie holding her wrap dress and then brushed it over her breasts, letting it sit on her hips.

I drew in a swift breath.

Her bra was black lace, her tits scrumptiously overflowing. I cupped them, trailing my fingers over the soft exposed flesh. Her nipples tightened against the lace, two hard berries begging to be touched. Sucked. Bitten.

"Has anyone else touched these breasts?" I asked gruffly.

She shook her head.

God, she truly was innocent.

"I'll be the first," I said, "and the last."

She widened her eyes, but in truth, the words probably surprised me more than they did her. Yeah, I'd thought about destiny. Yeah, I'd used the word soul mate. But to hear such words actually escape my throat was new. Very new.

And the words rang very true.

"I'm going to take off your bra now, Daphne."

She nodded.

I deftly unhooked the garment in back and let it fall over her arms to the floor in a black heap on the blue carpeting.

Then her breasts...

They fell against her porcelain chest, the pink-brown nipples hard and turgid.

For a moment, I thought I could be happy merely looking at her, letting my gaze drift over her perfection.

But only for a moment.

I cupped the soft mounds, her skin silken against my rough hands. Her nipples stretched forward, as if begging for my touch. I thumbed them both gently.

"Oh!" she gasped.

Truly untouched. And so very beautiful.

I bent my head—

"What are you doing?"

I met her brown gaze. "I want to kiss your breasts, baby. Suck on your nipples."

"O...kay."

"You'll love it. Trust me."

She nodded. I gently kissed one nipple. A soft sigh crept out of her throat.

"Good?" I said against her skin.

"Yes. Good." She sighed again.

I rained tiny kisses over both nipples and the tops of her breasts, getting her ready for what would come next.

Then I sucked one nipple between my lips.

A swift inhale squeaked from her throat.

Damn, this going slowly was more difficult than I ever imagined. I wanted to rip that dress the rest of the way off, shove her panties to the side, and sink my cock into her warmth. My already blue balls were going to be ready to fall off by the time

I got where I was going.

But she was worth it. Somehow, I knew she was worth it.

I continued sucking gently on her nipple despite wanting to bite it hard and make her scream.

I liked my sex rough. I liked my women to submit.

But Daphne Wade was so innocent. Her innocence went further than her being a virgin. I couldn't pinpoint exactly what it was about her, but I felt such an ache to protect her at all costs.

I'd never felt such a profound need before.

If possible, my desire to protect her was even stronger than my desire to fuck her.

Which meant...

Fuck.

I couldn't do this right now.

My cock was a massive aching rock inside my trousers. It had a mind of its own, and man, did it want to get laid tonight.

But I had to let my head prevail. Daphne, no matter what she said, wasn't ready for sex the way I knew it. I could be gentle, but gentle for me wasn't gentle the way Daphne needed it.

I let her nipple drop from my lips. "Daphne," I said softly.

"Yes?"

"I can't believe I'm going to say this."

"What?"

"This isn't right."

Her eyes misted over, laced with sadness. "Oh? I'm not pretty enough, am I?"

Was she bananas? "You're more than pretty enough. You're the most beautiful girl I've ever seen."

Her body was already pink and supple, but a visible shiver

raced through her. "Then why?"

"Sex isn't about being pretty enough or liking someone enough. Or even wanting someone enough. It's about being sure both people are ready for it, and I don't think you are, baby."

"I am. I told you I am."

I inhaled. Fuck. Her scent—that musky scent of arousal laced with a floral fragrance that was uniquely Daphne.

Her body was ready, no doubt.

But her mind was not.

"I *am*," she said again.

"Baby, you need to know something about me."

"I know all I need to know."

I chuckled. "You know next to nothing. I'm not the kind of guy who—"

I stopped abruptly. If Daphne weren't a virgin, I'd have fucked her six ways by now.

Or would I have?

It wasn't just her virginity that made me want to protect her. It was a sweet vulnerability. I could see it in her eyes. She'd been through something—something she hadn't told me about. Perhaps something had scarred her during her childhood. Perhaps she'd lost a loved one and hadn't told me. Perhaps she'd been bullied as a kid.

Something.

Something she'd have to tell me before we went any further.

I picked up her bra and handed it to her. "Put this back on."

"What if I don't want to?"

I shook my head, chuckling again. "Do it, because if you

don't, I'm going to fuck you so hard you won't be able to walk tomorrow."

That got her. She quickly snapped her bra into place. What a shame to cover up such perfection. Then she adjusted her dress back in place.

"Is this it, then?" she asked.

"What do you mean?"

"You don't want to see me anymore?"

"God, no. I want to see you. I just don't want to do this with you yet." That was a damned, damned lie. I wanted to sink into her soft body more than I wanted my next breath of air.

"Um ... okay."

"I don't think you're ready, and I'd never forgive myself if I did anything to hurt you."

"I told you I was ready."

"You're not, baby. I can see it in your eyes. I see something that ..."

"What?"

"I don't know. Something you're going to have to tell me before we have sex."

"There's nothing," she said.

"Daphne ..."

"I mean it. I don't know what you're talking about."

Okay. I'd play it her way for now. It was probably something that she considered nothing. Something she thought she was over. She didn't have to be over it for me to fuck her. I just had to know what I was dealing with.

She meant too much to me to be a quick fuck.

Damn.

What had I gotten myself into?

This woman had crept under my skin.

Into my heart.
And I hardly knew her.
Fate had brought us together. She was my destiny.
I'd do anything for her.

CHAPTER TWENTY-FIVE

Daphne

My body was in flames.

And Brad Steel just doused a bucket of water on them.

I wanted him. I wanted him in a way I didn't fully understand.

Which was why he'd stopped.

I should have thanked him, really. But I didn't want to thank him. I wanted to punch him and force him to make love to me.

"I'll drive you home," he said softly.

I nodded. "Thanks for dinner."

"You're welcome. Thank you for spending time with me." Then he laughed. "I've never said that to anyone before. But I mean it. Thank you."

"You don't have to thank me. I'm glad I met you. I just wish . . ."

"Wish what?"

"I wish it didn't have to be over."

He took my hand. "Who says it's over?"

"I know you say it's not, but come on. I may be a virgin, but I'm not a moron."

"It's over because we didn't have sex? Daphne, what makes you think all I want is sex?"

"You're a college guy, and Patty says—"

"Patty's right about most college guys. Even about me, for that matter. But it's not that way with you. You said it yourself. It's destiny."

"You believe that?"

"I do until something happens that makes me not believe it anymore."

"You think that will happen?"

"Anything can happen, baby, but I can tell you honestly, right now, I don't want that to happen."

Warmth bubbled through me. "I wasn't teasing you," I said. "I really did want to make love. I wanted it to be you, Brad."

"It *will* be me. Just not tonight." He pulled me close.

We stood, embracing, for several moments. I never wanted to let go.

"I should get you back," he said.

I nodded. "Okay."

"I want to see you tomorrow night, okay?"

"Yeah, o— Oh! No. It's first nighter."

"Shit, really? First nighter is a pain in the ass. Skip it and go out with me instead."

"I want to, but I can't. All the girls on the floor made plans to go together. Patty would be upset."

"Patty will be fine."

My mother and I had talked endlessly about college. I'd spoken to Dr. Payne as well. We all agreed that I should have the normal college experience—which included orientation... and first nighter.

"I should go."

"You realize they pair you off like ducks in a row, right?"

"I know what it is, but everyone says you don't *have* to spend the evening with your date."

"Whoever is lucky enough to be paired off with you will want to spend the evening with you," he said. "I guarantee it."

His words warmed me. "It doesn't matter. I won't be interested in whoever it is." I touched his stubbled cheek. "I'm interested in you. Only you."

He smiled, and his cheeks flushed a bit. He was a senior, twenty-two years old, and I made him blush.

It really was destiny.

"I can't talk you out of this, huh?" he said.

"I'm sorry. I don't want to disappoint the others. Plus, I honor my commitments. I feel strongly about that."

He kissed my forehead. "You're something, you know that?"

"I can meet you after," I said.

"You got it. Let's get you back to the dorm."

★ ★ ★

Brad gave me a searing kiss after he walked me to my room. Patty was still out with the girls, or maybe she'd met Sean. I had no idea. At any rate, I undressed, wrapped my robe around myself, and gathered my facial scrub and toothbrush, ready to head to the bathroom and wash up. I jerked when someone knocked on the door.

I sighed. Probably Ennis or someone else, saying another party was forming in the lounge. I was just too tired. These three days had been nonstop, and frankly, I wanted to lie in my bed and relive my time with Brad. I couldn't stop thinking about him. I decided not to answer the door. Who would it harm? As soon as whoever it was went away, I'd make my way to the bathroom.

Then a harsher knock. "I know you're in there," said a female voice. "I saw you come back with Brad."

I didn't recognize the voice, but I'd only just met all these people. It could easily be one of the girls from the floor.

If she saw me, I'd be a liar if I didn't answer the door. I wasn't a liar.

I opened the door.

Not one of the girls from the floor. Instead, it was a beautiful woman wearing jeans and a tank top with Candie's high-heeled slides. Her body was a perfect hourglass figure. Her hair was brown, lighter and shorter than mine, and her eyes a sparkling blue.

"Uh...hi," I said. "I'm sorry. Have we met? Do you live on one of the other floors?"

She eyed my room. "Cute," she said.

"What do you want?"

"Nice robe."

"Who are you?"

"I'm a friend of your brother's."

"Larry?"

"Yeah. Can I come in for a minute?"

Say no. But I no longer trusted my inner voice, not after I'd lost so much time junior year. I had nothing to fear from this young woman. She didn't seem dangerous. Even if she was, I was taller. Of course, I was no fighter. She could do some major damage with those wooden heels alone.

Something pulsed in my head. Something familiar, like I'd been in a similar situation before.

But I hadn't. I had no idea who this girl was.

"Who are you?" I said again.

"A friend," she said. "I'm here for one reason."

"And that is ... ?"

"To warn you to stay away from Brad Steel. You don't know what you're dealing with."

"I only just met—"

"I know. That's why I'm here, to help you. I know he's been with you the past three evenings. He'll hurt you, Daphne."

That feeling—that pseudo-memory of violation—pulsed through me again.

This person had been watching me?

My skin prickled with invisible insect bites. My heartbeat drummed in my ears. White noise clouded my mind.

"He uses women," she said. "I know how you're feeling. He's great-looking. You're new here and the most gorgeous guy on campus has the hots for you. I feel for you, but you're only going to get hurt."

"I don't believe you."

"I know you don't. You don't want to, and that's okay. If you keep seeing him, though, don't say I didn't warn you. I'll go now. Looks like you're ready for bed." She walked out of the room, closing the door behind her.

I quickly reopened the door. "Wait! I didn't get your name."

But she didn't hear me as she walked through the door to the stairwell.

My heart still thumped rapidly. Faster, faster, faster ...

I shouldn't be frightened. She hadn't done anything. But Brad ... Brad would never ...

Breathe in, breathe out.

Breathe in, breathe out.

Then the curtain fell.

CHAPTER TWENTY-SIX

Brad

Murphy came home with a woman who wasn't Patty Watson. Hey, none of my business.

"This is Sloane," he said, his voice cracking.

"Hey," I said.

He grabbed a few beers out of the fridge and then led Sloane and her big blond hair into his bedroom. I figured he was gone for the night, but he returned to the kitchen.

"Wendy's on the warpath," he said, his voice still off.

I rolled my eyes. "When is she not?"

"I'm serious. Sloane and I ran into her at the convenience store. She was buying a pack of Marlboros."

"She said she quit."

He cleared his throat. Then again. "Apparently not. Anyway, I tried to sneak us out of there before she saw us, but no deal. Sloane had to use the john."

"What happened? What's wrong, Murph? You're not acting like yourself, and you sound like a frog is living in your throat."

"She asked where you were."

"Fuck. What did you tell her?"

"I told her you were out, man. I'd never give up your locale. Except..."

"Except what?"

"You won't believe me if I tell you." He shook his head. "I can't even believe it myself. I'm lucky I didn't piss right there."

Not a good sign. My nerves jumped inside my skin. "Are you kidding? This is Wendy. I'll believe anything."

"She fucking pulled a gun on me!" He took a swig of the beer he was holding. "Held it at my head."

"A gun?" I raked my fingers through my hair. I'd taught her how to handle firearms. "Fuck, bro. I'm so sorry."

"Does she even know how to use that damn thing?"

I purposely didn't respond to his question, though the answer was *yes, all due to me.* "Don't you worry. I'll take care of this."

"That's not the point. I told her where you were. I'm sorry, man. I'm going to start carrying my own piece. This is ridiculous."

"This all happened in the store?"

"No, after I left the store. Sloane went to the bathroom, and I went ahead out to the car. Wendy followed me and pulled out the piece."

"Sloane doesn't know?"

"Hell, no. You know women. They take forever in the can. And thank God, because I really need to get laid now. If I tell her what happened, she'll bolt, and I wouldn't blame her."

"Wendy didn't show up at Tante Louise. Did you tell her I was with someone?"

"No. She didn't ask."

"Thank God. She's a loose cannon when she gets like this. She needs some help. I've tried to get her to go to therapy, but—"

"Therapy? She needs to be arrested, man."

"Why didn't you call the cops?"

"Because of you, Brad. I can still call the cops now."

I nodded. "Go ahead and call the cops. She deserves it."

"Man! I've got a woman with curves going into next week ready to spread her legs—"

"Oh, for God's sake. Call the cops tomorrow, then. I swear, Murph, your dick is your God."

"I won't deny it." He grabbed his crotch and walked out of the kitchen. Seemed okay for someone who'd recently been held up at gunpoint. Either that or he just wanted to get into Blondie's pants.

Fucking Wendy. I knew she wouldn't go quietly. At least she hadn't shown up—

Oh, fuck.

I knew Wendy like the back of my hand. She *had* showed up, and she had seen—

Daphne.

Damn.

I grabbed my wallet and keys off the counter and raced to my car.

* * *

Daphne's door was cracked.

I opened it. "Daphne? Oh, shit!"

She lay on the ground, her eyes closed, her burgundy robe open with her breasts spilling out. Next to her, her toothbrush, toothpaste, and some skincare products had fallen out of a bucket.

I knelt down and touched her cheek. "Daphne? Daphne, can you hear me?"

She opened her eyes. "Brad? What happened?"

"I don't know, baby. You're lying on the floor."

"I am?"

"Yeah. Can you sit up?" I helped her get into a sitting position and closed her bathrobe.

She twisted her lips, her forehead wrinkling. "I think . . . someone was here. A woman."

"Who?"

"I don't know. She didn't tell me her name. Yeah, now I remember. She told me . . . She told me you used women and that I should stay away from you."

Wendy.

Could only be Wendy.

"Did she hurt you?"

"No. She seemed nice. She sure doesn't like you, though."

"She didn't have a gun?"

Daphne gasped. "God, no!"

Thank God. "What did she look like?"

"Shorter than me, brown hair, blue eyes. Jeans and a tank top. Tight."

That was Wendy all right.

"I'm sorry, baby. I'll take care of this."

"How can you take care of it? Do you know her? She didn't tell me her name."

"Yeah. Her name is Wendy, and I won't let her bother you again."

"Why would she want to warn me about you?"

"She and I have history."

Her eyes widened. "Is she the one . . . ?"

"It's over, baby. I'm not interested in her."

"Are you sure? She's beautiful."

"She's nothing compared to you. Please don't believe anything she said about me. She's lying."

"She said I'd get hurt."

"I'll never hurt you, baby. I promise."

It was a promise I swore to keep, no matter the cost.

CHAPTER TWENTY-SEVEN

Daphne

Why did I feel so safe when Brad Steel's arms were around me? I barely knew him.

Fate.

That word kept humming its way into my mind.

"I guess I must have fainted," I said. "Or something."

"Are you sure? She didn't touch you or push you?"

I swept my mind for information. "No, I really don't think so."

"I should take you to the ER," he said.

"No." I hated hospitals.

"If you fainted, you might have low blood sugar or something."

"Then I'll eat a candy bar. There's a machine at the end of the hall."

"That's the least of my concerns. Fainting can mean other things. Worse things."

I'd fainted before a couple of times. The doctor at home had said it was due to my anxiety, which caused me to hyperventilate. Seeing the beautiful woman at my door warning me to stay away from a man I was sure was my destiny had caused me a lot of stress. It made perfect sense. I just wasn't sure I wanted to explain all this to Brad.

I also couldn't explain why I didn't want to go to a hospital.

I'd seriously have to be dying before I set foot in a hospital again. A hospital had taken nearly a year away from me. Yes, I understood physical ailments were different from mental ones, and I truly had no valid reason to fear a hospital, but I did anyway.

No one would steal time from me again. The faint was bad enough. That was stealing time as well, and I didn't want to lose any more of the precious commodity. Especially now that I'd met Brad Steel.

I wanted to spend all my remaining time—which was a lifetime—with him.

The thought frightened me more than a little, but I couldn't deny the truth of it. He was my destiny. I knew it so profoundly that I felt the knowledge had always been with me. I just hadn't accessed it yet.

I couldn't say these words to him, though. They'd scare him away. He was young, and I was younger still. Neither of us should be making decisions of such magnitude.

Of course, I wasn't making this decision. Fate was.

I forced a smile. "I'm fine. Really. It was just a shock."

"You did wake right up." He massaged the palm of my hand with his thumb. "I'm going to call you first thing in the morning, though."

"Okay," I said. "I'd like that."

He kissed me sweetly on the lips. "Tomorrow night. After you ditch your first nighter."

"Absolutely," I said.

★ ★ ★

As promised, Brad called me the next morning. I didn't have a lot of time to talk, so it was brief, but I smiled all day because he cared so much. By the time Patty and I were done with dinner—my first dinner ever in the cafeteria, as I'd been to dinner with Brad the last three nights—first nighter arrangements were underway.

The bathroom on our floor was crowded with women all scurrying to look their best for their "dates." I didn't care so much about that, but I did want to look my best for my real date after first nighter. I was meeting Brad outside my dorm at ten.

Ten used to be my bedtime. I'd been on campus for four days, and now my bedtime was midnight at the earliest. Once classes began, I didn't expect that to change. My guidance counselor had warned that college was not high school, and I wouldn't be able to slide by on intelligence alone. I'd have to actually study for several hours each night. Oddly, I was looking forward to studying. I loved learning.

I put on more makeup than usual but still kept to a natural look. Then I donned the new burgundy dress with the same shoes I'd worn last night with Brad.

"You look amazing!" Patty gushed.

"So do you."

She did. She wore an emerald prairie dress that flattered her green eyes. She was shorter in stature than I and wore higher heels, in gold. She'd painted her toenails and fingernails a neutral reddish brown that accented her coloring and clothing choice nicely.

I hadn't painted my nails or toenails. I almost never did, but now, looking at how polished Patty was, I wished I had. But it was too late. First nighter would begin in a half hour, and we needed to get moving.

"I'm so excited!" Patty gushed. "Aren't you?"

"Sure." I smiled. A little white lie wouldn't hurt. I was more excited about meeting Brad afterward.

"I hope I meet someone great."

"What about Sean?" I asked.

"Sean is also great," she said, "but he hasn't called me."

"After you..."

She laughed it off, though I wasn't buying it. "Slept with him? Yeah, twice. But you know, this is college. I plan to have loads of fun. No committing to one guy right away."

I didn't get the whole casual sex thing. Maybe because I'd never actually had sex, but I couldn't get myself to think of sex as a one-time thing. Maybe after I lost my virginity I would, but I doubted it. Not when I felt so strongly that Brad Steel was my ultimate destiny.

"You don't have any regrets?" I said.

"About screwing Sean? Heck, no. He's great-looking and a lot of fun. I hope I'll hear from him again."

"I'm sure you will."

"Maybe. You can always put in a good word for me with the roomie. What's going on there, anyway?"

"Not a lot." It wasn't exactly a lie.

"Not a lot? Are you kidding? You've been out with him the last three nights."

"And you notice I made it home each night." I twisted my lips. Foot in mouth. "I didn't mean—"

"No worries. I'm not insulted. It's pretty clear you don't have a lot of experience with guys, Daph."

My cheeks warmed, probably making them redder than the blush I'd brushed over them. "Not really."

"Brad seems like a good guy. I'm really surprised he hasn't tried anything with you."

"He says we can go slow."

"And you're okay with that? I've got to tell you—I couldn't wait to ditch my virginity."

I hadn't been okay with that last night. I'd wanted him to take me, and I'd been ready to let him. Brad had stopped it, and I still wasn't quite sure why. "Yeah, I'm okay with that. I appreciate him going at my pace."

"You're not horny for him at all?"

I laughed. "I didn't say that."

For sure, I'd been horny as all get-out last night, but Brad had probably done the right thing for me. How he knew what I needed, I'd never understand.

Or maybe it was all part of our destiny.

"Maybe you'll find someone great tonight," she said. "Let's go!"

CHAPTER TWENTY-EIGHT

B r a d

Driving to see Wendy wasn't what I'd had in mind for this evening, but she had to know what she'd done to Daphne and Murph was unacceptable and I wouldn't put up with it.

I was the one person who could control Wendy—in the bedroom, at least. I planned to exercise that control tonight, outside the bedroom. Early, before I met Daphne at ten.

Wendy attended a different college but cut class the majority of the time and stayed in Denver to be close to me. Her brilliant mind and photographic memory allowed her to ace classes she didn't even attend by speed reading all the textbooks. I'd never known anyone quite as brilliant as Wendy Madigan, but intelligence of that level seemed to come with some other issues.

From what I'd seen lately? A *lot* of crazy.

I'd never known Wendy to be violent. Pulling a gun on Murph yesterday was new, and something I needed to nip in the bud straight away—especially since I was responsible for her knowing how to wield a pistol.

I pulled into the driveway of the rental she used when she was in town, left the car, and pounded on the door.

The door opened, and Wendy stood there.

Buck naked.

"I've been waiting for you." She opened the screen door.

"For God's sake, anyone on the street can see you."

"Do you think I care?"

No, she didn't care. Wendy had a killer body, and she knew it. She loved showing it off... especially to me.

This woman had everything—beauty, brains, a family who seemed to love her. Why was she troubled?

The issues had emerged slowly in the six years since I'd met her. Little eccentricities that at first had added to her charm. Now? Pulling a gun on Murph and confronting Daphne in her dorm room? She'd graduated to the beginnings of insanity.

She needed help.

I walked in. "Put some clothes on."

"I don't think so. Drink?"

"No."

"Mind if I have one?"

"Actually, I'd rather you didn't."

"Don't be such a square, Brad. A few years ago, you loved to tie one on with me."

"A few years ago, I was a teenager."

"With the body and sexual prowess of a man." She raised one eyebrow. "I miss those days, don't you?"

No. I didn't say it, though. Getting her angry wasn't the best way to begin this conversation that I knew would end with her mad as hell.

"Sometimes," I said. Not a lie. I missed a few things about those days, just not anything having to do with her.

She poured herself a glass of wine. Red. Always red. Wendy said once that red wine reminded her of the deep red of blood as it ran through arteries. I'd brushed it off at the time.

Now it made me kind of nervous.

She took a sip. "To what do I owe the pleasure, Brad?"

I took the glass from her and set it on the table. "Go get dressed, and we'll talk."

She picked the glass back up and took another sip. "You want to talk to me? You'll do it now, and I won't be dressed. In fact…"

"What?"

"I don't think I feel much like talking. That is, unless you get undressed as well."

"No deal." I yanked the glass from her again, drips of burgundy splashing onto her naked torso.

"Well"—she batted her eyes—"the bedroom *is* your domain, and I'm happy to talk in there if you'd like. You still have to get naked, though."

Fine. If it took getting her into her bedroom to listen to me, that was what I'd do. I lifted my T-shirt over my head.

She sucked in a breath.

"Get in the bedroom. Now."

She trotted to the closed door and opened it. "You going to finish getting naked now?"

"This is my domain, as you've admitted. I give the orders in here."

She sat down on the bed, her body flushed with heat. "God, yes. You give the orders in here, baby. Always."

"That's right. Never forget it." A pair of handcuffs sat on the dresser. "Where's the key to these?"

"Top drawer."

I opened the drawer, found the key quickly, and placed it in my pocket. "Grab a rung of the headboard."

She moved slowly to the head of the bed.

"Faster!" I yelled.

She nearly jumped and grabbed a rung with her right hand. I quickly cuffed her wrist and clicked the other cuff into place around the rung.

"What are you going to do to me, Brad? I want juicy details."

"Shut the fuck up, or you'll get nothing."

"But—"

I grabbed a roll of duct tape, also on top of her dresser. I ripped off a piece and slammed it over her lips. "I thought I told you to shut the fuck up. Since you can't be trusted to obey me, I'll take care of it for you."

She moved her hips. Yeah, she was turned on. News to her, though. She wasn't getting any tonight. At least not from me.

"You will answer my questions with a nod or shake of your head. Do you understand?"

She nodded, her eyes wide.

"Are you wet right now?"

She nodded.

"Do you want me to fuck you hard?"

She nodded, this time quickly with jerky movements.

"I'm afraid I'm going to have to disappoint you, then. You've been a very bad girl, Wendy."

She undulated her hips. She knew what I usually did to her when she was bad. I spanked her or flogged her. She loved that.

Not tonight, though. Not ever again.

"More questions first," I said.

She nodded.

"Did you pull a gun on Sean Murphy?"

Her head remained still, and her cheeks went white.

"You must think I'm stupid. Did you really think he wouldn't tell me? Now answer me, or you'll get nothing. Did you pull a gun on Sean Murphy?"

She nodded slowly.

"Did you go to Daphne Wade's dorm and tell her I'd hurt her?"

Again, whiteness flooded her rosy skin.

"Answer me!"

She nodded again.

Not that I needed her nod to know the truth. I never doubted Murph or Daphne. But now that she'd admitted it, we could move forward.

"You ever go anywhere near either of them again, you'll regret it," I said between clenched teeth.

Now her cheeks reddened again, but this wasn't the turned-on blush of earlier.

I'd seen Wendy angry many times before. We were still in the bedroom, and in here, I was the boss. I moved toward her and unceremoniously ripped the duct tape from her mouth. "Don't say a fucking word," I whispered.

She kept her mouth shut.

"Let me tell you what's going to happen here," I said. "You're going to leave Sean Murphy alone. He can take care of himself, but stay the fuck away anyway. He's not your business."

She opened her mouth, but I silenced her with a gesture.

"I'm talking now. You're not to say a damned thing."

She nodded jerkily.

"Murphy, or anyone else I know at school. You stay the fuck away. Especially from Daphne Wade."

"You don't know everything about your sweet, innocent Daphne," she said.

"Did I tell you to talk?"

She shook her head.

"Right. I did not. Open your mouth again and I'll tape you back up and leave you this way. You can think about it all night while you're cuffed to the bed with no one whipping you or fucking you."

She remained silent.

"I know who she is. She's Larry's half sister. They're not close. Larry never lived with Daphne. He lived with his mother. Larry doesn't know shit about her, and neither do you. She's off your radar. Got it? You so much as go within a mile of her, and you'll be sorry."

She opened her mouth, but I motioned for her to keep quiet.

"You want a smack?"

Stupid question. She probably *did* want it. Wendy liked rough sex that pushed the boundaries. She was a masochist in that way, but in no way was she a true submissive. She liked the pain, but she'd never bow to anyone's will.

Anyone's except mine, that was.

I alone could control Wendy, and I meant to do it now.

"Any questions?"

She nodded.

"Go ahead."

"What's in this for me?"

The question I knew was coming, and the question for which there was only one answer.

Wendy needed nothing. She had her own money, thanks to her business acumen and my investments. She had a family who loved her and doted on her, though they seemed ignorant of her troubled ways. Perhaps because she was an only child.

They couldn't see her faults. She had a band of lackeys—Theo, Tom, and Larry—to carry out her business deals and other wishes.

She had no needs. Nothing I could offer her to keep her in line.

Except the one thing she coveted most in the world.

Me.

I was now taken, so I had to find another way.

To do that, I had to drive to the ranch.

Tonight.

CHAPTER TWENTY-NINE

Daphne

My first nighter date turned out to be a nice guy named Jason Durham, who was nearly as tall as Brad. He was a football player, very muscular, and pretty good-looking too. Any other time, I'd be thrilled.

But all I could think about was what he wasn't.

He wasn't Brad Steel.

He made no secret that he felt he'd hit the jackpot with me. I was flattered, but I didn't return the compliment. I couldn't.

Nine o'clock rolled around. Only an hour until Brad.

Still another hour to fill with Jason. Patty was happy with her date, and she came clamoring up to Jason and me. "We're going for ice cream. You guys want to come?"

"Sounds fun," Jason said. "You up for it?"

"I . . . don't think so."

"Come on, Daph," Patty said. "We're just going over to the Cage on campus."

"Oh, okay." That was different. I could get quickly back to the dorm. "Sure. I'm in."

We walked to the Cage. I didn't need to talk much, because Patty was always a lively conversationalist, and Jason and Patty's date, Rex, added to the talking as well. All fine with me.

We arrived and ordered our ice cream. Patty laughed

when I ordered vanilla.

"All these flavors, Daph, and you want vanilla?"

"It's my favorite." Which it was. I liked chocolate, but vanilla always seemed creamy and perfect to me.

Patty laughed. "You know? It fits you."

"What do you mean?"

"You know . . ."

Was she alluding to my virginity? If so, it was none of the guys' business.

"Don't tell me," Rex said. "We actually have a virgin here on campus?"

My cheeks warmed. I could deny it, but Patty would know I was lying. Why should I deny it anyway? It wasn't anything to be ashamed of.

"Yes," I said.

"Interesting," Jason said. "Why are you waiting?"

"I'm not waiting. I just haven't met anyone yet that I'm willing to do that with."

He smiled. "Maybe you met someone tonight."

"I don't think so."

"I thought we were getting along really well," he said.

"Could we please not talk about this here? My virginity is not up for debate."

"Yeah, of course," he said. "Sorry."

"I'm sorry too, Daph," Patty said.

Yeah, she should be, but I wasn't going to argue with her in front of two virtual strangers. We'd have words later.

"I'm willing to take that problem off your hands any time," Jason whispered in my ear.

"Not really in the mood after this conversation," I said quietly.

He nodded and took a seductive lick of his chocolate peanut butter in a waffle cone. Was that supposed to turn me on?

Because it didn't. In fact, it kind of made me want to puke.

"There's a big party at my dorm tonight," Rex was saying. "What do you say we all go over there after this? The RAs are getting us a keg."

"Sounds great!" Patty said. "You guys should come too."

"I'm up for it," Jason agreed.

I looked at my watch. Nine thirty. "I have plans."

"At nine thirty?" Jason asked.

"No," I said. "At ten, actually."

"For fuck's sake." Jason shook his head. "You got a boyfriend or something?"

"Not if she's a virgin," Rex said.

I stood. "I think I'm done here." I threw my uneaten vanilla cone into a nearby wastebasket.

Jason stood reluctantly. "I suppose I should walk you back."

"Please," I said, "don't trouble yourself."

"It's dark. I'd hate for something to happen to you."

Okay, maybe my first impression of him was right. He was a nice guy after all. Why did the subject of my virginity turn a nice guy into a jerk?

"Thank you," I said. "I appreciate it."

"Hey, just because I'm not going to get lucky isn't a reason to let you walk alone and get attacked."

Right. My second impression was definitely on the money. Still, I'd take the escort back to my dorm. I took self-protection seriously after Mariel's lecture.

He didn't try to hold my hand or anything. We just walked

back to the dorm pretty much in silence. When we got to the building, my nerves started to jump. What to say now? "Nice knowing you?"

"Nice meeting you, Daphne," Jason said.

"Yeah. You too."

"I have to tell you. I was thrilled when I saw you. You're the most beautiful woman in our class."

"You've actually seen *all* the girls in our class?"

"I've seen enough to know I hit the jackpot tonight. At least I thought I did."

"I'm sorry. I've already met someone."

"I kind of got that impression. He's who you're meeting at ten?"

"Yeah."

He nodded. "Lucky guy. I'm . . . er . . . sorry about the shit we gave you about . . ."

"My virginity?"

"Yeah. That was immature. I don't even know Rex."

"Probably not a bad thing."

He gave me a chaste kiss on the cheek. "If things don't work out with your other guy, give me a call. At any rate, I'm really glad we met."

Okay, back to first impression. Jason *was* a nice guy. He just acted like a jerk around Rex because that was what guys did. I still wasn't thrilled that Patty had broadcast my virginity to our dates. Most likely she'd be out late or all night again, so our words would have to wait until tomorrow.

"Deal," I said.

He smiled and walked away as I entered the building. It was nearly ten. I had to change into jeans before Brad arrived.

I was surprised to find him standing outside the door of my room.

He looked at his watch. "There you are. I was getting worried."

"I still have a few minutes," I said.

He grabbed me and planted a quick kiss on my lips. Sparks shot through me.

"Change of plans," he said. "I have to go home to the ranch tonight."

"Oh?"

"Yeah. It's important. Shit I have to do."

"Oh." I tried not to sound too disappointed, but inside I was devastated. I'd so been looking forward to more time with him.

"Hey," he said. "Come with me."

I widened my eyes. Had I heard him correctly?

"Yeah. Our house is huge. Plenty of room. You can meet my parents."

"Don't you live on . . ."

"The western slope, yeah. It's a five-hour drive from here, and I have to leave now so I'm not driving all night."

"Classes start next week."

"It's Friday. We'll be back Sunday evening."

"But there's—"

"More orientation?"

No. Orientation was basically over. Now we had the weekend to get settled before classes began on Monday. "Not exactly."

"Then come. Please."

"What will I do while you're doing whatever it is you need to go home to do?"

"You can hang out with my mom. You'll love her."

"Brad, no. This is too soon. It's . . . weird."

"I don't want to be away from you."

"It's only two days."

"I know." His eyes got a far-off look. "Seems like years. But I understand. How was your evening?"

"It was okay."

"Just okay?"

"Yeah. My date was a nice enough guy, he just wasn't..."

"Me?"

I laughed. "Well... yeah."

He stroked my hair. "Come with me, Daphne. I know it sounds crazy. It probably is. But I really want you to come."

Drive off in the middle of the night with a guy I hadn't yet known a week? Crazy. Completely crazy. I was batty to even be considering it.

But one look into his dark eyes, and I knew my answer.

"Okay."

CHAPTER THIRTY

Brad

Daphne fell asleep around midnight. We hadn't talked a lot, just mundane conversation, except that nothing was mundane with Daphne. She looked like a dream in her first nighter dress. I almost begged her to keep it on, but it probably wasn't the most comfortable thing to wear for a late-night road trip.

She wore jeans, flip-flops, and a Styx T-shirt, and she was sleeping peacefully in the reclined passenger seat of my truck.

She looked so peaceful and serene.

Had I made the right decision, asking her to join me? I had shit to do that I wasn't looking forward to, but I'd still have time to spend with her, show her my home, let her see the beauty of the western slope. Peaches and apples were in season, fresh off the trees from our orchard. It was perfect timing all around.

Except for the stuff I wasn't particularly looking forward to.

But that wouldn't take long. Wendy had an Achilles' heel other than me, and I had to take advantage of it.

Larry and Tom were already at school. As for Theo, I never knew when he'd show up. He might be around. Rodney Cates might be around. He and Theo's sister were a couple that started all the way back in high school, and they spent time in Snow Creek sometimes.

Those days seemed like another lifetime, but when I returned to Snow Creek, it all came back to me like it was yesterday.

That wasn't necessarily a good thing.

I'd had some amazing times in my hometown and on my ranch. I'd also had some dark times—times I wished I could take back, remove from my life.

Most of those times took place during my high school years as a member of the Future Lawmakers Club at Tejon Prep School in Grand Junction, a half-hour drive from Snow Creek.

The Future Lawmakers.

Not Future Lawyers, even though two of our members—Tom and Larry—had aspirations to attend law school. Future Lawmakers. At the time, I figured that meant helping to make laws, becoming legislators, or even judges, helping to interpret existing laws.

I looked down at my right ring finger.

The ring.

Our emblem, designed by Wendy.

She'd never told us its significance, and I never pressed her. Now? I hesitated to ask.

I had a love-hate relationship with the ring. It represented a time in my life where I was young and had all the possibilities in the world. It also represented people who'd changed, who were still changing, and not for the better.

I wiped my mind of the memories. Once I did what I had to do, this weekend was about new beginnings, not old high school memories and regrets. I'd brought Daphne on a whim, but I was determined to make this a nice weekend for her.

This would be the first of many times she'd come to my ranch, I hoped.

Yes, the first of many.

And if I was successful this weekend, she and I would never have to worry about Wendy Madigan again.

★ ★ ★

"Wake up, baby." I nudged Daphne softly. "We're here."

"Mmm." She opened her eyes. "What time is it?"

"A little after two. We made good time. Come on. Let's get inside so you can get some sleep."

"Yeah, sure. Okay." Daphne sat up and opened the car door on her side.

I got out as well and grabbed both our bags from the back. "Come on."

I unlocked the front door, and we walked in quietly. "Shh," I said to Ebony, giving her a pet.

"She's beautiful," Daphne whispered.

"Yeah, she's a sweetheart. Brandy's around here somewhere. Probably in bed with my dad. They sleep with him when I'm not home."

Daphne knelt down and let Ebony pepper her face with licks and kisses. "I love her. I totally love her."

"She'll lick you forever if you let her."

"I'm okay with that, I think."

I laughed softly. "I'm going to let her outside for a few minutes. Then I'll show you where you'll be staying."

She stood, letting go of Ebony and nodding. After the dog was safely outside, I grabbed our bags and led Daphne down the hallway to the guest room farthest away from my parents' master suite.

"This place is huge," she whispered. "I feel like I'm in a hotel."

I opened the door and flipped on the light. "Here you go."

Her eyes were still wide as she gaped around the room. She walked forward and opened the door to the walk-in closet, which was empty. "This closet is seriously as big as my dorm room. I'm not even kidding."

"I know. I lived in the same dorm when I was a freshman. It took some getting used to after having all the room I could ask for out here on the western slope."

"Where's your room?" she asked.

"Right next to this one," I said.

"And the bathroom?"

I nodded toward the second door in the room. "Right there."

She walked toward it and opened it. "My own bathroom?"

I nodded. "All our bedrooms have their own bathrooms."

She shook her head. "You actually live like this? I know the Steel ranch is successful, but just how successful *are* you, Brad?"

"I'm not overly successful at all. My father and mother are. But I'm their only kid, so I guess it'll be mine someday." I breathed in. "I love this place. It's in my blood. I know it like I know the back of my hand."

"You want to run the ranch someday?"

"I do. I really do. My dad isn't in the best of health, but it will still be a while before I take over."

"Kind of morbid, isn't it?" she said. "You love your parents, but you want the ranch to be yours."

Not as morbid as she might think. My father was a Grade A asshole whose arteries were hardening and lungs were failing because he'd smoked his whole life. My mother deserved better. He was a hell of a rancher, though. He'd taken this place from his father's dream to a multimillion-dollar operation. We'd recently passed into eight figures because of his shrewd investments. I planned to take it into the billions. Our cattle and our fruit were the best on the slope, our vineyards were starting to produce, and Dad was looking at hiring a winemaker.

I'd spent the last three years studying the business of agriculture, and I was going to take this place into the twenty-first century.

With Daphne at my side.

What?

Had I just thought that?

The words had fallen into my head as if they'd always been there and always would.

I still hardly knew this woman, but she was the one who'd used the word *destiny*.

Damn.

Daphne would be at my side as I ran this place.

I knew it as if it had been foretold by Nostradamus himself.

I kissed her forehead and then her lips. "Get some sleep. We rise early around here."

"What time?"

"Five, usually."

"In three hours?"

I laughed. "You don't have to get up that early. Sleep as late as you want to. But since I'm home, I'll be helping my dad."

"Don't you have ... I don't know. Cowboys to do that work?"

"Ranch hands you mean? We have lots of them, but Dad's a hands-on kind of guy, and frankly, so am I. I know how to do almost every job around here. Dad made sure of it."

"Your dad sounds like an amazing guy."

I kissed her lips again. "In some ways. Go to sleep." I walked toward the door.

"Brad?"

"Yeah?"

"Aren't you going to stay with me?"

"Baby, if I stay in here with you, neither of us will get any sleep."

CHAPTER THIRTY-ONE

Daphne

"I'm not asking for sex, Brad," I said. "But I'm in a strange house with people I've never met. I want something familiar next to me for the rest of the night."

"The rest of the night is three hours, baby. Then I'll be getting up."

"I know. Please?"

"You think I can sleep next to you, have your body next to mine, and not want you?"

"I think you're a grown man and you can control yourself. Just like I'm a grown woman and I can control myself."

"You're eighteen, Daphne."

"And you're twenty-two. If I can control myself, you should be able to."

He laughed then. "Men and women are different."

"Please, Brad?" I tried not to sound too needy, but I'd come along at his insistence, and now I felt ... well ... weird. His parents didn't know I was here. What would they think when they woke up and found he'd brought a strange girl home? A strange girl he'd known for less than a week?

I opened my mouth to say as much, but he finally relented.

"All right. I'll stay in here with you. I'm going to go to my room to get ready for bed because all my stuff is there. You get ready for bed as well, and I'll meet you back here in a few minutes. Okay?"

I smiled. "Thank you."

Already just knowing he'd be with me blanketed me in warm comfort. A warm comfort I'd never known. Not even my parents had given me such comfort and such a feeling of protection.

I might be imagining things, but oh, it was wonderful to imagine. In Brad's arms, I was safe, protected, comforted.

Loved.

I grabbed the small bag I'd packed and headed into the bathroom. The room was a full bath worthy of the most elegant hotel. Separate shower and bathtub, two vanities, and a toilet and bidet. I only knew what a bidet was from French class.

I washed my face and brushed my teeth. I usually only washed my private parts once a day, in the morning when I showered, but I ran the soapy cloth over them now. Just in case Brad couldn't control himself. I almost hoped he couldn't. But he most likely could, since he'd been the one who stopped before.

A giant yawn split my face. Better not to try anything tonight anyway. We were both exhausted, and he would be getting up in three hours or so. Still, being fresh down there felt nice. I was glad I'd done it for him. I slipped on my cotton tank and boy shorts pajamas and made my way over to the gorgeous queen-size bed. This would be a lot nicer than those twin bunk beds in the dorm.

Which reminded me. Crap! I hadn't left a note for Patty. Oh, well, she probably wouldn't be home tonight anyway. I'd call her in the morning to let her know where I was. Not that she called me all those nights she stayed at Sean's place. She probably wouldn't worry at all.

I turned down the covers and sat down on the cotton sheets. Now to wait for—

A soft knock on the door.

"Brad?" I said.

The door opened. "Yeah, it's me."

I drew in a breath. He was wearing nothing but navy-blue boxers. His chest was so perfectly sculpted with just a smattering of black hair over it. His nipples were brown circles against his tanned skin, and his abs . . . oh, my. That was actually an eight-pack, not a six-pack. His shoulders broad and bare, and his arms. Those strong arms that made me feel safe and sound were corded with muscles.

Muscles that came from hard ranch work, not from the gym.

Brad Steel was magnificent.

And he'd be sleeping with me tonight.

"You look amazing," he said.

I shivered. "They're just pajamas."

"You'd look even more amazing out of them."

I shivered again.

"I'll be good," he said. "I promise. Come on. Morning is nearly here. Let's get to bed."

I crawled between the sheets of the mega-comfortable bed. Brad slipped in beside me.

"Come here," he said.

I snuggled into his shoulder.

Before long, I was asleep.

★ ★ ★

I woke to the sun streaming through the blinds on the window. I sat up abruptly. *Where am I?*

Then I remembered.

Brad's ranch.

I gulped audibly. Did I really drive for hours in the middle of the night to spend the weekend with a guy I'd only just met? And was I here, now, in his parents' home? Lying in the most comfortable bed ever?

Talk about impulsive.

My therapist had told me I had a tendency to act on impulse. It wasn't necessarily a bad thing, he said, but something I needed to be aware of and curb when necessary.

I probably should have curbed it last night.

I smiled. I *had* tried. I'd said no at first, but Brad had really wanted me to come here with him. I still wasn't sure why. It was so early, and even though I felt seriously in my bones that I was destined to be with this man, I needed to act responsibly. It truly was too soon for me to be here.

But . . . I *was* here, so I had to deal with the situation.

I quickly checked the clock that sat on the bedside table. Ten thirty a.m.! Brad's parents would think I was the laziest person on the planet.

Brad was likely long gone. He'd probably risen at five and tiptoed out of here so he wouldn't wake me. I figured I'd wake naturally at seven or so. But ten thirty?

Granted, I'd gone to bed after two, but still, I'd slept a good portion of the drive. Brad hadn't, and he'd been able to get up.

Now what? Do I get dressed? Leave the room? My stomach growled. I needed food, but I couldn't go into the kitchen and just help myself.

Impulsive, for sure. I totally had not thought this through.

First things first. I headed to the bathroom for a shower. When I was squeaky clean and had dried myself with the most decadent plush towels in existence, I dressed in jeans, a tank top, and my sandals, applied some blush and lip gloss, and—

Flopped back on the bed.

Seriously, what was I supposed to do now?

My stomach growled again. If only I'd thought to pack some snacks. I had granola bars in my dorm room, but they hadn't made it into my bag. This really *had* been impulsive. I'd shoved clothes and toiletries into a backpack and just gone off with Brad.

I stood quickly. I was being silly. I'd been invited here. I walked to the door and tentatively opened it. The hallway seemed to stretch as I walked slowly toward the end of it. This was so surreal.

Lights from the large country kitchen loomed ahead. A woman stood at the stove.

I cleared my throat. "Uh . . . Mrs. Steel?"

The woman turned. She had dirty-blond hair, wore an apron, and had a big smile on her face. "Hi, honey. I'm not Mrs. Steel. I'm Belinda, the cook and housekeeper. Mr. Brad said you'd be up eventually."

"Hi. I'm Daphne."

"Can I make you some breakfast, Daphne? Eggs? Bacon? Toast?"

"Yeah, I guess. Thank you. Eggs, please. And toast. No bacon."

"Are you a vegetarian?" she asked.

"No. Just trying to cut down." I didn't want to explain my new humanely raised rules.

"Coming right up. Mr. Brad's out with his father this

morning. He'll be in around noon for lunch." She laughed. "But you probably won't be hungry by then."

I smiled. Sort of.

"Coffee? Juice? What would you like?"

"Could I have coffee *and* juice?"

"You may have anything you want. Strict orders to make you feel right at home and give you whatever your heart desires."

"Brad said that?"

"Maybe not quite in those words, honey, but yes, he said that. Between you and me, I've never seen him so smitten with someone."

I warmed all over and touched my cheeks. They were no doubt red as a beet.

Soon the kitchen was alive with the savory scent of frying eggs. When Belinda handed me a plate with two fried eggs and two pieces of thick toast, already buttered, I inhaled. This country breakfast sure smelled good. On the table were several mason jars holding different colored jams.

"All homemade," Belinda said. "Apple jelly and spiced peach preserves, right from the Steel orchard. The blackberry jam is from my own bushes."

"You made all of these?"

"Guilty," she said. "Try them all. The peach is my favorite."

"I'll begin with that, then." I spooned some of the bright-orange concoction onto my toast and took a bite.

Wow. Peach explosion! With a touch of cinnamon and nutmeg. "This is delicious," I said, my mouth still full.

"Thank you, honey. Like I said, it's my favorite. That wild blackberry is something too, though, and the apple is all Fuji with a touch of crabapple to give it a crisp tartness. You like apples, honey?"

"Love them. Love all fruit, actually."

"You sure you're not a vegetarian?"

I smiled after swallowing my second bite of toast with spiced peach. "No. I'm just trying to only eat meat that I know was raised humanely."

"Then you've come to the right place. The Steels have such a large ranch for a reason. All their beef is grass fed and pastured."

"I'm looking forward to trying it."

"You won't have to wait long. I'm fixing burgers for lunch at twelve thirty sharp. Mr. George likes his lunch early."

"Mr. George?"

"Mr. Brad's father. Mr. George and Miss Mazie, short for Mackenzie. Mr. Brad was named after his mother, Mackenzie Bradford Steel."

"His real name is Bradford?"

"It is," she said. "His middle name is Raymond for Miss Mazie's dad."

I nodded. "Do you get up at five to make breakfast?"

"No. I don't live here, but I do make sure all the breakfast fixings are in place before I leave after dinner, which is at seven. That's what I mean by an early lunch. It's a long wait for dinner."

"What are we having for dinner?"

"Thinking of your next meal already?" She laughed. "Mr. Brad says we're having rib eye steaks. Steel beef, so you can try the best cut."

"I'm not sure I've ever tasted grass-fed beef," I said.

"Then you're in for a treat. It's a little leaner but still very flavorful. More so, in my opinion. The Steels get a good marbling despite the grass feeding."

"A good marbling?"

"The way the fat is distributed through the muscle is called marbling, and marbling gives the beef its flavor."

"Oh. I guess there's a lot I don't know about beef ranching."

"I only know from listening to Mr. George talk. Stick around here, and you'll learn quickly."

I nodded, spooned some blackberry jam on my toast, and took a bite. Mmm. Deliciously wild and fruity. Tough call between that and the peach. Next, the apple. Oh my God. Crisp and amazing. The apple, hands down, was my favorite, though the other two were spectacular as well. This was true farm-to-table eating. Or rather, orchard-to-table. I couldn't wait to try more.

"When you're done, just leave your dishes in the sink. I'll clean up before I start lunch later."

"I'm happy to help in any way."

"Don't be silly. You're a guest here. Make yourself at home. The Steels have a marvelous library down the other hallway." She pointed.

"What about Mrs. Steel? Is she here? I don't want to step on any toes or anything."

"Miss Mazie is gone for the weekend. Went to Grand Junction to visit her mother. It's just Mr. George and Mr. Brad, and like I said, they won't be in until twelve thirty. The house is yours, honey."

"Oh. All right, I guess."

"Make yourself at home. Miss Mazie, if she were here, would say the same."

"Yes, she would."

I turned.

Brad had entered the kitchen.

CHAPTER THIRTY-TWO

Brad

Daphne looked like sunshine sitting at the table in our huge kitchen, sunlight streaming over her. Her hair was braided and fell into a dark rope over one shoulder.

"Hey, sleepyhead," I said.

Her cheeks pinked and she smiled. "Hey."

"Belinda taking good care of you?"

"The best," she said. "These jams are terrific."

"Only the best," I said.

"Do you need anything, Mr. Brad?"

"I've told you a million times, Belinda, just call me Brad. And no."

"Are you sure? Lunch isn't until—"

"Twelve thirty. I know. I figured I'd get back in here early to show Daphne around the place a little."

"Where's your dad?" she asked.

"He's still out on the northern quadrant."

"Northern quadrant?" Daphne queried.

"This place is huge," I said. "He'll make it back by lunch."

"You guys work like this all through the weekend?"

"Stock still needs tending. Fruit needs picking."

"But you have . . . ranch hands."

"We do. We take time off whenever we want to, but I like

working when I'm back here. It's good for my head."

No truer words. My father might be an asshole who pushed my mother around, but he did teach me a lot of important stuff, such as good hard work keeps you sane. I knew every aspect of this business, from contract negotiation and financials to how to clean out barns and care for stock. We weren't too good to get our hands dirty. Frankly, I liked it that way.

"I'm going to take a quick shower. I'll be ready in ten minutes, and then I'll show you around a little before lunch. Sound good?"

She nodded. "I'll be fine. I may just get a spoon and eat these jams right out of the jars."

That got a laugh out of Belinda. "Honey, I've done the same thing myself."

I left the kitchen and traipsed to my bedroom. I'd come in here when I woke up to shower this morning because I didn't want to wake Daphne.

She'd slept so well, like an angel in my arms.

Crazy, these feelings I was having. I wanted her so badly, wanted to push her down onto a bed and fuck the daylights out of her, but my need to protect her from everything, even myself, superseded all that. These feelings were new to me. New . . . and pleasant.

I would be the one to take her virginity, and it would happen soon. It wouldn't happen under my parents' roof, however. Not going there.

Wendy and I had fucked on my parents' bed once. It had been her idea, of course. Also her idea to use two of my father's neckties—he only owned three—for me to bind her to the antique headboard.

Admittedly, the bondage and discipline aspect of our

relationship used to thrill me, but I felt like I'd outgrown it. I scoffed. Outgrown something at twenty-two? Sounded ridiculous, but it was true. I'd dated other women when Wendy and I were in one of our "off-again" periods, and though our sex had been rough and hard, I'd never bound or spanked any of them. Other than Wendy, I was about hard vanilla fucking.

No matter how often we broke up, though, we'd always found our way back to each other. Yeah, she was my kryptonite.

Or she had been.

Daphne Wade had neutralized the kryptonite.

I no longer had any desire for Wendy. The thought was odd, as Wendy had been such a huge part of my life for so long. I'd been drawn to her despite her flaws—and they were many. When we first met, though, she was a sixteen-year-old girl. A sweet sixteen-year-old girl who'd just become a cheerleader. She was pretty and perky and smart. A great match for me.

But even then, she'd had a darkness about her—not a darkness so much as an edge that unnerved me.

And as these years passed, that edge became more and more a part of who she was.

Not only Wendy, but Theo, Tom, and Larry had changed too—especially Theo. I expected him and Wendy to end up together eventually. They both shared that edge of insanity that creeped me out.

I'd put it off for too long, but now that I'd met the woman who was my soul mate, I had to take care of Wendy once and for all. It would be for her own good, as well as mine and Daphne's.

★ ★ ★

"My father's a little gruff," I said to Daphne after I'd spent the last hour showing her some of the ranch. "Don't let him scare you."

Her eyes widened. "Scare me?"

"Maybe not the right word. He might not seem overly friendly at first, but that's just who he is."

"Do you have any brothers or sisters?"

"No, it's just me. My mom was in a car accident when I was a toddler. She had really bad internal bleeding, and the doctors did a total hysterectomy to save her life."

"Oh!" Daphne clasped her hand to her mouth. "How awful. I'm sorry."

"It was hard for her but good for me." I smiled. "I don't have to share this place with anyone. I'm the sole heir."

She swatted me on the arm. "I'm serious."

"I know. Having a brother or sister would have been nice. My father especially never got over it. It changed him."

My mother had been driving, so as far as my father was concerned, the accident had been her fault. Once she'd recovered, he started using her for a punching bag, but I didn't want to lay that on Daphne quite yet. She was so sweet and angelic. She shouldn't have to deal with something so horrible. By the time I was sixteen, my muscles were bigger, and they were younger than my father's, so I'd put a stop to it. I'd been worried about living outside the home for college, but my father never touched my mother again.

Instead, he ignored her, treated her like a cow patty on his shoe.

I wasn't sure which was worse.

"I'm so sorry," Daphne said.

"Don't be," I said. "I'm his only child, so he was hard on me, but I'm more than ready to take over this place when it's time."

"You're so young yet."

"Like I said, he was hard on me."

"And your mother?"

"What do you mean?"

"Is she ... okay?"

A loaded question. Physically, yes, she was okay. Emotionally? She held her own, but she'd been beaten down for years by my father. When I was fifteen, I tried to get her to leave. Said I'd go with her, and I'd take care of her. But she wouldn't. She said marriage vows meant something to her, and she would stand by her commitment. Then she got a dreamy look in her eye and said she and my father had been happy once, and one day, she felt sure, they would be again.

It hadn't happened yet as far as I could see.

Again, when I hit sixteen, I'd stopped the abuse—the physical abuse, anyway.

But when I was seventeen, she lost it and had to be hospitalized for several months.

She was better now. She got through her days and had hobbies that gave her joy. Her greenhouse, for one. She loved flowers, especially tulips.

Still, though, her relationship with my father was icy. The tension was palpable when they were in the same room.

Part of me was glad she was gone this weekend. Daphne would be spared any unpleasant interaction between my parents. My father would be polite to her, in his own way. He'd be glad to see me move on from Wendy. He never liked her, always thought she had some kind of ulterior motive.

If he only knew ...

If things didn't go well today, he *would* know. I'd go to my father for help.

The mouthwatering smell of burgers wafted in from the kitchen. I took Daphne's hand. "She's okay. Come on. Lunchtime."

Belinda set the plate of burgers on the table. "Hot off the grill," she said. "Where's your father?"

"I have no idea."

Then the door slammed, and my father's cowboy boot footfalls clomped through the corridor.

Dad was home.

CHAPTER THIRTY-THREE

Daphne

Mr. Steel was a big man. He was the same height as Brad and only slightly broader, but something about his presence filled the room.

"Hey, Dad," Brad said. "This is Daphne Wade. Daphne, my father, George Steel."

Mr. Steel didn't smile but held out his hand. "Daphne."

"Nice to meet you, Mr. Steel." I took his hand. It was big and rough and calloused. A lot like Brad's, only more so. And his grip didn't seem nearly as friendly. "Thank you for opening your home to me."

He nodded. "Happy to."

His attitude negated his words. Brad had said he was gruff, so I decided to go with the flow.

"It's a nice day," Mr. Steel said. "Let's eat outside, Belinda. I'm going to wash up."

"Of course. I'll set it up."

"Can I help you with anything?" I asked her.

"Aren't you a dear? Yes, take this plate of lettuce, tomatoes, and onion. I've got the burgers."

"I'll grab the condiments," Brad said.

In a few minutes, everything had been transferred onto a glass-topped table on a sprawling redwood deck. I gaped at the huge backyard. In the distance, another house stood.

"That's the guesthouse," Brad said.

"Oh?"

"Yeah, though it's nearly as big as this one." He laughed and held out a chair. "Have a seat."

I sat down. Should we wait for Mr. Steel?

Brad answered that question for me when he grabbed a bun. "Help yourself."

I took a bun and topped it with a freshly grilled burger. I inhaled the savory scent of grilled beef. I hadn't eaten meat in a few days due to my new restrictions, and boy, had I missed it. I topped it with lettuce and tomato. I loved onion, but I passed on it. I didn't want onion breath for kissing Brad later.

Of course, when Brad added a huge slab to his burger, I wished I'd done the same.

Mr. Steel joined us a few minutes later. "Well, what do you think?" he asked me.

I swallowed my bite of burger. "About what?"

"Steel beef?"

"Oh, it's delicious, of course."

He smiled. Sort of. "She's a smart one, Brad."

"Daphne only eats humanely raised meat," Brad offered.

Mr. Steel nodded. "What are you two going to do for the rest of the day?"

"I have some business to attend to," Brad said.

"And you?" he said to me.

"I'm taking her into town," Brad answered for me.

I nodded. First I'd heard of any of it.

"You'll love Snow Creek," Brad said. "You can explore the town while I'm taking care of some stuff."

I swallowed another bite. "Sure. Sounds good."

I'd grown up in a Denver suburb. A small town might be fun.

"You really taking care of it this time?" Mr. Steel asked Brad.

Brad simply nodded.

I had no idea what they were talking about.

And I got the distinct impression I didn't want to know.

★ ★ ★

Brad and I drove into Snow Creek after lunch. He showed me around a little and then left me to my own exploration while he took care of whatever business awaited him. He didn't volunteer any information, and I didn't ask. I was horribly curious, but I didn't feel it was my place. If he'd wanted me to know, he'd have told me.

The town was adorable. I walked down the main street and spent time in an antique shop. When I was done browsing there, I stopped at an ice cream shop and tasted a couple flavors before deciding on my standard vanilla cone. Who cared if Patty and our first nighter dates had laughed at my favorite flavor? I was hardly alone. Everyone loved vanilla.

I took my cone to the nearby park and sat on a bench, watching some kids play Frisbee. When I'd polished off the ice cream, I walked back to the main street to explore the other side.

A small café and coffee shop, a hardware store, a tattoo—

Oof!

A guy exiting the tattoo parlor nearly knocked me off my feet. He grabbed my arm and steadied me. "I'm so sorry. Are you okay?"

"Yeah, just a little startled."

He had dark hair and tan skin, quite attractive, and his eyes were a fascinating blue that looked almost ... unreal.

"Can I buy you a coffee or something? By way of apology?"

"Oh, no. That's okay."

"Come on. I insist." He pointed to the café. "Best coffee in town. I'm Theo, by the way. Theo Mathias."

"Daphne Wade."

He cocked his head. "Wade. Not Larry Wade's sister?"

I nodded. "Guilty, though I hardly know Larry. We didn't grow up together. I'm here visiting Brad Steel."

"Steel's in town? I just saw him a few days ago. Where is he?"

"He's here somewhere. Said he had some business to take care of."

"He did?" Theo's weird blue eyes took on a strange look.

"Yeah, but I don't know anything about it."

Theo didn't reply for a few seconds. Then, "I went to high school with Brad and Larry."

"Really? Maybe you can tell me about my brother, then. Like I said, I hardly know him."

"Good guy. He's planning to go to law school."

I laughed. "That much I know."

When he didn't say anything again, I cleared my throat. "Did you get a tattoo?" I nodded toward the tattoo parlor.

"Not yet, but I'm thinking about it."

"What kind of image?"

"I'm not sure. I looked through the books today, but I didn't find anything that spoke to me."

"Oh." Now what?

"So about that coffee ... ?"

I looked at my watch. "I suppose so. I'm not supposed to meet Brad for a half hour yet."

"Where are you meeting him?"

"By the library."

"That's only a block away from the coffee shop. Plenty of time. Come on."

CHAPTER THIRTY-FOUR

Brad

"Wendy's not here," Warren Madigan said after he opened the door.

I cleared my throat. "I'm actually here to see you."

"Oh? Come on in. It's always good to see you."

"Is your wife home?"

"Yeah." He turned. "Marie! Brad Steel's here."

Marie Madigan, nearly a dead ringer for Wendy but with a few gray hairs and wrinkles, came running. "Oh, God, is Wendy all right?"

"She's fine," I said.

"Thank goodness," she said. "How are you, Brad?"

"I'm good."

"What can we do for you?" Warren asked.

"Can we sit?"

The Madigans lived in town. Townies, to a rural kid like me. I was the odd man out of our little group in high school. The country kid with money. The others, except for Wendy, all lived in the city—what we in Snow Creek called Grand Junction. Warren Madigan owned an auto repair shop, and Marie was the local school secretary. Wendy had gone to Tejon Prep by way of a large scholarship due to her genius IQ.

"Sure." Marie led us into the small living room and gestured to the sofa.

I sat down, and they sat across from me in two chairs.

"What is it?" Warren asked.

"It's Wendy," I said. "I think she needs . . . help."

Marie sighed. "We've tried, Brad."

"I know you have."

"You're the only one who can get through to her, son," Warren said. "Maybe if you tell her."

"That won't work," I said. "I've tried as well. I think you may have to consider having her committed."

"How can we do that?" her mother asked. "She's over eighteen."

"Besides," Warren said, "what has she done this time?"

"She's stalking my new girlfriend, for one."

"Oh." Warren shook his head. "So it's really over this time, then?"

"I'm sorry, Warren," I said, "but it's been over for a while."

"Not according to Wendy."

"Wendy sees things in her own way," I said. "You both know that."

"It's her high intelligence," Warren said. "The child psychologist who tested her when she was little told us to expect some differences in her."

Marie sniffled. "I always hoped, Brad, that you and she . . ."

"I'm sorry, Marie, but Wendy and I aren't in love."

"Maybe *you* aren't in love," she said. "Wendy is."

I shook my head. "She's not. What Wendy and I had was never love. It was infatuation, puppy love. We were kids. We've grown up, and what we had no longer works."

"This new girl you've found," Warren said. "Is she anything like Wendy?"

Interesting question. Daphne was intelligent, though I

doubted she was a crazy genius like Wendy. "I don't see how that's any concern," I said.

"Brad," Warren said, "Marie and I have always liked you. We know our daughter. She's a handful. But you were always so good at handling her."

"She's more than I can handle now. I'll graduate in May and begin the process of taking over the ranch. I can't do that and continue to deal with Wendy."

"We can't expect him to take over our problems, Warren," Marie said.

"That's not what I'm saying," he said. "Wendy's a grown woman. She's no longer anyone's problem but her own."

"That's the way we all need to think of it," I told them. "She and I no longer have a relationship. I wanted to come here and tell you in person, because I know she won't tell you. I ended it for good."

"I'm sorry for anything she did to your new girlfriend," Marie said sadly.

"Daphne is okay, and she'll be fine, but Wendy needs to keep her distance."

"There's nothing we can do," Marie said. "Wendy's an adult. Unless she commits a crime..."

"She pulled a gun on my roommate."

Marie went white.

Warren cleared his throat. "When?"

"A couple nights ago. Outside a convenience store in Denver."

"Did he file charges?"

"I urged him to, but as far as I know he hasn't."

"How on earth does Wendy even know how to handle a gun?" Marie asked.

So much they didn't know. I said nothing.

"She's still an adult," Warren said. "If your friend doesn't file charges, there's nothing we can do."

I cleared my throat. "That's where you're wrong. I've done some research. In Colorado, a person can be detained for up to seventy-two hours if a professional feels she's a danger to herself or others because of her mental state."

Marie's eyes widened. "She can?"

"Yeah. We can easily find a licensed professional to testify, if my friend will tell his story. After a court hearing, the detention can be lengthened."

"No," Marie said. "Wendy doesn't need that kind of help."

"Marie," Warren said softly, "she pulled a gun on another person."

I nodded. "Murph may still press charges. I want him to. But Wendy needs professional help that she won't get through the criminal system. She's guilty of assault with a deadly weapon, but no one was harmed. She has no previous record, so she'll get probation and community service if she has a good lawyer. That won't help her in the long run. She needs professional psychiatric treatment. Plus, I'm not sure Murph will file the report."

"Good," Marie said. "I can't bear the thought of my baby in jail, even for a minute."

"Why won't he file?" Warren asked.

"Frankly, he's a little afraid of your daughter and what she's capable of."

"Are you, Brad?" Warren rubbed his chin. "Are you afraid of her?"

Loaded question if there ever was one. I felt certain that I was the one person Wendy wouldn't harm, but she could easily harm me through others. Murph was only the beginning.

"In some ways I am," I finally replied.

"I'm sorry," Marie said. "I won't have my daughter committed."

"Marie..." Warren began.

"She's a genius, Warren. She can do whatever she wants. She can be a nuclear physicist, a rocket scientist, a biomedical engineer."

"Her major is journalism," I reminded them.

"A Pulitzer Prize-winning reporter, then," Marie said.

"Please," I said. "Wendy needs this."

"No." Marie shook her head vehemently. "No, no, and a thousand more times, no."

"Warren?" I looked to Wendy's father. Could he talk sense into his wife?

"I'm sorry," he said. "She's our only child."

"Then you should want what's best for her."

He stood then. "I need you to leave, Brad. You've upset Marie enough."

"Your friend is probably lying." Marie wiped a tear that fell from her eye. "Wendy wouldn't even know how to get a gun."

I said nothing. She knew well how to get a gun.

Thanks to me.

My biggest mistake so far in my short life had been teaching her how to shoot. I reiterated my promise to myself that I'd never teach another human being to handle a gun. Never, no matter the circumstances.

"My friend isn't lying," I said calmly. "Thank you for your time."

I walked out of the Madigan house. I'd known going in

that it was a long shot, but still I'd hoped her parents might take the reins. They weren't strong people, though—definitely not strong enough to handle the child they'd created. They hadn't kept her challenged, so she'd found challenges elsewhere.

To all our detriment.

The next conversation about Wendy Madigan would be with my father.

CHAPTER THIRTY-FIVE

Daphne

Theo Mathias turned out to be a talker once he got comfortable, which was fine with me. I was learning a lot about Brad, plus I didn't have to make conversation.

"We formed a club in high school," he was saying. "The Future Lawmakers. Though it was more of a business enterprise. I'm not sure how we came up with that name. Anyway, it became a school club, but Brad, Larry, and I plus one other guy were always the principal members. We added two others eventually. A cheerleader who had the hots for Brad and a guy who had the hots for my little sister. We all still keep in touch, and four of us are still in business. My sister's engaged to the guy now."

"Is Brad still in business with you?"

"Sort of. He's our financial backer. You must know that the Steels are loaded."

"I got that impression."

"He never wanted to get involved in the operations. He's a rancher at heart. That's his real business, and he's good at it. We're just an investment for him."

"What kind of business are you in?" I asked.

"We're diverse, but sales, mostly."

"What do you sell?"

"What don't we sell? We specialize in buying up popular products in bulk and then selling them individually to make huge profits."

"So Brad fronts you the money."

"Yeah. That's how it began, anyway. We don't need him as much anymore, but he's still a silent partner, and he's made all his money back plus some."

"A good deal for him, then."

"A great deal for him."

I finished my coffee and checked my watch. "I should go. I need to meet him at the library in ten minutes."

"Absolutely. I'll walk over with you and say hi."

"Sure. Okay." What could it hurt? This guy was a friend of Brad's.

Brad was waiting outside the library when we got there, his eyes wide when we approached.

"Theo," he said, "what are you doing here?"

He didn't sound overly happy to see his friend. Odd.

"I stumbled into Daphne in town, nearly knocked her over coming out of the tattoo place, so I bought her a cup of coffee to make it up to her."

Brad eyed Theo, squinting. "What the hell did you do to your eyes?"

Theo laughed. "Oh, I almost forgot. Colored contacts. They're not available to the public yet, but I got my hands on a pair. I'm trying them out to see if I can use them for Halloween."

So they weren't his real eyes. No wonder they'd looked so *un*real.

"Halloween's over a month away," Brad said dryly.

"Never too early to start planning," Theo said. "That's my motto. For everything."

Brad took my hand. "Let's go, Daphne."

"Okay. Thanks for the coffee," I said to Theo.

"Any time. Any friend of Brad's is a friend of mine. Especially a sister of Larry's." He winked, turned, and headed in the other direction.

Brad turned to me, his eyes intense. "How much time did you spend with him?"

"About a half hour. Why?"

"What did he tell you?"

I cocked my head. "Are you angry?"

"No. Just concerned."

"Why? He said you were friends."

"We are. Sort of."

"So it's just business, then?"

"He told you about that?"

"Well... yeah. He said you all met in high school and started some club, and my brother was in it. How well do you know my brother, Brad?"

He didn't answer.

"I'm interested. I hardly know him at all. Maybe I can get to know him better through you."

He turned to me and gripped my shoulders. "Daphne, I didn't know you were Larry's sister when I took an interest in you."

"I ... know that."

"Good. You and I have nothing to do with Larry. Or Theo. Or my stupid high school club."

A sliver of fear edged into me. "O ... kay."

He loosened his grip. "I'm sorry. It's just... High school was a long time ago for me. I made some decisions that I regret."

"Brad, no one's going to judge you for what you did in high school."

I believed those words. I had to. I didn't want to be judged for my high school years, a year of which I'd spent hospitalized.

"I hope not," he said.

"Did you do something . . . bad?"

"No, baby. I didn't."

He looked past me, toward the Rocky Mountains. Was he lying? Brad usually looked me in the eye. If anything, I was the one who had a problem making eye contact. I was a little bit shy by nature, and everything that had happened since I got to college was so very new to me.

Finally, I broke the silence. "What were you doing today?"

"Just business, baby. That's all." Again, he looked past me.

I felt in the marrow of my bones that meeting Brad had been fate, that he was my destiny. I still felt that way, standing here with him refusing to meet my gaze.

I'd had enough of people refusing to meet my gaze last year, when I returned to high school after my year-long hiatus.

I wasn't going to take it from my boyfriend.

"Look at me, Brad. Look me in the eye."

CHAPTER THIRTY-SIX

B r a d

I hated talking to Daphne about this. She was innocent. A gorgeous flower swaying in the wind. I didn't want to be the tornado that uprooted her.

I should take her back to school and end whatever this was between us. Bringing her innocence into my world could lead to disaster, and that was the last thing I wanted.

But as I dropped my gaze back to her big brown eyes, I knew I couldn't give her up. She was it for me—the woman I'd bring home to Steel Acres, the woman I'd devote my life to, the woman who would bear my children.

Fuck! I hadn't even known her a week.

I knew next to nothing about her. She was so young, too. Only four years separated us, but at our age, that might as well be a lifetime, especially after the life I'd led so far.

I did as she asked. I looked her in the eye. Right in her gorgeous and warm brown eyes. "Let's go back to the coffee shop."

"I don't want any more coffee."

"Tea? Water? I just want to sit with you and talk."

"Water. Or a Coke maybe."

I took her hand, and we walked the block back to the coffee shop. We grabbed a table in back, and I got our drinks quickly and sat down next to her.

"I don't know much about you," I said, "except that you love animals and want to eat ethically sourced meat."

"I don't know much more about you," she said.

"Not true. You've seen my home, met my father. Met Theo. I haven't met any of your friends."

"You've met Patty and Ennis."

"You just met them yourself, baby. Tell me about your friends at home."

She got quiet. "I don't really have friends at home. My best friend, Sage, moved after sophomore year. I spent my junior year . . . away, and most of the friends had forgotten me or moved on when I returned."

"How is that possible? Who could forget you?"

"A lot of people, apparently."

"Just because you spent a year in London?" I smiled. "That's why Prince Charles appeals to you."

"Ennis? No, not really. He was the first person to speak to me when I went down to the lounge party that first night."

"He's also the one who got you drunk."

"He didn't get me drunk, Brad. He didn't pour the drink down my throat. I did that."

Her self-awareness was refreshing. She didn't try to blame anyone else for her own mistake. I liked that. "He should have warned you about the Everclear."

"He probably didn't know. He's been nothing but kind to me."

"You don't think he's interested in you?"

She blushed. "I didn't say that."

Jealousy spiked in my gut. "I knew it."

"Relax. I told him I wasn't interested in him romantically."

"And what about your first nighter date?"

"I'm definitely not interested in him romantically. He seemed nice at first, and I think he is, but he's really immature."

"Most freshman guys are," I said.

"Were you?"

"I'd seen a lot more by the time I went to college than most guys have."

"What had you seen?"

"Nice pivot. We're talking about you now."

"Why do we have to talk about me?"

"Because I know so little about you. Tell me about your year in London."

She looked down at her soft drink and swirled it in the glass. "I stayed with a distant relative. I didn't get into the heart of London very often."

"Where did you go to school?"

"She's an educator. She schooled me at home."

I widened my eyes. "Really? Wouldn't going to London be more beneficial if you went to school with British people and learned the culture and stuff?"

"I don't know." She still stared at the brown liquid in her glass. "My parents set it all up. I don't really like to talk about it."

"Why?"

"I don't know. Do you like to talk about your high school days?"

Point and match. No, I didn't. I took a sip of my coffee. "Tell me something else about yourself, then."

"What do you want to know?"

"I don't know. What's your favorite color?"

"Yellow."

"Really? Not pink or red or blue?" Was yellow really anyone's favorite color?

"No, yellow. It's the color of the sun. Of brightness. Of happiness. It chases the dark away."

Chases the dark away? That was deep. What was going on inside Daphne's head? I wasn't sure how to respond.

"How about yours?" she asked.

"Brown," I said without hesitation.

"Really?" She smiled. "Not red or blue?"

"Nope. Brown. My first dog, Misty, was brown. My horse is brown."

"You have a horse?"

"I do. Do you ride?"

She laughed. "I'm from the suburbs. When would I have learned to ride?"

"London maybe?" I grinned.

"Still not going there. What's your horse's name?"

"Sebastian. Next time you visit the ranch, I'll introduce you. Take you on a ride if you want."

"With you?"

"Not on the same horse as me."

"Why not? People do it all the time on TV. In movies."

I laughed. "That's not reality. There's a limit to how much weight a healthy horse can handle."

"Are you saying I weigh a lot?"

"Of course not. I'm saying *I* weigh a lot. My weight plus the saddle is quite a bit. But we have a great mare you can ride. She's really gentle."

Daphne took a sip of her drink. "I'd love to meet Sebastian and the mare. What's her name?"

"The one I was thinking about for you is Daisy. She's

technically my mom's horse, but my mom doesn't ride much anymore."

"Why not?"

"Just lost interest, I guess."

"Does your dad ride?"

"Oh, yeah. He's the one who taught me."

"Your dad seems nice."

"He can be." I really didn't want to talk about my father. "Tell me about your parents."

"My dad is a highway engineer for the state. My mom stays home now. She used to be a teacher."

"Oh? Why did she quit?"

"To stay home with me."

"That must have been nice for you."

"She only quit two years ago."

"To stay home with you? But if you were gone that first year, why didn't she keep working?"

Daphne's rosy cheeks went pale.

I'd hit a nerve.

CHAPTER THIRTY-SEVEN

Daphne

Uh-oh.

I truly hated lying, and this was why. A lie wasn't *just* a lie. Soon you had to tell other lies to cover up for the initial lie, and if you forgot to, you'd get caught in the lie.

I should have been truthful with Brad and told him I'd been hospitalized for most of my junior year of high school.

But I couldn't. He'd run away screaming—not that I'd blame him—and I couldn't bear to lose him.

"She was burned out on teaching," I said.

"Daphne."

I met his gaze.

"If we're going to have a relationship, we have to be honest with each other."

"Good point," I said. "What did you do in high school? Tell me about my brother."

He chuckled. "I will, if you really want to know. There's some stuff I wish I hadn't gotten into."

"I've told you before, I'd never judge you based on high school. I wouldn't want to be judged based on high school either. Who would?"

"Baby, I know you won't. I won't judge you either."

"High school was months ago for me. For you, it was years ago."

"So? High school is high school. People who look back on high school as the best years of their lives are pretty sad, don't you think? Eighteen years old, and it's all downhill from there. I'd hate to think my best years are behind me."

His words struck me. I had to believe my best years were in front of me. I'd lost nearly a year of my life. I didn't want to lose any more.

"Tell me," he said. "No judgment. Then I'll tell you anything you want to know."

Trust him.

That was what my heart was telling me.

My head was a different matter. My head had learned to be cautious.

Trust him.

Sometimes, my therapist once said, you have to take a leap and the net will appear. Perhaps this was one of those times.

I drew in a deep breath. "I lied to you, Brad. I wasn't in London during my junior year, but if I tell you where I was, you have to promise to never tell anyone."

He covered my hand with his. "I promise, Daphne. You can tell me anything."

Another deep breath. "All right. Here goes." Pause. "I spent most of my junior year in a psychiatric hospital."

His eyebrows twitched, but at least he stopped himself from looking completely surprised. "Why, baby? What happened?"

"Honestly, there's a lot I don't remember. But my diagnosis was severe anxiety and depression."

"Did you . . . try to . . ."

I heard the words he couldn't bring himself to say. "No. I didn't try to commit suicide."

"Thank God. I can't bear to think of you in that much pain."

I smiled weakly.

"Why don't you remember a lot of it?"

"Mostly because of the medication. That's what my therapist says."

"What kind of meds did they have you on?"

"I . . . don't know, really. It was like trudging through a thick fog sometimes. I was in a dark place."

He smiled and squeezed my hand. "Your choice of yellow as your favorite color is making more sense to me now."

"I love the sun," I said. "I like to watch it rise when I get up in time. There's nothing more beautiful than the dawn of a brand-new day."

He reached toward me and trailed a finger over my cheek and jawline. "I think there's one thing in the world that's more beautiful than a sunrise."

I warmed and turned my cheek into his hand. His touch gave me so much comfort—more comfort than my mother's embrace. Even more comfort than a sunrise and a new day.

Scary, but in a good way.

Fate.

Always fate.

My therapist would question my thought process, but there wasn't a doubt in my mind.

Brad Steel was my destiny.

"Do you still see your therapist?" he asked.

"No. I saw him all last year. He said it was cool for me to go to college. I have his number but haven't needed to call. He said I could use the university counseling center if I need to."

"But you haven't needed to," he said.

"No, but school hasn't even begun."

"True." He smiled. "Do you still feel depressed sometimes?"

"I get sad, but everyone does. It's just regular sadness, not the depression I went through before."

"And medication?"

"Not anymore."

"Did your doctors ever figure out what caused your depression?"

"It's hereditary. My mother suffers from it as well."

He nodded. "I'm sorry you had to go through that."

I smiled. "What doesn't kill you makes you stronger. Or so people tell me."

"I think that's true," he said. "If it didn't, no one would live after the bad stuff."

I hadn't lied to Brad. I'd never considered suicide. In fact, I didn't even remember the worst of my depression. One day I woke up in a hospital and had no recollection of how or why I'd gotten there. That was what bothered me the most. I felt good now, and I was optimistic about life. I was optimistic about Brad. But that lingering fear in my mind that I'd never remember such an important part of my life disturbed me.

Dr. Payne had said I probably had a repressed memory. My mother assured me I was okay. I'd failed a test at school and then a couple girls had bullied me and punched me a few times, all of which sent me into depression. I didn't remember any of it, but it certainly sounded like something that would depress a person, although I'd always been an excellent student. The girls who bullied me had apparently both moved away by the time my senior year rolled around. Not that I wanted to confront them, but if I could have at least seen them, maybe I'd remember the trauma.

Then again, who wanted to remember trauma?

I cleared my throat and told Brad the story.

"You really don't remember?"

"I don't. Sometimes I wish I could, but other times I'm glad I can't."

"Why would anyone bully you?"

"Why does anyone bully anyone? I have no idea."

"Usually because they're weak or jealous," he said. "In your case, it was probably both. They were weak, and they were jealous of you."

"Why would anyone be jealous of me?"

"Because you're the most beautiful girl in the world."

I smiled. His words made me feel warm and cozy inside. Special. Protected. His words were like a suit of armor that would conceal and protect me so no one could ever hurt me again.

"You didn't have any problem when you went back to school?"

"No. Those girls were gone, and everyone else was nice, though most were distant."

"Why?"

"I don't know. I'd been gone for a year. My few friends and I had grown apart, and my best friend had moved. It was different. Not great, but I made it through."

Brad stared at me, his eyes meeting mine as if he were searching for something.

Something I couldn't put my finger on.

CHAPTER THIRTY-EIGHT

Brad

I should drive her back to campus. See her safely to her dorm room and never set eyes on her again.

But that wouldn't happen. She was inside me now, a part of me, almost as if I'd grown a new limb. It sounded crazy even to me, but I couldn't deny the truth.

Daphne Wade was like a beautiful castle fashioned out of sand. One tide could come in and topple everything. She was fragile. So fragile yet so strong. Not everyone could get through such a year and come out swinging, ready for college.

Daphne was the ultimate paradox—and she was mine.

From the first time I laid eyes on her, I'd wanted to protect her. I didn't know why then, but I knew now. She needed me.

And I needed her.

I needed something sweet and good in my life.

But could I in good conscience bring this fragile woman into my fucked-up universe? I'd done things I could never take back, things that could have consequences far into the future. I could mitigate the fallout. Indeed, I had and would continue to. But some things were beyond my control.

I had to believe. I had to believe in the goodness of humankind. I deserved happiness, and so did Daphne. We could find it together.

She needed me, and I needed her.

A life with her would never be easy or simple, but then a life with me wouldn't be either.

I reached forward and touched her silken cheek.

She smiled into my hand. "You didn't run away screaming."

"Why would I?"

"Because I just told you I spent time in a mental hospital."

I smiled. "You're not the first person I've known who spent time in a mental hospital."

"Oh?"

"My mother was hospitalized while I was in high school."

"I'm so sorry. Why?"

"It's a long story. Her relationship with my dad has been strained since the accident. My dad . . . Well, he's not the best husband in the world." I didn't want to lay all the details on Daphne yet.

"Is she okay now?"

"She is. She has things in her life that make her happy."

Daphne smiled. "I bet you're one of them."

Just when I thought I couldn't adore her more. "Let's go back to the ranch," I said. "It's nearly dinnertime, and then I want to take you someplace special tonight."

★ ★ ★

My mother's greenhouse was about a mile away from the main ranch house. She kept her favorite flower, the tulip, in bloom all year long. I cut a bright-yellow bloom from one of the bulbs and handed it to Daphne.

"It's beautiful. I've never seen a tulip in the fall."

"To say my mom has a green thumb is an understatement.

She has a way with all plants, but she especially loves spring flowers."

"Your mother must be an amazing woman."

"She is. She's strong. Getting help doesn't make you weak, Daphne. It makes you strong."

She nodded. "This is a beautiful place."

"I thought you'd like it."

"Is that why you brought me here?"

"Yeah, but also because it reminds me of you. The way you said you love the sunrise. This place, where flowers bloom all year round, is like a constant sunrise."

"It is. It's wonderful." She walked toward another cluster of tulips, the palest green. "These look sad."

"Those are my mother's favorite."

"Really?"

"Yeah. What do you mean when you say they look sad?"

"It's almost like nature forgot to finish their color."

"I never thought about it like that." I cut a bloom and handed it to her. It did look pale and sad against the bright yellow of the first flower.

"Night and day," she said, holding them both. "One is the moon, the other the sun. The light drives out the dark."

"You have a way with words," I said. "Have you thought about majoring in English? Maybe doing some writing?"

"I have, actually." Her cheeks reddened. "I'm taking freshman year to sort things out, figure out what my dreams are."

"That must be nice," I said.

"I suppose so. Didn't you do that when you began college?"

I shook my head. "I know where my future lies. Here. The ranch. It'll be mine someday, and I need to know how to run it. My father taught me everything he knows, and college has taught me more about the business side of things."

"You never had a dream, then? Other than the ranch?"

"No," I said truthfully. "I never did."

Her eyes took on a faraway look, a look laced with sadness. Was she feeling bad for me? I slid my finger over her hairline and down her silken braid that fell over one shoulder.

"I have a dream now," I said softly.

"Do you?"

"I do." I leaned down and pressed my lips to hers. "Do you still want me to be the one?"

She nodded shyly.

"I want that too." In fact, I never wanted another man to touch this beautiful flower—a flower that had wilted from lack of sun but now was blooming in full color.

What had she done to me? I was no poet, yet here I stood, thinking of her metaphorically as a flower . . . and it seemed so truthful and right.

I could make love to her right here in the greenhouse. My mother wasn't home, and my father never set foot in here. It seemed apt . . . but no. No one's first time should be on the cold floor of a glass house. Surrounded by flowers and greenery? Maybe, but not here.

Her first time would take place in a bed in the arms of a man who truly cared.

The guesthouse was fully furnished. We'd go there.

And we'd go now.

CHAPTER THIRTY-NINE

Daphne

Brad Steel was going to make love to me.

He was the man of my dreams...and he wouldn't stop this time. I wouldn't let him.

We drove to the guesthouse behind the ranch house.

"What if your father comes over here?"

"He won't."

"How can you be sure?"

"I'm sure."

"Okay." I had no reason to disbelieve Brad. He knew his father better than I did. I wrapped my arms around myself, easing the nervous chill inside. I wasn't frightened, exactly—just apprehensive. I didn't know anything about lovemaking, but I had a feeling Brad knew a lot.

That fact unsettled me more than a little. He'd been with loads of women, including the beautiful one who'd shown up at my dorm room.

I wanted to be special to him, as special as he was to me. I could only give my virginity once, and while I knew Brad was the one, part of me wished we could experience this together.

Dr. Payne had told me to go slowly in relationships, that adult love was something that didn't happen overnight. I'd believed him.

Until I met Brad Steel.

I didn't know what love was, other than the love I felt for my parents. What I felt for Brad was brand-new to me—brand-new and so intense.

Was I in love?

Could a person fall in love in a week's time?

In fairy tales, maybe, but in real life?

Brad led me into the guesthouse. It was nearly as big as the main house.

"Just how many guests do you have?" I asked.

"Not a lot."

"Then why such a big house for them?"

He laughed. "I have no idea. The house has been here my whole life. Sometimes family stays here. Other times, friends. But honestly, it doesn't get used that much."

"Amazing. I can't even imagine growing up the way you did."

"Big houses don't make happiness, Daphne."

"I didn't mean it that way. Just never having to worry about money, is all."

I had a few pairs of designer jeans. Before I'd gone to the hospital, my mother always said we couldn't afford designer jeans. After I got out of the hospital, my mother and father had spoiled me. We weren't a rich family, and things were especially tight after my mother stopped working. My hospitalization must have cost a ton, though they never talked to me about it. The only time I asked, they told me it was nothing and not to worry.

I worried anyway.

I walked over to the baby grand piano in the living room. "Do you play?"

He shook his head. "If I did, we'd have a piano in the main house."

Good point. "Why here, then?"

"Heck if I know. Whoever decorated the house brought it in, I guess."

I walked to the gorgeous instrument and sat on the bench. Middle C. How did I know that?

"I always wanted to learn piano, but my parents couldn't afford lessons." I touched the key and played the note.

"There you go," he said.

"That's middle C." Next was D, and then E, F, and G. I laced my fingers over C, E, and G and played a chord. This was getting weird.

"That's pretty," he said. "What is it?"

"Just a chord. C major." I played the chord again, the CE inversion.

"You said you didn't have lessons. How do you know that?"

I wasn't sure how to answer. Would he believe me if I said I didn't know? Because that was the truth.

"Music class." I stood quickly.

Good answer. A big lie, but he'd buy it.

He did.

"You want anything? I'm pretty sure there's some soda and wine in the fridge."

I inhaled. "Just some water would be great."

"You got it."

I followed him to the kitchen, where he poured two glasses of water and handed one to me. Then he clinked my glass. "To us."

"To us," I echoed and took a long drink to ease my dry mouth.

"We don't have to do this," he said.

I put my glass down on the counter. "I want to."

"You just seem a little . . . hesitant."

"It's my first time, Brad. I'm a little nervous. Wouldn't you be?"

He smiled but didn't respond. I picked up my glass, took another long drink of water, and then set it back down.

"Now what?" I said.

"Funny thing," he said. "I wasn't nervous at all my first time or any time after, but I'm nervous as all hell right now."

I lifted my brow. "Why?"

He smiled and fingered my braid again. "Because it's you."

"I don't want to make you nervous."

"That didn't come out right, but I don't know how else to say it."

I broke through with courage and reached toward him, touching his stubbly cheek. His skin was warm, so warm. "I don't want either of us to be nervous."

"Me either." He placed his hand over mine, turned his head, and kissed my palm. "You're the most beautiful woman I've ever laid eyes on."

"You're the most beautiful man I've ever laid eyes on."

"I don't want you because you're beautiful, Daphne. I want you because you're *you*. I know that doesn't make any sense."

I smiled, warming inside. "It makes perfect sense."

He kissed my palm again. "I'm going to take you to the bedroom. We'll go as slow as you need to go."

I nodded.

But I wasn't going to go slowly.

CHAPTER FORTY

Brad

The master suite in the guesthouse was large and decorated in neutral colors. Not that I was an expert in decor, but Daphne brightened up the boring room.

Hell, Daphne brightened up the most intricately decorated room.

I took her in my arms and pressed my lips to hers. I was hard as a rock but determined to go slowly. For Daphne, I'd do anything.

She surprised me when she opened instantly and pushed her tongue out to meet mine. Yes, we'd done quite a bit of kissing in the week we'd known each other, but I'd planned to go a bit more slowly.

Instead, I decided to follow her lead. I took her soft and sweet tongue and twirled it with my own, deepening the kiss until a soft groan hummed from the back of her throat.

I broke the kiss and inhaled a much-needed breath. Then I slid my lips over her cheeks and jawline and then to her neck. "I'm going to undress you."

"Please," she whispered.

I lifted her shirt over her head and tossed it onto the floor. Her breasts were already swelling inside her bra. I made quick work of the undergarment and tossed it as well. Then I stared.

Though I'd seen her breasts before, they were even more beautiful to me now. Her brown-pink nipples were hard and taut and surrounded by tight, wrinkled areolas. I cupped each breast and flicked my thumbs over her nipples. She closed her eyes and jerked slightly, sighing.

Quickly I removed my own shirt and crushed her into a hug. God, her skin, her flesh. I'd wanted to feel her against me, and it was heaven. I tilted her chin upward and kissed her again, even harder and deeper this time, showing her with my tongue what I'd do to her virgin pussy.

My dick strained against my jeans. I wanted to go slow for her, but I wasn't sure how much longer I could hold out. I needed to get inside her, needed to feel every part of her.

I wanted everything. I ached to feel her swollen lips on my cock, but I couldn't ask that of her, not when she was so inexperienced.

Then the words I'd said to her the first time we tried this edged into my mind.

I want to rip your clothes off your body, shred them into tiny pieces if that's what it takes. Then I want to sink my cock so far into you that our bodies never come apart.

I'd been blunt then, and she'd wanted to keep going. I'd stopped because I felt she wasn't ready.

Her body was responding to me now. When I inhaled, I could already smell the musk of her desire. This was going to happen tonight, and this time, I wouldn't stop.

I broke the kiss, panting. "Sit on the bed, Daphne."

She obeyed me without question.

I met her gaze. "Remember when I said I wanted to rip your clothes off and sink my cock into you?"

Her eyes went heavy. "Yes."

"I want you even more now, baby. I have to have you this time, so if you're going to stop me, do it now. If we go further, I won't be able to stop."

But please don't stop me.

She cupped my cheek, her flesh so warm. "I don't want to stop. I want it to be you, Brad. Only you."

"Thank God." I pulled off her shoes and then unsnapped and unzipped her jeans. I yanked them over her hips and off her body. She was naked now, save for pink lace panties.

I inhaled again, this time closing my eyes.

"What are you doing?" she asked.

"Smelling you, baby." I opened my eyes.

She'd gone slightly rigid. "Smelling me?"

"Yes. You're wet, and it's the sweetest perfume in the world."

She closed her eyes. "Oh," she sighed, her body flushing all over.

Such pure beauty. For a moment, I thought I could be happy just feasting on her with my eyes—and what a gorgeous feast she was. Skin the color of creamy milk, a tiny spray of freckles over her nose and shoulders. Breasts like alabaster globes, and nipples so hard and sweet. Between her legs, the paradise I longed for.

"Daphne."

She opened her eyes.

"I'm going to undress now."

Her eyes went wide. "Okay."

"I don't want to scare you. Have you ever—"

"Only in pictures."

I nodded. I kicked off my boots and unbuckled my belt. My cock ached as I freed it from my jeans and slid them over my hips.

Her eyes went wider, and I still had my underwear on.

I stepped out of my jeans. "You still with me?"

She nodded.

"Sure?"

"Brad, I've never been so sure of anything in my life."

That was all I needed to hear. I slid the briefs over my hips. My dick sprang up, bigger and harder than ever.

I waited. Waited for her to ask if it would fit. Waited for her to say she changed her mind. Waited for her to say anything.

She didn't speak, though. Just regarded me, eyes heavy-lidded, body flushed and shuddering slightly.

I sat down next to her on the bed and eased her onto her back. "I'm going to make this good for you," I whispered. "I promise."

"I know you will."

She trusted me, and I hadn't done anything to earn her trust. Not yet. But I would. I'd earn all the trust she was instilling in me at this moment if it took a lifetime.

I started at her forehead and placed a kiss on her soft skin. Then I rained kisses down her face, stopping at her lips and diving between them with my tongue. We kissed deeply for a few minutes, but my cock was aching so badly, I had to move forward. I kissed down her neck to her breasts, sucking on each nipple and relishing her sweet moans. I didn't want to leave her breasts, but my dick had other ideas. I moved downward, trailing my lips over her flat abdomen to her nest of black curls.

I inhaled.

Sweet Daphne.

Her panties still separated me from paradise. I was determined to be gentle, but when I slid my fingers under the band of her panties, I acted on instinct. I ripped the string bikini and pulled them off her.

"Brad!" she gasped.

"I told you the first time I wanted to rip your clothes off."

"I remember."

"I'll buy you more panties."

"I don't care. I don't care, Brad. Just… Please, just…"

I gazed between her legs. Her glistening pussy was beautiful. I blew on it softly, and she squirmed. "Please what, baby?"

"I want you. I want something. I just want… Please…"

"Tell me," I said softly against her hot flesh. "Tell me what you want, baby."

CHAPTER FORTY-ONE

Daphne

What *did* I want? How could I describe it? I could say I wanted him to fuck me. True, but so crass. I could say I wanted the moon and the stars. Also true, but metaphorical and ridiculous. I could say I wanted him to cherish me, but we'd known each other for only a week.

I cherished him, though. I cherished him more than I had anything so far in my eighteen years.

"Tell me, baby," he said again.

"I feel so...warm and delicious inside. I want to feel everything, Brad. I want you to show me."

He spread my legs farther apart and kissed the insides of my thighs. "I knew it," he said. "So sweet."

Then he stroked between my legs with his tongue.

And I burst into flames.

Such intense physical and emotional pleasure coursed through me, and we'd only just begun. I inhaled swiftly and sharply, letting the delicious tingle flow through my veins and out my fingertips, as if I were setting it free into the universe.

He glided his tongue over the entrance to my vagina again and then again. I squirmed on the bed, my hips moving of their own accord, searching for, searching for...

"Oh!"

He touched his tongue to my clitoris, and I nearly shattered. Such intensity! I'd never masturbated. I had no idea what pleasure awaited me.

He would show me. Brad would show me.

"Do that again," I begged.

"I have to ... God, Daphne, I need to get inside you."

"Do it, then. Make me feel everything. Please."

"I want you to come first. I don't want to hurt you."

"I don't care. I need you inside me. I need it, Brad. Please."

"Are you sure?" he asked once more. "It might hurt. You might bleed."

"I know all that, and yes, I'm sure. Take me. Take me now."

He fidgeted for a few seconds and then crawled up my body, took my mouth with his, and thrust into me.

I moaned softly, relishing the fullness. No more empty ache. Only Brad. And me. And Brad inside of me.

He broke the kiss. "I'm sorry," he whispered against my ear. "I went quickly to get the pain over with."

Pain? Right, there was supposed to be pain. I didn't feel any pain. Only fullness. Only the strong knowledge that he was supposed to be there, inside me.

"I'm okay," I said. "It feels good."

"Thank God, because I have to do that again." He pulled out and then thrust back in. "I couldn't wait any longer, but I swear, Daphne, I'll take care of you after this."

"It's okay. I want this. I love this."

He pulled out and pushed in once more and then again. And again and again. His thrusts became quicker as his groans became louder, and somehow in the mass of quivering feelings bubbling through me, something clicked.

My clitoris. He was hitting it somehow, and oh my God,

something big was coming. Something big.

"Fuck!" He thrust into me, and instead of pulling back out, he stayed there, embedded so deeply. His dick pulsated inside me.

Several seconds later, he pulled out and rolled over onto his side. "Baby, you're amazing."

I hadn't done much, but I wasn't going to argue with him. "So are you. It was wonderful."

And oh, it had been. Just the fullness. The beauty of it all. The joining of two bodies. The joining of two people who cared so much for each other.

He pulled a condom off his dick—when had he put it on?— rose, and threw it into the wastebasket. I lay on the bed, basking in the afterglow. Had I come? I wasn't sure. All I knew was that this was the most important thing that had ever happened in my life. Brad walked into the bathroom for a moment and returned with a washcloth.

He sat on the bed. "Let me take care of you." He spread my legs and placed the warm cloth between them. "Any pain?"

"No, none."

"Amazing. Doesn't look like you bled, either."

"Is that strange?"

"Probably not. I've only been with a virgin once before, and she screamed bloody murder but only bled a little."

I closed my eyes, basking in his care of me.

"Daphne"—he smoothed the warm cloth between my legs and over my inner thighs—"I'm sorry I couldn't wait longer. Did you come?"

I warmed with embarrassment. "Honestly? I'm not sure."

He smiled. "Then you didn't."

"How do you know?"

"Because you'd know if you did."

"How would I know if I've never experienced it before?"

He removed the cloth and kissed the top of my vulva, smiling. "Just trust me."

"It doesn't matter to me," I said truthfully. "It was wonderful the way it was."

"It matters to me. I'm going to take care of you." He lay down beside me and pulled me into his arms.

"You don't have—"

He quieted me with a deep kiss. I opened to meet his tongue. My sex was still aroused, still pulsing with ache and need. My body moved of its own accord. I undulated beneath Brad's touch, still reaching for something just beyond my grasp.

He broke the kiss and slid his lips over my cheeks, neck, and chest before he sucked one nipple between them. In tandem, he trailed fingers over my abdomen to my vulva and then to my clitoris and circled it gently.

And then not so gently.

The tugging on my nipple and the sensation below swirled together in a shuddering mass of feeling. Every one of my senses went on overload. The sight of his firm lips around my nipple, the taste of him lingering on my lips from our kiss, the smell of our arousal in the air, the sounds of his moans and of mine—all so overwhelming.

Still, I needed more, wanted that fullness inside me, that sensation that I'd never be empty again. Brad let my nipple drop with a soft pop and replaced his lips with fingers. He kneaded and pinched it while moving downward, his lips forging a trail to the hidden spot between my legs. He replaced his other hand with his mouth and sucked on my clitoris. Hard.

Waves of pleasure rippled through me, and that ultimate

peak in the distance that I couldn't quite reach came nearer and then nearer still . . .

I lifted my hips off the bed, chasing his mouth, chasing his tongue, chasing after that elusive precipice that teased me with its nearness.

"That's it," he said. "You're getting there. Relax and let it happen, baby."

Then he shoved a finger into me.

"Brad!" My feet landed on the elusive peak, and then I jumped off into the euphoric clouds of bliss. Sparks pulsed from my core outward, through every cell in my body, as I floated in ecstasy. Words left my throat, but I had no idea what they were.

Brad's voice wafted through the air, low and raspy, a symphony to my ears as electricity coursed through me and I drifted through the clouds, my speed decreasing.

I landed on the softness of the bed, Brad's face between my legs, his chin glistening and his eyes full of fire. His finger was in me still, slowly moving in and out, in and out, until he removed it.

I sighed.

"Well?" he said.

"Well, what?" I murmured.

"See what I mean? Now you know."

"God, yes. Now I know."

He crawled upward and pulled me into his arms. "I'm so happy I was the one to do that for you."

"Me too." I closed my eyes and snuggled into his shoulder.

CHAPTER FORTY-TWO

Brad

She fell asleep in my arms almost immediately.

Her tall height made her perfect for me. She melted into my body as if we'd been cast to fit together, the perfect yin and yang.

My thoughts about her scared me a little. I'd fallen, and I'd fallen fast and hard. That wasn't like me.

Maybe I'd never met the right girl.

Daphne was my future.

What I felt for her was something I'd never felt before. I wanted to protect her from all the cruelty in the world. I wanted to lie with her every night for the rest of my life. I wanted her to live with me here on the ranch and be the mother of my children. I wanted to grow old with her, laughing and enjoying life, bringing her bright-yellow tulips every morning.

I wanted a life with this woman—a long and prosperous life.

I wouldn't tell her yet. I'd only scare her away. No one fell in love in a week. No one except me, apparently. No way could she possibly love me yet, but she would. I knew in my heart and soul that she would.

She'd given me her virginity. To her, that was huge. She was definitely feeling something profound. She'd talked about fate and destiny, but she hadn't mentioned love. That was okay. Love would grow. Just like the blossoms in my mother's greenhouse, our love would grow and live during all seasons.

I should wake her and take her back to the main house, but I didn't want to leave this heavenly place we'd created tonight.

★ ★ ★

An hour later, I left the guesthouse. I scribbled a quick note to tell Daphne I'd be back soon just in case she woke up and found me gone.

Then I walked to the main house.

Time to talk to my father.

I found him in his study, as usual. I knocked on the open door. "Dad?"

"Yeah?"

"I need to talk to you."

"It's late."

"I know, but it's important."

"Come in, then," he said gruffly.

I entered and sat down in one of the chairs opposite his desk. I was here to ask for a favor. A big favor. He'd act like it was a big pain in his ass, say "I told you so," but in the end, he'd come through for me.

My father had warned me about Wendy early on, when I first brought her home. At the time, I didn't listen. My father had become so harsh to my mother over the years that I no longer valued his opinion.

That one will be your undoing, son. Mark my words.

He'd been right about Wendy, though, and now I wished I'd heeded his warning.

One thing was certain. Wendy would *not* be my undoing. I'd take care of it any way I had to. I needed to be free of her, not just for my own sake but for hers as well.

And for the sake of the beautiful, innocent woman lying asleep in the guesthouse.

"Did you come in here to stare at the wall?" my father asked.

I drew in a breath. "No. I need help, Dad. It's about Wendy."

I braced myself for the yelling. The "I told you so." The "I have better things to do than clean up your messes." The harsh criticism of my decisions.

To my surprise, all he said was, "It's about time."

He listened, he made plans, and for the first time since I was a kid, I believed in my father again.

Then I walked back to the guesthouse.

★ ★ ★

I jerked upward at the shrill screech.

Daphne sat on the edge of the bed trembling, her arms wrapped around her body.

"Baby?" I said tentatively.

"No!" she screamed again, this time standing.

I blinked to adjust my eyes to the darkness. "Daphne, what's wrong?"

"Get away from me! Help! Help!" She raced toward the door of the bedroom.

I scrambled out of bed quickly, grabbed her, and pulled her into my arms. She struggled against me, but I held her firmly. "Shh. It's okay. You're here with me. No one is hurting you. Shh."

She continued to struggle for a few seconds more and then melted into me. "Brad? What happened?"

I kissed the top of her head. "You were screaming, telling me to get away from you."

"No, no. I wasn't."

"You were."

"I mean . . . I wasn't telling *you* to get away."

"What was going on?"

"I'm so sorry you had to see that. It's a nightmare. I have them sometimes."

"Come on." I led her back to the bed. "Tell me."

"I can't."

"Daphne, you can tell me anything."

"That's not what I mean. I actually *can't*. I never remember the nightmares."

"You don't remember who was trying to harm you?"

She shook her head. "Never. I don't have them as much anymore. I guess I should have warned you, but I didn't know we'd sleep together."

"You fell asleep, and I didn't want to wake you. You looked so serene and peaceful."

"It's not your fault. I should have—"

"Baby, it's not anyone's fault."

She nodded. "I'm a little embarrassed."

"Don't be." I kissed her forehead. It was moist with sweat. "I won't let anyone hurt you. Ever. I promise with everything in me."

CHAPTER FORTY-THREE

Daphne

"Daph, where have you been? I've been worried sick!" Patty grabbed me in a hug after Brad dropped me off the next day.

"I meant to call, but time got away from me. I went to Brad's ranch for the weekend. I should have left a note. I'm sorry."

"I was really close to calling your parents."

"Oh, God. I'm glad you didn't."

"If you didn't show up today, I was going to. I actually went over to Sean's place. He had another girl there!"

"I'm sorry, Pat." Except I wasn't surprised. Sean didn't seem the one-woman type, though Patty didn't seem the one-man type either.

"Yeah, he's a pig. But he said Brad was away for the weekend as well, so I thought maybe the two of you were together. Didn't seem like you, though."

"It wasn't really like me, but I never gave it a second thought. As soon as Brad asked me, I knew I'd go. His ranch is gorgeous, and the little town is so quaint and lovely. I met his dad and one of his old friends. I saw another side to him, and I loved it."

"So are the two of you..."

"What? Dating?"

"Well... yeah. And..."

My cheeks warmed, and though what had occurred between Brad and me was private and I didn't especially want to confide in a girl I'd only known for a week, I couldn't help a small smile.

"You did!" Patty exclaimed.

I nodded shyly.

"No longer a virgin. That's great! And for Brad Steel to be the one. Yum!"

"It was amazing," I said.

"It's great, isn't it? Once you get past that initial pain."

"I didn't have any pain."

"Really? I didn't have huge pain. Some of my high school friends said it was the worst, though."

"Is it normal to not have pain?" I asked.

"Oh, probably. Did you ride a bike a lot?"

"When I was younger I did."

"You probably broke your hymen on a bicycle seat a long time ago. No biggie. Plus, you use tampons, right?"

I nodded.

"Just consider yourself lucky. Brad Steel and no pain. I'd say that's a winner!"

"I don't have any complaints. It's happening so fast, though. I never imagined it this way."

"It *is* fast, but go with it, Daph. Enjoy it while it lasts."

"Do you think it won't last?"

"He's young."

"He's twenty-two. That's older than we are."

"It's still young, especially for a guy. Don't get me wrong. It's obvious he adores you. I wish a guy would look at me the way Brad looks at you."

I smiled.

"I don't mean to get too personal, but . . ."

Too personal? I'd already shared the most personal thing that had ever happened to me with her. "Go ahead."

"What did you use for birth control?"

"He used a condom."

"We need to get you to the university health center. You should go on the pill."

Chills erupted on my skin. The health center? Patty had no idea how I felt about hospitals or doctors or health centers. "Why?"

"So he doesn't have to use a rubber anymore. Men hate them."

"Oh." I didn't want Brad hating our time together. "Okay. I'll go over sometime next week."

"The sooner the better. I'll go with you if you don't want to go alone."

I was tempted to take her up on it. I hated the idea of going alone. But if I was mature enough to have a sexual relationship, I had to be mature enough to take care of birth control on my own. "I'll be fine."

For the first night since I'd been at school, I didn't see Brad. He called and told me he was taking care of some business for the ranch, so I went with Patty and two of the other girls on the floor to dinner at the cafeteria and then to a movie on campus. Afterward, we went to the Cage for a drink.

After a round of Cokes, Flo, one of the girls, said, "How about something better, ladies? I have two sixers in my mini fridge."

Sixers? I had no idea what a sixer was, though I assumed it was alcohol. Classes began the next morning, so I didn't want to stay up too late. I went along, though. I needed to stretch my wings and make friends other than Brad, Patty, and Ennis.

A sixer turned out to be a six-pack of beer. I wasn't crazy about beer, but I took a can, determined to drink only one.

"What do you guys want to do?" Flo asked.

"Truth or dare!" her roommate, Stacey, offered.

"Yeah, let's do that!" Patty agreed.

I'd never played truth or dare before. My social life had been nonexistent the past two years. At least I'd heard of it. I wasn't that much out of the loop.

"You go first, Stacey," Flo said.

Stacey took a long swallow of beer and eyed each of us. "I choose . . . Patty. Here's your question. Did you fuck your first nighter?"

Patty nearly spewed her mouthful of beer on me but luckily caught herself in time. "What kind of question is that?"

Funny. I was the most inexperienced girl on campus— well, maybe not anymore—and even I saw that one coming.

"Truth or dare," Stacey said teasingly.

"Geez, all right." Patty took another drink. "Yeah, I did."

Really? She slept with that asshole, Rex? I liked Patty, but she needed to be a little more selective.

"Patty . . ." I said.

"I know. I know. You don't like Rex. He wasn't very nice to you that night, but he was really sweet to me after you and Jason left."

"Why didn't you like him, Daphne?"

"He seemed like a pig to me is all," I said.

"He's one hot-looking pig, though." Patty laughed. "I guess it's my turn. Flo, you're the one. Truth or dare. Have you ever done drugs?"

Flo reddened. "I've smoked pot, and once I did a line of coke."

Who were these women? I must have had that written on my face, because Stacey said, "What's the matter, Daphne?"

"Nothing. I just wouldn't even know where to get pot or coke."

"Such a sheltered babe," Patty said.

"Yeah? What drugs have you done?" I asked.

She giggled. "Actually, none, unless you count alcohol."

"Such a sheltered babe," I mocked.

Flo laughed. "Okay, okay. My turn. Daphne, you're the one."

I went rigid. No reason to be nervous. *Just go with it.*

"Where were you over the weekend?"

I wasn't ashamed of what I'd done or where I'd gone, but I hardly knew Flo and Stacey. My weekend with Brad had been so special, and I didn't want to taint it. If I told them, they'd make a big deal out of it, tease me for spending the weekend with a guy I hardly knew.

It was too beautiful to share just yet.

"I ... I'll take the dare, I guess."

Flo's eyebrows shot up. Clearly she wasn't expecting that. "Okay, a dare. Hmm ... I know." She smiled mischievously. "You have to go downstairs to the guys' floor and take off your shirt for one minute."

Was she kidding? No way. Except I'd taken the dare. I thought quickly.

"One minute. Anywhere on the guys' floor?"

"Yup. And you'll need a witness. Patty, you go with her and time her."

I drew in a deep breath and let it out slowly. "Okay."

CHAPTER FORTY-FOUR

B r a d

I hadn't lied to Daphne. I was attending to business tonight, just not ranch business.

I had to tell Murph what was coming. My father had made arrangements with a licensed psychotherapist to have Wendy committed. The psychotherapist would be calling Murph about the assault.

I threw Murph a bottle of beer. "Let's talk, dude," I said.

"What about?"

"First of all, are you okay? After the incident with Wendy?"

"Yeah, I'm good."

"You sure? Getting threatened like that is kind of a big deal."

"I know, but it was Wendy. I know her."

"Wendy can be pretty scary, Murph."

"No shit. It's got me thinking about stuff. But I'm good. I'm good."

I nodded. "All right. Then I need you to talk to a guy. He'll be calling you."

"I'd rather not."

"Why? Did she threaten you?"

"No."

"Then let's do this. A psychotherapist is going to call you about what happened. Just tell him the truth. He's on my dad's payroll. We're going to get Wendy committed."

"No shit?"

"No shit. It's been a long time coming. She'll be gone for good, and neither one of us will have to deal with her anymore."

He didn't say anything.

"This is good news, Murph."

"Yeah. Yeah it is." He hedged a little. "Like I said, though, I've been thinking... I found a new place. I'm moving out."

Brick to gut. I hadn't seen that coming.

"Wendy's a part of your life," he went on. "I love you, man, and we'll always be brothers, but I can't live with you anymore."

"Murph, you're safe here. Wendy's days as a free woman are numbered."

"My safety's not the issue. You've got baggage, Steel. Major baggage, and I can't be around it anymore."

"Look, I'm taking care of the Wendy situation."

"It's not just Wendy. Your friend Theo, well ..."

"Well, what?"

"He strikes me as kind of psycho. He creeps me out."

"He's just... different."

But who was I kidding? Wendy, Theo, all of them. They'd changed since high school.

Maybe Murph was right to want to get away from all of it. Who could blame him? If I could get away from it, I'd go running myself.

"When are you leaving?"

"I'll be out by the end of the week," he said. "My new place isn't nearly as nice as this, but I can't deal with the nutcases that come around."

"You don't think I'm a nutcase too, do you?"

He laughed at that one. "Of course not. Except so far as you hang around those other nutcases."

I let out a laugh as well. "You can still come around. Have a beer."

"I know that, and you're welcome at my new digs anytime. I'll get you the address. And Brad?"

"Yeah?"

"I hope things work out with you and Daphne. She's gorgeous and hot, but I think she's genuine as well. I think she'll be good for you."

I nodded. "I hope things work out with you and Patty. Or Sloane. Or whoever."

He laughed again. "I'm not even close to wanting a relationship. Patty and Sloane are both great. Why should I choose?"

"I suppose you don't have to, until one of them forces you to."

"I don't like ultimatums. I'm young. I'm still sowing my oats. Maybe you should do the same."

I shook my head. "I'm going to see how things go with Daphne. I've never met anyone like her."

"Good luck with it."

"I'm not seeing her tonight, though. You want to get a drink?"

"Sorry." He polished off his beer. "I have plans."

"Patty?"

"No."

"Sloane?"

He smirked. "No."

"Dude, you're going to hell. You know that, right?"

He laughed. "What a way to go, though."

Murph was a heck of a guy. He and I had been roommates all last year. He'd put up with a lot of Wendy bullshit, but he'd never left. Of course, she hadn't pulled a gun on him last year.

Daphne was out with the girls tonight, and now Murph was gone, so I was free.

I could do anything.

I checked my watch. Nearly eleven.

It was the last evening before classes began, and there was only one person I wanted to see.

She might be back at the dorm by now, and if she wasn't? I'd wait.

CHAPTER FORTY-FIVE

Daphne

"I can't believe you agreed to this," Patty said as we walked down to the guys' floor. "Why didn't you just answer the question?"

"I didn't want to. If I'd told them I was at Brad's ranch, they'd have pounced on me with a million questions, and I didn't feel like talking about it to two people I hardly know."

"Okay, I can understand that, but Daph, you have to take off your shirt on the guys' floor!"

"I don't have to. You can just say I did."

"Daph…"

"Don't worry. I'm not going to ask you to lie."

"Then how are you going to pull this off?"

"Remember when I got Flo to agree to *anywhere* on the guys' floor?"

"Yeah."

"I'll find a closet, and you can stand watch and time me."

Patty laughed. "You're devious!"

"Not devious. I just pay attention to wording." I paid attention to everything these days because I didn't want to forget anything that happened to me ever again. I'd grown very observant.

"What if we can't find a closet?"

"The laundry room."

"Good call. Guys don't do laundry. But what if they do? Plus, it's the night before classes begin. Someone will probably be doing a load."

"Then we'll knock on Ennis's door. He'll let me do it in his room. Then I take off my shirt for sixty seconds, you time me, and we're done. No lies."

"You're such a schemer!" Patty said. "I love it."

"It's not a scheme, Pat. I'm following the rules." I smiled.

"You're one smart cookie."

We walked onto the guys' floor. A few guys passed us and said hi.

"Where do you suppose a closet is?" Patty whispered.

"I have no idea. Let's try the laundry room."

We walked to the end of the hallway where the washers and dryers sat. Crap. Someone was using them. The little room was vacant at the moment, but a guy could walk in at any time and check on his laundry.

"I guess it's Ennis's," I said.

"I hope he's there," Patty said.

We arrived at Ennis's room and knocked. No one answered.

"How can he and his roommate both be out?" Patty said. "It's eleven."

I looked around. The room to the left of his said *Dirk and Gene* on the front. Dirk the jerk—the one who thought life wasn't worth living without bacon. I hadn't been a fan when I met him, but at least I knew him. "Let's try Dirk and Gene," I said to Patty.

"Okay." Patty knocked on the door.

Dirk opened it, dressed in a T-shirt and boxers.

"Sorry," Patty said, "did we wake you?"

"Nah. What's up?"

"Is your roommate here?"

Dirk shook his head. "He should be back soon, though. You want to leave a message for him?"

"No," Patty said. "We're actually here to see you. Daphne needs a favor."

Dirk smirked. "Sure thing. What do you need?"

"We need you to leave your room for one minute so we can do something."

"Say what?"

"It's silly, really," I said. "We're playing truth or dare, and Flo dared me to come down here to the guys' floor and take my shirt off for one minute. Technically, the inside of your room is on the guys' floor, so if you'll step out for a minute, I can take my shirt off inside your room and make good on the dare."

Dirk's lips curved upward in a sly smile. "Sure. You can use my room."

"Great," Patty said. "We'll just be a minute. Literally."

"One condition."

"What's that?" she asked.

"I stay."

I lifted my eyebrows as Patty said, "Sure, you can stay."

"Pat—"

"You just have to turn around so you don't see Daphne."

"Sorry. I get to look. Either that or no room."

"You're a perv. We'll find someone else," Patty said. "Or we take our chances in the laundry room. Come on, Daph."

I sighed. "No, let's just get it done. I don't have to take off my bra."

"You want this guy ogling you?"

"No, I don't, but if we don't get back up there soon, Flo and Stacey are going to come looking for us. Ennis isn't home, so what other choice do I have?"

"Good thinking," Dirk said.

"You shut up," Patty said.

"Come on. Let's get it done." I entered Dirk's room. "Close the door, Dirk. And for God's sake, put some pants on."

He pulled on a pair of jeans and smirked again. "Satisfied?"

"Let's get this over with. Patty, start timing." I pulled off my shirt.

Dirk sucked in a breath. "Nice."

I still had a bra on, but it was a lacey black one. I should have changed first.

I closed my eyes. If I didn't have to see Dirk seeing me, I could deal with it better. "For God's sake, Pat, how much longer?"

"Forty-seven seconds."

A minute was supposed to be short. I opened my eyes. Dirk was still looking at me, but at least he wasn't salivating. I zeroed in on his crotch. If he was hard, I couldn't tell. That made me squeak out a giggle.

"Thirty more seconds," Patty said.

Only halfway there? This was the longest minute in history. I crossed my arms over my chest. No rule against that. I wished I'd thought of it at the beginning.

Dear Lord, how long could a minute take?

"Fifteen seconds," Patty said.

I closed my eyes again and inhaled. Almost done. Almost done.

"Ten," Patty said. "Nine, eight, seven, six, five, f—"

"Daphne!"

I dropped my arms to my side. "That's Brad!"

"What's he doing here?" Patty said. "Three, two, one. Get your shirt on. Quick."

I threw my shirt back over my head and tucked it into place.

"Thanks for the peep show," Dirk said.

"This isn't for public broadcast," Patty said. "You keep your trap zipped."

"Maybe I will and maybe I—"

"Daphne! Where are you?"

I opened the door to Dirk's room and stepped out. "I'm right here, Brad. What are you doing here?"

"Your friends upstairs told me where to find you. What are you doing down here?"

"Patty and I were just talking to Dirk." Thank God Dirk had put jeans on. "Dirk, this is Brad Steel."

"Hey," Dirk said.

Brad ignored him.

"I'm going back up," Patty said. "I'll tell Flo and Stacey you did it."

"Did what?" Brad asked.

"Nothing."

"She stripped, man," Dirk said.

"I did not! Shut up, will you?"

Brad went rigid. "What were you doing in his room?"

"It was a dare," Dirk said.

"I told you to shut up!"

"No," Brad said. "I want to hear this."

"She took off—"

"Be quiet, Dirk. I'll handle this." I turned to Brad. "It was a stupid truth or dare game. I took the dare, so I had to come down here to this floor and take off my shirt for one minute. I did it in Dirk's room with Patty timing me. No big deal."

His face turned red. Was he really angry about this? It was so minor.

"We couldn't find a closet to use, and someone was in the laundry room. I just had to do it somewhere on the guys' floor. The other girls didn't think it through."

"You saw her topless?" Brad said through clenched teeth.

"No, no," I answered for Dirk. "I had my bra on. Ask Patty."

Brad advanced on Dirk. "I ought to—"

"Brad, please." I stepped in front of him. "He was a perfect gentleman." A little white lie, but he hadn't tried to touch me, so I'd give it to him.

Brad turned to Dirk. "You breathe a word of this to anyone, and I'll crush your skull. You hear me?"

"You don't scare me," Dirk said, though his demeanor said otherwise.

"Good. Don't be scared. Be confident. I don't give a shit. But if you tell anyone you saw her in her bra, you'll get scared real quick. Come on, Daphne." He grabbed my arm and yanked me to the stairs.

Halfway up the stairs, he stopped and gripped my shoulders. "What were you thinking?"

"It was just a stupid game."

"I don't want any other guys looking at you."

"Brad, I'm on a campus full of guys. They're going to look."

"Not at your bra."

"I told you, it was—"

"Truth or dare. I get it. Why didn't you just answer the question, Daphne?"

CHAPTER FORTY-SIX

Brad

"It was too personal," she said, "and it would have invited a lot of other questions I didn't want to answer."

"What was it?"

She blushed. "They wanted to know where I'd been this weekend."

"Why didn't you tell them? Are you embarrassed?"

"Of course not. I loved this weekend. But it was so special to me, and if I'd told them, they'd have wanted to know all about you, whether we... you know. I don't know them well enough to let them into that part of my life. It's too personal. Too special."

Her lips trembled a bit. Had I frightened her? Granted, the thought of her taking her shirt off in front of that degenerate unnerved me more than a little. Okay, it pissed me off and sparked a jealous anger. In my heart, I knew she was innocent of any wrongdoing, but still, I was livid.

I grabbed her in the stairwell and crushed our mouths together.

Mine, I said with that kiss. *You're mine. You'll always be mine.*

She opened for me, and in a fit of jealous rage, I groped her breasts through her shirt.

She pulled back. "Brad..."

"I'm sorry," I said. "It's just... I can't deal with the fact that he saw them."

"He didn't. I had my bra on."

"Still. I hate it, Daphne. I hate it."

She cupped my cheek. "I have no interest in Dirk. I actually think he's kind of a dick."

"Then why—"

She covered my lips with her fingers. "It was a stupid game. That's all. If it means that much to you, I'll never play it again. It was awkward, anyway. I hardly know these girls."

Yes. That's what I want. Never play the game again.

But I couldn't say the words. For the first time, the four years' difference in our ages became crudely apparent. She was barely out of high school, and I was almost through college. Games like truth or dare and spin the bottle seemed like a lifetime ago. In fact, I'd never played either.

"It's okay," I said. "You were just trying to get to know the people on your floor. I understand." *Sort of.*

"I did the best I could. I made her say it could be anywhere on the guys' floor, which meant I could minimize who saw me."

"Why him? Why not Prince Charles?"

"Ennis? He wasn't home. He was my first pick, after a closet or the laundry room, but we couldn't find a closet, and someone was using the laundry room."

I let out a breath I'd only just noticed I was holding. "All right."

"I don't want anyone else, you know."

I smiled like a moron. "I don't either."

"I meant it when I said I thought fate had brought us together."

"I meant it too, even though I never really believed in fate."

"You don't?" She smiled. "I do. I have to."

"What do you mean?"

"My life has been...a struggle in some ways. I have to believe fate has something better in store for me from now on, and when I met you, I had the strong feeling that I'd found my destiny."

I kissed her forehead. "I'm sorry you've had a struggle. That year couldn't have been easy."

"Parts of it weren't. But parts of it I just don't remember. I've promised myself I'll never go down that rabbit hole again. I'll stay happy. I'll find the sunrise in everything in my life."

The warmth of a sunrise glowed in her. *She* glowed. She dazzled. Daphne Wade was so innocent, yet she knew so much more about life than anyone I'd met so far in my twenty-two years. This woman was my destiny, my soul mate. She was right. Fate *had* brought us together.

I trailed my finger over the apple of her cheek and down her jawline. "Daphne."

She met my gaze. "What, Brad?"

"I love you. I love you so much."

She widened her eyes. "Oh."

"I know it's ridiculous. We've known each other for a week. It doesn't make any sense."

She reached up and laid her soft hand over mine. "It makes perfect sense. I love you too."

"You're so young," I said.

"So are you."

I chuckled softly. "You're right. I am. I didn't expect this so soon in my life."

"I didn't either, but it feels right, doesn't it?"

"God, yes," I said, relishing the warmth of her hand on mine. "It feels so right."

I wanted to drop to my knees then and there and ask her to spend her life with me, but I didn't want to scare her away. We had a lifetime ahead of us—a lifetime of love and children and happiness.

I didn't need to hurry.

She'd be mine forever. I knew that now. One day, we'd marry and have children, but that didn't have to be today. It could be years from now, after we knew each other better, after she'd finished her education.

I'd wait however long I needed to.

I'd wait forever.

I lowered my head and pressed my lips to hers. It was a soft kiss, a kiss of meaning. A kiss of love. A kiss full of promises of a future to come.

This was what I wanted more than anything.

Which meant damage control—things I needed to deal with before I could make a life for Daphne and me on the ranch. I'd already set things in motion with Wendy, but other baggage remained.

At least I had all the time in the world. Daphne was young. We could wait years to begin our life together. Yeah, we had time.

I'd need it to find a way to put some things in their graves.

CHAPTER FORTY-SEVEN

Daphne

I grasped my campus map in my hand as I trudged to my first college class. We'd had several tours during orientation, but how was I supposed to remember where each building was? I was determined that after today, I'd no longer need the map. My first class was in Majors Hall, and of course it was the farthest classroom building from my dorm.

Not a problem. It was a beautiful day. Patty and I had gotten up early to hit the cafeteria for a light breakfast and some coffee. Her first class wasn't for another hour and a half, so she was sitting in the student center gossiping with Flo and some other girls I didn't know. I was on my own now, and I was okay with that. After the debacle last night, I needed some space from the girls.

I finally made it to my classroom with five minutes to spare. I took a seat in the middle of the classroom.

A few minutes later, Ennis strolled in. "Hey, Daphne." He sat down next to me.

Never had I been so thrilled to see a familiar face. "I'm so glad you're here."

"Sorry I wasn't in last night to … uh … help you out."

"Crap. Did Dirk tell you?"

"Yeah, but he swore me to secrecy."

"He'd better not tell anyone else. Brad will kick the tar out of him."

"Oh?" Ennis wrinkled his forehead. "You don't say?"

I recognized sarcasm when I heard it. Ennis's jaw was still slightly bruised from Brad's punch the first night of orientation.

"How serious are you two anyway?" he asked.

"We just met," I said.

We *were* serious. We loved each other. It sounded ridiculous to say it, but it was fate. And it was right. I had the same feeling I'd had during the game last night. I didn't want to talk about it. It was too personal.

"A guy doesn't go around threatening other guys over a girl he's not serious about."

"I wouldn't know," I said truthfully. Brad was my first boyfriend.

Wow. Brad was my first boyfriend. I replayed the words in my mind like a broken record.

What did I know about love? For that matter, what did Brad know about love? Sure, he was more experienced than I was, but he was still pretty darned young.

The class began to fill up, so I was spared talking about it anymore.

Thank goodness.

I knew in my head and my heart that I was meant to be with Brad.

But I had no way to explain that knowledge to others. They'd all think I was wacked.

I'd been sure before, but now I was even more sure, if that was possible. Brad hadn't run away screaming when I told him about my hospitalization and my lack of memory of that time. In fact, he'd shared his mother's issues with me. He understood.

He was definitely the one.

★ ★ ★

Classes went by in a flash the first week. I saw Brad about every other evening. We didn't sleep together again, as we were both busy with studies. Neither one of us was interested in a quickie. Besides, we had all the time in the world, and I was determined to focus on my classes. The vast amount of material we were expected to learn on our own nearly overwhelmed me, but I took the time I needed to study and read.

I actually kind of enjoyed it. English was my favorite class, and I began seriously considering a career in creative writing.

Before I knew it, three weeks had flown by.

"Have you taken care of things yet?" Patty asked me one day during lunch.

"Taken care of what?"

"The health center. You need to get on the pill."

"Oh." I warmed. "Brad and I ... We haven't ..."

She widened her eyes. Was that shocking?

"We've both been really busy," I said.

"Daph, you're never too busy for good sex."

I couldn't help a smile. The sex with Brad had been amazing, but what did I know of good sex? It hadn't hurt, and I hadn't bled. Did that make it good? Brad and I had an amazing connection. Did that make it good? Our physical chemistry was also off the charts. Did that make it good?

Patty, on the other hand, had slept with two different guys in the three weeks since we'd been at college. Was her sex the same as mine? How could it be, without the emotional connection?

"Earth to Daphne," she said.

"Oh, sorry. I was just thinking."

"About sex?" She guffawed.

I warmed more.

"You're blushing! You *were* thinking about sex."

I stood. "I'm finished. I have some time before my next class. I'll go to the health center now and get a prescription."

"I'd go with you, but I'm meeting my lab partner to go over notes."

"It's okay. I can take care of it myself."

Though I'd have liked to have her there. Hospitals and anything like them gave me the nerves. I breathed in and out slowly as I got rid of my tray.

No biggie. This was a student health center, not a psychiatric hospital. No one would shove drugs down my throat. No one would make me sit in therapy when I didn't feel like it. No one would force me to write in a journal and then take it away from me.

I shook my head to clear it. I couldn't go there. Not now. That part of my life was over. Kaput. I was in college, and I'd met an amazing man. *New life. New life.* I repeated the words to myself over and over.

Still, my nerves were in shambles.

The building housing the student health center loomed in the distance as I walked toward it. It seemed to pulse with a heartbeat of its own.

Just your imagination, Daphne. Do this. Do this for yourself and for Brad.

I grabbed my courage, opened the door to the building, and approached the reception desk.

"May I help you?"

"Hi. I'm here to . . . I'd like to get some oral contraceptives, please."

"Sure. No problem. You're lucky we're pretty slow today. The nurse practitioner can see you without an appointment. Have a seat, and I'll tell her you're here."

An appointment? Yeah, that made sense. Why hadn't I thought to call in advance?

"Thanks." I sat down in the waiting area.

No one else was waiting. No eyes to feel on me.

Tick. Tock. Tick. Tock.

I had plenty of time before my class, but I was hyperaware of the seconds ticking by. This was worse than timing my shirtless experience in Dirk's room.

I picked up a magazine from the table next to my chair. *Seventeen.* I was no longer seventeen. I was eighteen. An adult. Did this magazine even apply to me anymore? Why was it here, on a college campus? I perused the articles.

"The Ten Best Acne-Fighting Masks."

I was lucky. I didn't have acne. Not interested.

"How to Give a Hickey."

Seriously?

"How to Tell if He's Right for You."

That one got my attention. I flipped through the pages to find the article.

"Daphne?" A tall woman in a white coat stood by the reception desk.

"Yeah. That's me."

"Come on back."

She led me to an exam room and closed the door. "I'm Kathleen, the nurse practitioner here." She glanced at a chart. "You're here for oral contraceptives?"

"Yes, please."

"How long have you been sexually active?"

"Not long. I only did it once a couple weeks ago."

"And what method of birth control did you use?"

"A condom. I mean ... he used a condom."

"Good. Good. When was your last pelvic exam?"

Pelvic exam? "I'm not sure what you mean."

"No one has examined your pelvic organs manually?"

"No."

"That's okay. A lot of women don't have one until they're eighteen. I'll need to do an exam before I can give you the contraceptives. Just to make sure there aren't any problems. Not that I expect any."

"Okay."

"Do you have any questions?"

"Not that I can think of."

"The exam is invasive. I'll insert a speculum into your vagina to take a look at your cervix. I'll do a pap smear too, since you've never had one. Then I'll insert my fingers into your vagina to feel your uterus and ovaries."

"Okay." It sounded intrusive and awful, but what else could I say?

"I need you to undress from the waist down. If you'd prefer, I can leave you a gown and I can do a breast exam as well, though at your age it's not really necessary."

"Just the pelvic, please," I said. Being groped below the waist was enough for today, thanks.

"Perfect. I'll just take your blood pressure first." She placed the cuff on my upper arm and inflated it. "Good. One twenty over seventy." She handed me a paper blanket. "Go ahead and undress from the waist down. Cover yourself with this and sit on the exam table. I'll knock in a few minutes."

"Thank you."

She left, and I quickly undressed from the waist down, covered myself, and waited.

At least no one was staring at me.

CHAPTER FORTY-EIGHT

Brad

I had a bad case of senioritis. Classes were interesting enough, but I didn't have any desire to study. Daphne invaded my mind constantly, and when I thought about her, I had to think about other things.

Things I didn't like to think about.

Things I'd kept on the back burner far too long because I thought I had more time to deal with them.

Things I had to deal with sooner rather than later, now that I'd made a commitment to a woman.

Daphne and I saw each other a lot in the evenings. We usually studied together, though I spent a lot of time staring at her over my book. We hadn't made love again. Even though I was constantly hard in her presence, I didn't want to pressure her.

We never ate lunch together, as our schedules didn't allow it. I sat with Murph in the cafeteria. Patty approached us.

"Hi, guys," she said.

"Hey," Murph said. "Want to join us?"

"Thanks, but I already ate with Daphne. I was supposed to meet my biology lab partner after lunch, but she blew me off. Just thought I'd say hi."

"You're welcome to sit down," I said.

"No, that's okay. See you guys around." She walked away and out of the cafeteria.

"That was slightly awkward," I said. "You haven't called her, have you?"

"No. I haven't called Sloane either. I'm pretty into Lorraine right now."

"I've said it before, Murph. You're going to hell."

"And I've said it before. What a way to go!"

"How's the new place working out?"

"It's good. A lot less drama."

While I enjoyed having someone else around the condo, I'd decided not to get a new roommate. This way, Daphne and I could be alone whenever we wanted to be. I really wanted to ask her to move in with me, but she was so young and it was way too soon. Waking up next to her each day would be like waking up to sunshine. Granted, in Colorado, we usually woke up to sunshine anyway, but Daphne was sunshine times a hundred.

A lot less drama.

Murph's words invaded my headspace.

I'd never thought of my life as "drama," but he had a good point. I'd gotten myself into a mess six years ago, and it was still a huge part of my life. I compartmentalized it. Didn't think about it.

Except now I *had* to think about it. Had to deal with it.

Time to call a meeting of the Future Lawmakers.

All except Rod Cates. He hadn't been involved since high school, and now he and Theo's sister were engaged. How I wished I'd gotten out long ago.

Hindsight was always twenty-twenty.

I finished my meal quickly and excused myself. I didn't have a class this afternoon, so I went back to my condo to make the requisite phone calls. Tonight I'd be dealing with some major shit.

I opened the door, and—

"Good, you're here."

Wendy's voice.

"How the hell did you get in here?"

"You gave me a key, remember?"

"Yeah, and I've changed these damned locks two times since then."

"Brad," she cooed, "surely you know by now that I get whatever I want."

Mental note: Call locksmith again.

"I'm busy. What do you want?"

"A pound of flesh," she said. "You went to my parents behind my back."

I cleared my throat. That was the least of what I'd done, as she'd soon learn.

"You're damned right, I did. You've always been a little crazy, Wendy, but you've gone mental now. You pulled a gun on Murphy."

"That little thing? I wasn't going to hurt him."

"Do you think that matters? He moved out. I lost a roommate because of your shit."

"You don't need a roommate, Brad. You're worth millions."

"Maybe I like having a roommate. Did you ever think of that?"

"I—"

"No, you didn't, because you never think of anyone but yourself, Wendy. You're a classic narcissist. Everything's about you."

"You're a shrink now? Diagnosing me?"

"I'm no shrink, but I don't need a medical degree to recognize a crazy person when I see one. Sane people don't go around waving guns."

"Tell you what," she said. "I promise never to pull a gun on anyone again."

"Good." Though I didn't believe her.

"If . . ." she continued.

"I'm no longer making deals with you."

"Sweet, sweet Brad," she snarled. "What makes you think you have a choice?"

"There's always a choice, Wendy," I said. "Always."

CHAPTER FORTY-NINE

Daphne

"Come in." My voice was unsteady after the knock on the exam room door.

Kathleen marched in with a smile on her face. "All set?"

I nodded.

"Okay. I need you to scoot to the edge of the table and put your feet in the stirrups."

The stirrups weren't actually stirrups at all. They were metal notches. I'd been wearing sandals, so my feet were bare, which made me feel all the more exposed. I secretly wished for a pair of socks, even though that made no sense.

Kathleen washed her hands at the sink and then put on a pair of blue rubber gloves. "Since this is your first pelvic exam, I'm going to explain to you what I'm doing as I do it so you're informed."

Please, don't. "Okay."

She squirted something onto her fingers. "This is a lubricant. I'm going to put it on your vaginal opening so I can insert the speculum."

A glob of cold hit my vagina. I tried not to shudder.

"Relax," she said.

So much for not shuddering.

"Now I'm going to insert the speculum. It shouldn't hurt, but it will be cold."

The lubricant was already cold, so I didn't worry too much.

Right. Should have worried. The speculum was colder than the lube, and it stretched me open.

"Everything looks good in there. Now I'm going to do the pap smear. You might feel a little bit of cramping."

I sucked in a breath. A little bit of cramping.

"Relax," she said. "This only takes a few seconds."

After what seemed like a lifetime, she withdrew the speculum. "Now I'm going to examine you manually to make sure your uterus and ovaries are the normal size for a woman your age." She inserted her fingers into me, stretching me. It felt strange, but it wasn't painful.

"Ovaries look good." *Pause.* "Uterus is normal." *Pause.* "Hmm."

"What is it?" I asked, my heart speeding up.

"Probably nothing. You say you used a condom?"

"Yeah."

"Your cervix feels a little soft."

"Is that bad?"

"I want to do a pregnancy test."

"But I can't possibly be pregnant. Brad used a condom. I saw it."

"I'm sure he did. And you're probably not pregnant. But your cervix feels softer than usual, which could indicate pregnancy."

"I ... I don't want the test."

"Daphne, I understand your apprehension. Condoms are effective most of the time, so there's probably nothing to worry about. But I want to check this out. I can't give you oral contraceptives if you're pregnant, so I need to rule it out."

My heart was beating like a herd of galloping stallions. *I'm not pregnant. I can't be pregnant.*

"I'll need a urine sample," she said. "Go ahead and get dressed. The bathroom is right next door. You'll find wipes. Wipe front to back, please, and then begin your urine stream into the toilet. Once you've begun, give me a small sample in the cup, all right?"

"Yeah. Sure." My voice was robotic.

She smiled. "Relax. There's most likely nothing to worry about, okay?"

"Okay." *Breathe in. Breathe out. She's a medical professional. She knows what she's talking about.*

She left the room, and I quickly got dressed, even though I could barely feel my legs. Whether it was from having them in the stirrups or from nerves, I had no idea. Probably nerves. I walked robotically out of the exam room and into the bathroom. The cups sat on a small table next to the sink with instructions to write my name on the cup with the permanent marker sitting next to them. I did so quickly, my hand shaking. Then I followed the instructions and peed in the cup. I washed my hands and took the cup out to Kathleen.

"Okay, Daphne, go ahead back into the exam room, and I'll be with you when I have your results."

I nodded, numb all over.

Back in the exam room, I sat down in a chair.

Another waiting game.

And this one was slower than the minute I spent in Dirk's room without my shirt on.

Tick.

Tock.

Tick.

Tock.

Nothing to worry about.

Brad used a condom.

Condoms were effective most of the time.

Most of the time ...

Most.

Not all.

Not *all*.

Ten minutes passed. Twenty. Thirty.

Then Kathleen's knock on the door.

I cleared my throat. "Come in."

She wasn't smiling.

CHAPTER FIFTY

Brad

"You may think there's always a choice. You'd be wrong."
Wendy eyed my hand. "Still wearing your ring, I see."

I looked down at my right hand.

Yeah, I was, but it had nothing to do with any fucked-up loyalty to Wendy or the Future Lawmakers. I couldn't get the damned thing off. I'd put on a lot of muscle and broadened since I was in high school, which evidently extended to my fingers.

I'd paid for these stupid rings that Wendy had designed. Her distorted symbol that had no meaning as far as I could tell.

"I won't be wearing it much longer." *Mental note: Go to a jeweler, have the damned thing sawed off, and sell it for junk gold.*

"You're still wearing it, though. That says more than a thousand words, Brad."

It says only that I can't get it off. But I didn't tell Wendy that. Let her think she still had some kind of bizarre hold on me. I could use that to my advantage.

"No more deals. Figure out how to finance your future some other way, Wendy. You're cut off as of now."

She smiled. "You'll never cut me off, Brad. You and I both know that."

I chuckled. "You're wrong. The bank is closed."

She sauntered forward and trailed her index finger over my lower lip. "Close the bank if you want to. We no longer need your money. But that's not what I'm talking about when I say you'll never cut me off."

"Yeah? What are you talking about, then?" Though I already knew.

"You and I, Brad. We're connected. We'll always be connected. Someday, we'll have that baby that was stolen from us in high school."

"No, we won't."

Her miscarriage had been tragic, but it had also been a blessing in disguise. I didn't want to be bound to Wendy through a child. If I could excise her from my life with a sharp scalpel, I would, and I'd live with the scar, no matter how deep.

And it would be deep.

"Oh, we will. You can't avoid destiny, Brad."

"My destiny lies with someone else."

"Daphne?" She shook her head. "There's so much you don't know."

"I know everything."

"About her year in London?"

I didn't want to discuss Daphne with Wendy, but I couldn't resist shoving it in her face. "She told me all about it."

"Then you know she wasn't actually in London."

"As I said, she told me all about it."

"That's sweet. Really. But there's no way she told you *all* about it. There are things even she doesn't recall."

"What the hell are you talking about? If you know something, you better fucking tell me."

"Sorry, you set the rules, so you get to live by them. You

said no more deals. You want to know the truth about your sweet little slut? You won't get it out of me. Besides, it's not my story to tell." She turned and flounced toward the doorway. "Oh! Looks like you have another visitor." Wendy walked away.

And Daphne stood in my doorway.

CHAPTER FIFTY-ONE

Daphne

Nausea coiled in my belly like a snake. Slowly it wound its way up my esophagus.

Why was *she* here?

Why was *I* here?

Why was life so complicated?

Why couldn't I just be happy watching the sun rise and set?

Why couldn't Brad and I have the chance to get to know each other?

"Hey, baby," he said. "Sorry about her. What are you doing here? Don't you have class?"

I nodded. "Yeah. I'm cutting. I . . . I need to talk to you."

"Sure. Come in. What's wrong?"

Oh, God. What *wasn't* wrong? I was about to ruin this man's life.

Positive.

The test had been positive.

Condoms are effective most of the time.

Most *of the time.*

Should I go out and buy a lottery ticket now? Of course not. I'd already used up my "one-in-a-million chance." Though it was more like a three-in-one-hundred chance. Kathleen had informed me, after I nearly fainted with shock, that condoms, when used properly, were about ninety-seven percent effective. Had Brad used it effectively? How hard was it to use a condom correctly?

I walked slowly into Brad's condo. "You're alone, right?"

"Yeah. Sorry about Wendy, but she's out of our hair now."

I nodded. I didn't care about Wendy. In light of my present situation, Wendy was the least of my worries.

"Can I get you anything? A drink?"

I nodded again. "Water would be good."

"Sure. Have a seat." He walked into his kitchen.

I looked around the living area. The leather furniture seemed to reprimand me. *See us? See his good life? Don't ruin it for him.*

If only...

Kathleen had talked to me about my options. Abortion. Adoption. I didn't have to become a mother at eighteen. Or nineteen. Technically I'd be nineteen when the baby came.

I understood all that. But this wasn't just any baby. It was Brad's baby. Brad's and my baby. The man I felt in the depths of my soul was my destiny. The man who would be the father of all my babies.

Brad came back from the kitchen and handed me a glass of water. "Sit down, Daphne."

Reluctantly, I took a seat on the leather couch that had been mocking me moments ago. He sat down next to me. I took a long drink of the cool water, letting it ease my parched throat.

How could I do this to him?

How?

And what if...

What if he wanted me to have an abortion? Could I do it?

I set the glass of water down on the end table and then turned to him, tears welling in my eyes.

He cupped my cheek. "Oh my God. What is it?"

I melted into him, and his strong arms cocooned around me. If only I could stay here, stay like this, protected within his embrace forever.

I sniffled into his shoulder.

I'd put this off long enough. My therapist wouldn't have sent me off to college if he didn't believe I was strong and capable, so I'd be strong and capable.

I'd look the man I loved in the eye and tell him the truth.

I pulled away and sniffled again. I met his gaze. "Brad?"

"Yeah, baby. What is it? What's wrong?"

"I'm..."

"Yeah?"

"I just came from the health center. I went to get the pill so you wouldn't have to use condoms."

He smiled. "That's sweet of you. So what's wrong?"

"Turns out, we don't need condoms anymore, and I don't need the pill."

"Oh?"

"I'm pregnant, Brad."

He cocked his head, as if my words hadn't quite registered. "Did you hear me?"

"I don't understand. I used a rubber."

"I know. I told them that."

"So how...?"

"No birth control is a hundred percent effective."

"One time? After one time?"

I nodded. "I gave the health center your name and told

them they could talk to you about it if you called them. I mean, if you want to be sure. I'll do the test again if you want. I'm not lying."

"No. No. I mean . . . no. You don't have to do the test again."

"So you don't think I'm lying?"

"No." He cleared his throat. "Of course I don't. I just . . . I've used condoms lots of times, and this never happened."

"Please," I said. "I really don't want to hear about all the other women you've fucked right now."

I shuddered at my use of the word *fuck*. It wasn't like me.

"I didn't mean it like that."

"That's what it sounded like. How do you think I feel? I have sex one time, and this happens. Did you use the condom right?"

"For God's sake, Daphne, I know how to use a damned condom."

"You might as well have used nothing."

Then I burst into tears.

I was completely inexperienced. It was my body. I should have taken care of it.

He touched my face. "Honey, please. This isn't anyone's fault. Now we have to decide what to do."

"I know what you want. You want an abortion."

"Only if that's what you want."

"I don't know what I want, Brad. I'm eighteen years old. I don't even know what I want to major in yet. I'm not ready to be a mother."

"I'm not ready to be a father, either. Are you saying *you* want an abortion?"

"No. No. That's not what I'm saying. I've known about this for an hour. How can I make any kind of decision that quickly?"

"It's not your decision," he said. "It's *our* decision."

"Our decision? You can't be serious. It's in my body."

"It's part of me, too."

"Stop, just stop!" I stood. "Why is this making us fight? I don't want that."

He rose and put his arms around me. "I don't want that either. I love you, Daphne."

God, more tears. "I love you too."

"We'll work this out one way or another."

"I don't think I can do it, Brad."

"Do what?"

"Have an abortion. It's not that I'm some pro-life activist or anything. I just don't like the idea. This is our baby. Yours and mine. A part of you and a part of me. There's something special about that. This baby was conceived in love."

"There's everything special about that."

"I suppose we could have the baby and put it up for adoption," I said.

"Could you do that?"

"I have no idea. Right now, I feel like maybe I could, but as the baby grows, and after I see him and hold him ... I just don't know. What do you want?"

He smiled and kissed my forehead. "This messes up my life. It messes up your life. But as I stand here and look into your beautiful eyes, I'm certain of two things."

"What are they?"

"I love you. And I want this baby."

CHAPTER FIFTY-TWO

Brad

I want this baby.

My words surprised me, but I couldn't deny their truth. I wanted this child with Daphne. She was so young. Hell, I was young too. But we could do it. We could do it together.

I was financially stable. I'd be almost done with college by the time the baby came, and then we'd move to the ranch after I graduated. Daphne could complete the first semester. She'd have to put off school for a semester or two, but she could go back later if she wanted to. Grand Junction had colleges. We could get a nanny for the baby. I'd build us our own house on the ranch or renovate one that was already there. Our ranch was huge. There was plenty of room, and it would all be mine someday anyway.

My mother would love a grandchild. We might not need a nanny. My mother could help with the baby.

All these thoughts whirled in my head, until Daphne's soft voice interrupted them.

"You do?"

"Yes, Daphne. I do. I want you, and I want this baby."

"Oh, Brad." She fell into my arms again. "Can we really do this?"

"Honey, people do this all the time with a lot less than

we have. We'll be fine. I promise you." I kissed the top of her head.

This beautiful woman was carrying my child. It was early yet. Anything could happen. But it wouldn't. She was right about fate. I believed now. How else could a condom have failed? Fate. Daphne would have this baby, and we'd have a family of our own.

Just the thought made me want her. Already I was hardening inside my jeans.

Great timing, Steel.

But she pushed into me, her body responding to mine.

I lowered my head and took her lips with mine.

We kissed with passion and need. With urgency yet tenderness, exploring each other's mouths.

I wanted to make love. Weeks had gone by since that perfect first time. I broke the kiss with a loud smack. "Can you?"

She nodded, her lips red and swollen from just one hard kiss. "Yeah. The nurse practitioner said it won't hurt the baby."

"Thank God." I lifted her into my arms and carried her into my bedroom.

Our bedroom.

This was our bedroom, now. She'd have to move in, let me take care of her. Finally I saw the good in Murph moving out. Daphne and I needed this time to get to know each other. Truly know each other—and prepare for our family while I finished college.

I undressed her slowly, revealing each new inch of flesh and then gazing at it as though I were unveiling a perfectly preserved Renaissance painting.

Except that Daphne was more perfect than any painting. She was warm flesh and blood.

She was mine.

All mine.

When she stood before me naked, I feasted on her with my eyes. Such pure beauty. Her dark braid fell over one shoulder, curving over the swell of her breast. Her pink-brown nipples were hard and taut, protruding from their fleshy mounds. Her belly was flat with a slight sexy curve. I trailed my finger over it, imagining it swollen with my child.

Then the triangle of darkness between her legs, and the paradise that lay between them. The paradise that had brought us where we stood today. Two people who loved each other and who had created another person from that love.

Yes, it was too soon.

Yes, we were too young.

Yes.

Yes.

Yes, to all of those things.

None of it mattered, though, because this woman was my soul mate. Fate had brought us together, and destiny would keep us together. We would make a family for our child.

I removed my own clothes a bit more quickly than I'd removed hers. I could think about serious and loving topics all I wanted, but I couldn't deny my ache to be inside Daphne's body.

Her eyes widened at my hard cock.

"You okay?" I asked.

"Yes, of course. I just can't believe it didn't hurt."

"It won't hurt this time either. God, baby, I want to go slow, but—"

She lay down on my bed. "It's okay. Take what you need."

I groaned as I lay down next to her and spread her legs. I stroked her soft folds to make sure she was ready.

Oh, yes. She was ready.

I rolled on top of her, bracing my arms on the bed to hold my weight, and slid gently into her heat.

"Ah…" I groaned. She was the perfect glove for me. Without a condom, I felt every ridge, every crevice, inside her. Sensation coiled in me. Each slide of my cock rippled through my whole body.

I was seventeen again, this time losing my virginity to the girl who was my future.

Nothing had ever felt like this—being inside Daphne. Being inside the woman I loved with no barriers to my pleasure.

I pulled out and thrust back in, savoring her welcoming warmth again. Again. Again.

I wouldn't last long. I knew this, but it didn't matter. This was the first of many times I'd make love to the mother of my child.

The first of many.

The first of so damned many.

"Baby, I'm sorry. I have to come."

"No, wait. I'm… I feel something… Oh!"

The walls of her pussy clamped around me, and that was the end for me. I thrust hard, and my cock released into her. Each pulse brought me closer to her, and her own climax sent me through the roof.

We rode the stars together, our bodies slick with sweat, and when I finally came down, I rolled off her, turned my head, and gazed at her flushed body.

So fucking beautiful.

Emotion lay thick between us, and before I knew it, words popped out of my mouth.

"Marry me, Daphne. Marry me, please."

CHAPTER FIFTY-THREE

Daphne

Marry me.

The words I wasn't sure I'd ever hear came tumbling from Brad's lips.

Who would want me? I was a mess. I'd spent a year hospitalized, for God's sake. I still had nightmares of things I couldn't remember when I woke up.

Sometimes, I felt I'd never be whole.

But lying here in Brad's arms, I was. I was whole. Did love make a person whole?

My therapist always said healing must come from within oneself.

I believed that. Truly I did, and I rose each morning looking for the best and brightest things each day had to offer.

One of those best and brightest things was the man whose arms I now snuggled in.

But...married at eighteen?

That wasn't me. That was never me.

I smiled and kissed his moist cheek. "Yes. I'd love to marry you, Brad. I want to give our baby a proper home with a mother and a father who adore him."

Brad smiled and pressed his lips to mine. "We'll do it at the ranch. Next weekend."

I jerked upward. "Next weekend?"

"Well... yeah. It's perfect. You can move in here with me and finish the first semester. Maybe the second, too, if you're up to it. What's the due date?"

What's the due date? Yeah, Kathleen had told me.

"May third."

"That's perfect. We'll arrange for you to take your second semester finals early, and..."

His words stopped making sense. They swirled around me, like blurred images made of sound waves.

I'm getting married. I'm moving in with my boyfriend. I'm having his baby.

Married. Moving. Baby.

"Daphne!"

Brad gripped my shoulders.

I met his dark gaze. His eyes. His gorgeous brown eyes. They steadied me. Brought me back into focus.

"Are you listening to me?"

I nodded. "It's a lot to think about."

"I know, sweetheart. I know."

"There's one other thing."

"What?"

I gulped. "I have to tell my parents."

"I know. I'll go with you."

"We can't get married next weekend, Brad. I have to go home. Tell them."

"You're right. I should meet them."

"This is crazy. They're going to think we're both crazy."

"It is a little crazy, but you didn't get pregnant on purpose. We used protection. It just happened."

It just happened. That was what I'd tell my parents. It just happened.

After all they'd been through with me, how could I say something just *happened*?

"What if they won't let me marry you?"

"Daphne, you're eighteen years old. You don't need their permission."

He was right. I knew he was right. But eighteen wasn't that much different from seventeen. I didn't feel like an adult a lot of the time.

You were adult enough to have sex.

The words in my mind made me chuckle out loud.

"What's funny?" he asked.

"I was just thinking how I don't feel eighteen. I don't feel like an adult at all sometimes, but I felt ready to have sex with you. That's pretty adult."

"I suppose. Although a lot of teenagers have sex."

"I just don't know how to tell them, Brad. They had such high hopes for me, after ... well, you know."

"Marrying me isn't exactly slumming."

"Come on. You know I didn't mean it like that. They want me to go to college. There was a time they didn't think I'd be able to do it."

"Daphne"—he met my gaze, his own laced with seriousness—"just how ill were you?"

That question—the question I couldn't answer because I didn't actually know. I didn't actually remember a lot of stuff.

"Severe anxiety and depression," I said. "I told you."

"I understand it can be debilitating," he said, "but you're healthy now. Right?"

"Yes." I wasn't lying. Not really. I was healthy. I was at college.

At college ... and pregnant.

"We'll visit your parents this weekend. I'll meet them. They'll see I'm a good guy with a lot to offer."

I nodded.

"Then the weekend after next, we'll go to the ranch and tell my parents."

"They'll hate me," I said.

"Why would they hate you?"

"Because I'm ruining your life."

"Baby, you're not ruining my life. I knew the first time I saw you that my life would be with you. Yeah, it's a little sooner than I expected, but my life is with you. Now and always."

His words warmed me.

"Besides," he continued, "I took you home the first week I met you. My dad knows I'm serious about you. And my mom will love you."

His mom. The mom who took care of the beautiful greenhouse on the ranch—the place where blooms abounded and new life occurred daily. The greenhouse was like a metaphor for a happy life. A life of sunrises and yellow tulips.

The pale-green tulip popped into my mind.

It had been a sad bloom, as if the fairies who visited the garden had forgotten to give it color.

It reminded me of my year away.

Those are my mom's favorites, Brad had said.

Why would her favorite be such a sad bloom?

I erased the thought from my mind.

My life would be the bright yellow tulip.

The tulip of a sunny day.

I'd marry Brad Steel. Have his child. Live a wonderful life with a wonderful man.

Never again would I be a colorless flower.

CHAPTER FIFTY-FOUR

Brad

My father wouldn't be pleased. Neither would my mother, but for different reasons.

Then there was Wendy.

But Wendy was no longer an issue.

It was happening today. My father had offered Wendy's parents a nice chunk of money, and finally they'd agreed to speak to the psychologist. Their testimony plus Murph's had been enough for the psychologist. The paperwork had been filed, and I knew exactly when the deed would be done this morning.

I cut classes so I could see it happen. I had to make sure she was going away. The psychologist had promised my father she'd be hospitalized for at least a year.

Perfect. For now, at least. Time for me to marry Daphne. Time for our baby to be born. Time for me to deal with the remaining Future Lawmakers without Wendy's influence, to get them back on track so they could all lead successful lives.

Time for me to make up for mistakes I'd made years ago. Mistakes I could finally undo.

I drove to the condo Wendy rented in Denver, parked a few doors down, and waited.

Wendy's car sat in the driveway. Good. She was home.

Shouldn't be long now before the psychologist came accompanied by the police. She wouldn't go quietly.

Time passed slowly, and thoughts of my past with Wendy formed in my mind in vivid color.

The day I'd met her… She was a cute cheerleader with a killer body. Who could resist? Not a seventeen-year-old horny high school guy. We were inseparable that first month, and when we finally had sex, she'd screamed like a banshee the first time. She'd bled too.

My mind soared to Daphne. Yeah, much better. My first time with her had been everything the time with Wendy wasn't. No screaming. No pain. Pure perfection, as if we were meant to be together, to create another life. Granted, we hadn't meant to do the latter, but I couldn't bring myself to be overly upset about it. It was fate.

I chuckled out loud. I had to tell my father. After he'd agreed to help me deal with Wendy, I had to tell him I'd screwed up again. It was hardly a screw-up, though. I'd used a condom. Again, fate.

Daphne and I and this baby were meant to be.

I closed my eyes, picturing our future child in my mind. A little boy. This one would be a boy. Maybe one day we'd have a girl, but this one was a boy, I felt certain. What would we name him? I had no idea. I didn't want to name him after my father. Yeah, he'd come through for me this time, but all those years he tormented my mother… I'd never forget that.

Daphne could name him. She'd pick the perfect name.

He'd be big and strong and wonderful, and I'd teach him to work the ranch as my father had taught me. I'd—

I jerked when sirens shrieked. A police car whizzed past me and stopped in front of Wendy's condo. An ambulance followed.

An ambulance? That was a surprise. My father told me it would be the police.

An officer exited the car along with a man in plain clothes. The psychologist, of course. I started my engine and drove forward until I had a good view of Wendy's door.

The officer knocked. Even in my truck, the loud pounding resonated in my ears.

The door opened.

Wendy.

Christ, she was freaking naked! Was she always naked at home? She seemed to be every time I went to see her.

Words were exchanged, but they were only a jumble to me. Wendy closed the door, and a few minutes later, the officer and the psychologist entered the home.

I waited. A couple guys in white got out of the ambulance and brought a stretcher to the front door. God, they were going to strap her down. My father had gone all out.

She wouldn't go quietly.

Or would she?

Would they subdue her with a sedative? *Could* they?

More moments passed. My heart raced. *Please, let this work. Please get her out of my life.*

Finally, the door opened. The officer led Wendy out in handcuffs, the psychologist at her side. She was eerily quiet... until she saw the guys in white waiting for her.

"Fuck no!" she shouted. "You aren't putting me on that thing!"

The men went to work strapping her down anyway, despite her protests. I made out most of her words because she was screaming.

"What the hell? I have rights, you know! I have money!

I'll sue the hell out of all of you! I want a lawyer! I have a right to a—"

My truck. Her gaze settled on my truck.

"You!" she yelled. "You're behind this! I'll never forgive you, Bradford Steel. I'll fucking see you in hell!"

My blood chilled.

Maybe I shouldn't have come, but I had to see this event for myself. Had to make sure she was truly gone.

Wendy was brilliant, yes.

But she was no match for my father.

Or for me.

From now on, I'd make sure of it.

CHAPTER FIFTY-FIVE

Daphne

Telling my parents that I was pregnant, moving in with the father of my baby, and getting married wasn't going to be easy. I went over and over in my mind how to tell them during the half-hour drive to my home. I'd called earlier to tell my mother I was coming and bringing a friend.

They were ecstatic that I had a friend.

Of course, they didn't know the friend was actually a lover who had gotten me pregnant.

I cleared my throat. "This is it," I said to Brad.

He pulled up next to my parents' modest suburban home and parked on the street. Then he turned to me. "Doing okay?"

Not even slightly. "Yeah," I said.

"Do you want me to wait out here for a few minutes?"

"No. I need you to be with me."

"Absolutely," he said. "Whatever you need."

We left the car and walked up to the door. Oddly, I felt like I should knock or ring the doorbell even though this was my home. Why did I feel like such a stranger here?

Easy. I *was* a stranger here. I was a completely different person from who I was when I left this house a month ago.

I reached toward the doorknob when the door opened on its own.

My mother stood in the entryway. "Daphne, honey. Welcome home." Then her eyes turned to circles.

I cleared my throat again. "Mom, this is Brad Steel. He's . . . my boyfriend."

"Oh, my." She held out her hand to Brad. "It's very nice to meet you. I'm Lucy Wade."

"Nice to meet you, Mrs. Wade."

"Lucy, please. Come right on in."

I entered and Brad followed me. My father sat in his recliner, reading a newspaper.

My mother cleared her throat. "Jonathan, Daphne's home, and she's brought her"—another throat clear—"boyfriend."

The paper dropped, and my father nearly stumbled getting out of the recliner before he put the footrest down. "Boyfriend?"

"Daddy," I said, "this is Brad Steel."

"Good to meet you, sir," Brad said.

"Brad Steel. Not the Steel ranch heir?"

Brad nodded. "One and the same."

"Oh. Well, this is a surprise. Have a seat. Make yourself at home. Tell me how you two met."

"At an orientation function," Brad said. "We went out that evening, and we've seen each other regularly since then."

"Goodness," my mother said.

I wasn't sure what she meant by that.

"It was kind of a whirlwind thing," Brad said, smiling at me.

God, he was so handsome. How did I ever get so lucky?

"I hope you like Italian food, Brad," my mother said. "I made spaghetti. It's Daphne's favorite."

"I eat anything," he said, still smiling.

"Would you like something to drink?" my mother asked.

"I'm getting Jonathan his beer."

"Sure, a beer would be great," Brad said.

"Brad's twenty-two," I said.

"I wasn't going to card him, Daphne." My mother walked to the kitchen.

What a stupid thing to say. What was wrong with me?

Silly question. I had serious breaking news to share. That was what was wrong.

My mother returned with two beers. "Daphne?"

"Just water, Mom."

She left again, returning momentarily with two glasses of water. She sat down opposite my father. "I figured Daphne's friend would stay in her room. She has a pull-out couch. But of course that's not appropriate now. I'll make up the guest room for you, Brad."

"You don't need to bother. I can just drive back to campus for the night."

"I wouldn't hear of it. You'll stay here. We'd like to get to know you."

I held back a sarcastic laugh. My mother had no idea that Brad and I had already been intimate and I was carrying the product of that union.

After dinner. I'd tell them after dinner.

Then they'd probably be happy to have Brad drive back to his place. In fact, they might never let me out of their sight again.

You're eighteen, Daphne.

Again, I didn't feel very adult sometimes.

My father kept Brad busy talking about the ranch and about my half brother, Larry. I listened with half an ear, until my mother began talking.

"Have you made any girlfriends, honey?"

"Yeah. My roommate, Patty, is nice. We get along well."

"Oh, good. I didn't expect you to find a boyfriend so soon. After all . . ."

"I've never had a boyfriend?" I finished for her.

"Well, no, you haven't. And then there's the other stuff."

"I've been honest with him, Mom. He knows about junior year."

"And he's okay with it?"

"Why wouldn't he be? I'm fine now, right?"

My mother nodded, smiling but looking past me. "Of course."

But did she truly believe I was fine? I often wondered. They'd been thrilled when my therapist thought college was a good idea.

"I'm happy for you," she continued. "He seems like a very nice boy."

"He's a man, Mom, and I'm a woman."

"Of course." Again with the smile.

This was going to be more difficult than I ever imagined.

CHAPTER FIFTY-SIX

Brad

Jonathan Wade was a good man, from what I could tell in the fifteen minutes we'd been conversing. He was smart, and he asked intelligent questions about the operation of the ranch. He seemed happy that Daphne and I were together.

Of course, he didn't know the whole story yet.

These were Daphne's parents, and I would let her take the lead on telling them while supporting her a hundred percent.

Wendy was gone. Committed for at least a year. Still, she wouldn't be put away forever. She'd use her smiles and wiles to get what she wanted, and after a year, she'd be back.

And I'd have to up my game.

Either that or find a way to silence Wendy forever.

Just the thought gave me the shivers. I wasn't a killer.

I certainly knew people who had the potential, though.

Theo was too smart to kill. Larry not smart enough.

But Tom Simpson...

He was the future lawmaker I understood the least. He had an iciness about him—something that made me think he was capable of just about anything.

He'd gotten married recently to his college sweetheart, Evelyn Rogers. She was working as a secretary while Tom attended law school. Frankly, with the money Tom brought in from the club's investments, Evelyn didn't have to work.

Which meant Tom hadn't told her about his other source of income.

Fine. Not my business.

I probably wouldn't tell Daphne about the Future Lawmakers either. It was a part of my life that I compartmentalized. Chose not to think about except when I couldn't avoid it. Besides, after telling my parents about Daphne's pregnancy, my next course of business was to bring the club members together and put it all in the past once and for all. With Wendy out of the picture for now, it would be a much easier task.

All these thoughts invaded my headspace while I robotically explained the operations of the ranch to Jonathan Wade.

Funny. Larry looked a lot like him except for the receding hairline. Jonathan still had a full head of hair while Larry's hairline was already moving backward. I read somewhere that male pattern baldness was passed down through the mother on the X chromosome. I knew nothing about Larry's mom. He'd grown up with her in Grand Junction, and she kept to herself. I wasn't sure any of the Future Lawmakers had ever met her.

Daphne favored her mother. Lucy Wade was a lovely older version of her daughter, with shorter hair and some crinkles around her eyes. Daphne would retain her beauty as she aged. Lucy was proof of that. Not that it mattered. Daphne was my destiny no matter what.

Lucy and Daphne stood and went to the kitchen, presumably to get dinner on the table.

"You're the sole heir, then?" Jonathan said.

"Yeah. My mother couldn't have any more kids after me."

"That's something. I'm sorry."

"Yeah, it was hard on her."

"I'm sure it was. I guess it'll all be yours then. You think you can run the place like your dad?"

"Better, to be honest. My father's not a businessman. He's a great rancher, and he's made millions. My goal is to take it into billions."

Jonathan chuckled. "Billions raising beef. That would be something."

"Not just beef. We have a huge functioning orchard, and our vineyards have just begun to produce. We'll begin selling wine before long."

"You know anything about wine?"

"I took an oenology class last year, but I still have a lot to learn. I'm looking forward to it, though."

"That's a lot of cash to get a winery up and running."

"True, but I'll make it work. Plus, my father has outside investments in stocks, precious metals, and foreign currency that have done really well. And I'm determined. Especially now."

"Why especially now?"

Shit. I hadn't meant to say that. "I'm nearly done with college, and I'll be working the ranch full-time soon. I'm determined to do the best I can and make the ranch better than ever."

Would he buy that?

He nodded.

Good. He seemed to.

Lucy walked back into the living room. "Dinner's on the table."

Jonathan and I both stood, and I followed him into the

dining room. Four places were set.

"You sit here, Brad." Lucy indicated a chair across from Daphne.

"Thank you."

Jonathan said a quick word of thanks, and then we filled our plates.

Daphne covered her spaghetti with the red sauce but declined the platter of meatballs.

"Honey?" her mother said. "No meatballs? They're your favorite."

"I . . . uh . . . I'm not eating much meat anymore."

"Why not?"

"I want to make sure the meat I consume is humanely raised."

Jonathan let out a chuckle. "Sounds like college drivel."

Daphne reddened a bit. "My roommate and I have discussed it. Her parents own a pork farm, and they humanely raise their pigs. And Brad's cattle are humanely raised."

Jonathan looked to me. "Did you put this idea in her head?"

"No. You can see I took several meatballs. But we do raise our animals humanely. All pastured and grass fed. They're not force fed and they're not confined to small spaces, like a lot of animals are."

"Daphne has always loved animals," he said.

"Yeah, I do," she agreed, "and it dawned on me that I shouldn't be contributing to animals in pain."

"Why not just go vegetarian?" Lucy asked.

"Because I love meat. I believe we need meat. I just don't believe we need to abuse animals to get it."

Lucy smiled. "That sounds just like you, sweetie. Always

so caring. You do whatever makes you happy. Next time I make meatballs, I'll be sure to buy only meat that's humanely raised."

"Thanks, Mom."

The two women exchanged a smile, and it struck me that Lucy Wade would do anything for her daughter.

Anything.

Even accept a marriage and pregnancy at eighteen.

We were going to be okay.

CHAPTER FIFTY-SEVEN

Daphne

My dinner tasted like dirt.

Yeah, it was my favorite meal, but I could barely produce enough saliva to get it down. After dinner, I had to tell my parents about my pregnancy and my impending marriage.

I hated to disappoint them.

The good news was that my father already seemed to adore Brad. They continued to talk animatedly about the ranch during dinner.

My mother served up her signature chocolate cake for dessert, and I ate mine deliberately slowly, trying to draw out the evening.

More time.

Needed more time.

I was so not ready for this.

"Care for a nightcap?" my father asked Brad when I'd eventually eaten the last crumb of my cake.

"No, thank you," Brad said, eyeing me.

No more drinking. We have something to do, his eyes said.

"Why don't we go out on the deck?" Lucy suggested. "It's a beautiful evening."

I loved the deck. Did I really want to do this out there?

Yes, I did. We'd be outside, so my parents wouldn't yell.

Not that I thought they'd yell. They'd treated me with kid gloves since junior year. Still, being outside, in the beauty of a Colorado evening, would be nice. Maybe would make what I had to do a little easier.

"Coffee?" my mother asked.

"That I'll take," Brad said.

I agreed as well. I didn't want to be kept awake tonight, but coffee bought me a few more minutes while my mother prepared it.

Brad sat next to me on the patio couch. I desperately wanted him to hold my hand, and I wanted him not to just as desperately. How affectionate were we allowed to be in front of my parents? I had no idea.

Except that I did.

I was an adult. I could be affectionate with the man I loved in front of whomever I wanted.

I exhaled slowly and grabbed Brad's hand. It was warm in my own, and so comforting.

Brad and Dad continued to chat about college and the ranch until Mom came out with the coffeepot and cups. She poured us each a cup, offered cream and sugar, and then sat down.

It was time.

The bell was tolling.

And it was tolling for me.

Brad squeezed my hand.

And I opened my mouth.

Then shut it just as quickly.

I took a drink of my coffee and burned the roof of my mouth. Great.

I put the coffee down and inhaled sharply.

You're an adult, Daphne. You did nothing wrong. You're in love with this man, and he's in love with you. All is good.

I opened my mouth once more. "Mom, Dad...?"

"Yes, honey," my mom said.

"Brad and I have some news."

This perked my father up. "Oh?"

"Yeah. We realize we haven't known each other that long, but..."

God, please help me.

Brad squeezed my hand once more.

"We're in love," I said.

"So soon?" my mother asked.

This time Brad spoke. "Yes, we are. I love your daughter very much."

I smiled and met his dark-eyed gaze. He was so confident, so self-assured. He made me believe we could actually do this.

"Anyway, we didn't mean for this to happen, but—"

My mother went pale. "Oh my God. Are you all right, Daphne?"

"Yes, yes. I'm fine."

"Thank goodness. You're feeling good, then? No... dreams?"

I'd had the nightmares a few times since I arrived at school, but I didn't want to worry my mother. "No, Mom. No dreams."

She smiled weakly.

"We... Well, the truth is..."

"I love her," Brad said again, squeezing my hand.

"And I love him," I said. "We're getting married."

My father regarded us sternly. "I hope you're planning a long engagement. Say three or four years?"

Brad spoke again. "More like three or four weeks."

My father lifted his eyebrows. He was a smart man. Surely he knew what was coming.

I gathered my courage. "I'm pregnant."

My mother's hand flew to her mouth. "Daphne, *no.*"

"Just so you know," Brad said, "we did use protection. We weren't irresponsible."

"Not irresponsible?" my mother shrieked. "She's eighteen! You took advantage of her."

"No, he didn't," I said. "I knew exactly what I was doing."

"How could you know what you were doing? You don't—"

"Lucy!" my father roared.

My mother stopped midsentence, her face still white, and pressed her lips together into a straight line.

"Young man," my father said to Brad, "you and I need to have a conversation."

"Of course," Brad said. "I'll listen to anything you have to say. Daphne and I didn't plan this, but I love her. I can give her a good life on the ranch. She can still finish her first year of college and then go back later. We'll make this work. We're both determined."

"I don't doubt the sincerity of your words, Brad." He stood. "Come with me."

CHAPTER FIFTY-EIGHT

Brad

I stood and followed Jonathan back into the house.

"About that nightcap," he said.

"No, thank you."

"You don't have to have one, but I do, and we're not having it here."

"You want to go somewhere?"

"A little Irish pub about a mile away from here. I want to talk to you in private."

★ ★ ★

Jonathan ordered an Irish whiskey, and I decided to join him. One drink wouldn't hurt, and I could use a little relaxation. Jonathan seemed so serious.

I took a drink of the liquor and let it burn a trail down my throat. Then I turned to him. "I really do love her, Mr. Wade."

"Jonathan, please."

"All right. Jonathan."

"I know you love her, son. She's a very special girl."

"She is."

"It's soon, but I see it in your eyes. You want to take care of her."

"I do. And I will."

"I believe you want to. I truly do. You certainly have the means, and I believe that you used protection."

"I did. A condom, like I said."

"Things happen," he said.

"Yes," I agreed, not sure where he was going.

"So you love her, but you haven't known her long, and you're both so young. Is this really what you want?"

"It is, sir. I've thought of nothing but Daphne since I first laid eyes on her. Would I have liked to go a little slower? Of course. But what's done is done. It can't be undone."

"Well, it could be."

"Neither of us wants an abortion."

"I understand. And adoption?"

"We talked about it. But I love Daphne, and I want her to be my wife. I'd hate knowing we had a child out there who wasn't in our home."

He nodded, took a long drink of his whiskey, and set the glass down on the wooden bar. He turned to me and met my gaze. His blue eyes were stern. "I think you're a good man, from what I can tell by only talking to you for a couple hours. I do think you mean well."

"I do. I love her, and I already love this baby."

"I want you to succeed. I want Daphne to be happy."

"That's what I want as well."

"Then there's something about Daphne that you need to know."

EPILOGUE

Brad

Present Day...

Thank God for that faulty condom, or I wouldn't have my son Jonah. He was perfect, and as he grew, he became strong and determined. Of all my children, my firstborn resembles me the most, not only in looks but also in personality.

Today, he refuses to speak to me.

I've tried.

I've tried with all of them.

I thought for sure my baby girl would come around, but she hasn't yet.

Oddly, the one who speaks to me now is the one I failed in the worst way. My second born. Talon.

He's visited a few times, and we've had some deep conversations about guilt and blame. Wendy told Talon a fabricated story about Joe's conception. She said I had a one-night stand with Daphne during one of our off-again periods, and that I was dating another woman at the time.

All lies, except for the fact that Wendy and I were off at the time.

I wasn't seeing anyone else, and I loved Daphne from the moment I saw her. She was never a one-night stand.

Wendy told so many lies over the years. So many.

I may have a chance with Ryan and Marjorie. But my firstborn, the one whose conception led me down this path, will never forgive me. I know that now, and I must accept it. He's quick to anger, quick to judge, and even quicker to draw his weapon.

I didn't teach him to use a gun. I never wanted to—not after what teaching someone else had cost me.

I didn't know until much later in life that Tom Simpson had taught him, and that Jonah had taught his younger brothers.

Now? After all they've been through? I'm glad they know how to handle weapons. I'm glad they can protect themselves and their families, even if Tom had something to do with it.

Tom . . .

That iciness I identified in those early years was colder than even I thought possible, though I didn't know the extent until much later.

I spend a lot of time thinking. But I've stopped counting my regrets. Even I don't have time enough for that—and all I have is time.

So I think. I think about the past, let myself fly backward in time and relive what I cannot change.

I remember the legacy I vowed to create after Daphne and I wed.

A legacy for my wife.

A legacy for my children.

A legacy for my grandchildren.

A legacy born in heaven.

And in hell.

CONTINUE THE STEEL BROTHERS SAGA
WITH BOOK FOURTEEN

#1 *NEW YORK TIMES* BESTSELLING AUTHOR

HELEN
HARDT

A STEEL BROTHERS NOVEL

LEGACY

MESSAGE FROM HELEN HARDT

Dear Reader,

Thank you for reading *Fate*. If you want to find out about my current backlist and future releases, please like my Facebook page and join my mailing list. I often do giveaways. If you're a fan and would like to join my street team to help spread the word about my books. I regularly do awesome giveaways for my street team members.

If you enjoyed the story, please take the time to leave a review on a site like Amazon or Goodreads. I welcome all feedback. I wish you all the best!

Helen

Facebook
Facebook.com/HelenHardt

Newsletter
HelenHardt.com/SignUp

Street Team
Facebook.com/Groups/HardtAndSoul

ALSO BY HELEN HARDT

The Steel Brothers Saga:
Craving
Obsession
Possession
Melt
Burn
Surrender
Shattered
Twisted
Unraveled
Breathless
Ravenous
Insatiable
Fate
Legacy
Descent

Blood Bond Saga:
Unchained
Unhinged
Undaunted
Unmasked
Undefeated

Misadventures Series:
Misadventures with a Rock Star
Misadventures of a Good Wife (with Meredith Wild)

ACKNOWLEDGMENTS

Ever wondered how the Steel family saga truly began? *Fate* begins that story. I hope you enjoyed reading about how Brad and Daphne Steel met.

Huge thanks to the following individuals whose effort and belief made this book shine: Jennifer Becker, Audrey Bobak, Haley Byrd, Yvonne Ellis, Jesse Kench, Robyn Lee, Jon Mac, Amber Maxwell, Dave McInerney, Michele Hamner Moore, Keli Jo Nida, Chrissie Saunders, Scott Saunders, Celina Summers, Kurt Vachon, and Meredith Wild.

Thanks also to the women and men of Hardt and Soul. Your endless and unwavering support keeps me going.

To my family and friends, thank you for your encouragement.

Thank you most of all to my readers. Without you, none of this would be possible.

Stay tuned for more Brad and Daphne in *Legacy*!

ABOUT THE AUTHOR

#1 *New York Times*, #1 *USA Today*, and #1 *Wall Street Journal* bestselling author Helen Hardt's passion for the written word began with the books her mother read to her at bedtime. She wrote her first story at age six and hasn't stopped since. In addition to being an award-winning author of romantic fiction, she's a mother, an attorney, a black belt in Taekwondo, a grammar geek, an appreciator of fine red wine, and a lover of Ben and Jerry's ice cream. She writes from her home in Colorado, where she lives with her family. Helen loves to hear from readers.

Visit her at HelenHardt.com